LONE LAKE ROAD

Witches on Whidbey Island

Ted Mulcahey

TED MULCAHEY

For Patte
Muse, Hero, Partner

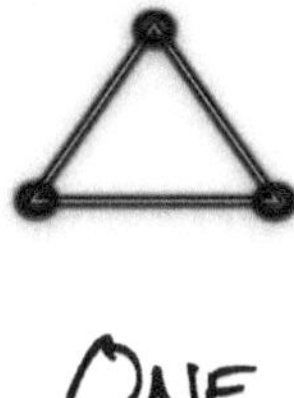

ONE

Every time I drove through the curves at the north end of the three-and-a-half-mile ribbon of asphalt carved through the Putney Woods forest on South Whidbey Island, I got the chills—literally.

In mid-summer, when the temperature was seventy-five in Langley or Freeland, it would drop at least five to ten degrees when I hit that stretch of Lone Lake Road. In the winter, during the dark and rainy season, it was the first and last place the frost visited. Though accidents were rare on that stretch of road, it was always within that quarter mile when they did happen.

Most thought it was purely a function of the dense woods and lack of shade and perhaps a slight dip in elevation. To those of us in law enforcement ... well, we knew otherwise.

My name is Roger Wilkie, and I'm the head sheriff's deputy for the island's south end. I've been in the job for six years, and although it's essentially a quiet, relaxed place to live, I've seen some wacky shit. After over a dozen years as a detective with LA's finest, I moved to the island to find a quiet spot to regroup after my wife died.

Whidbey Island is far from the sprawling population and rampant senseless crimes that infect large metropolitan cities like LA. Still, I gotta say, some bizarre happenings occasionally crop up. There was the time two knuckleheads tried to burn down Sharon Waffle's house and then ended up being heroes. Then there was the severed foot in the derelict boat on O'Malley's property—and please, don't get me going on those two.

Just last year, there was that Hogan character who tried to kill an entire community, but thanks to Andie Saunders, a world-renowned microbiologist, we averted disaster. And yes, O'Malley had his fingers in that one, too. Through some miracle of fate, that famous scientist is now my wife, and while I hate to admit it, the O'Malleys also helped with that.

But about those curves ... here's why I know there's more to it than climate and geography ...

Six months ago, just after things were settling down after the Harry Hogan fiasco, I got a call to check out a dead deer on the north end of Lone Lake Road.

For those unaware, Whidbey Island's Columbian black-tailed deer population numbers north of 2,000 animals. Combine this with a citizenry of 70,000 and the number of deer–car accidents ranks among the highest anywhere. Not a week went by without several such occurrences—so often that the county contracted with some locals to pick up and dispose of the carcasses.

It was a weekend when the person responsible for that section of the county was away on holiday, and I was just around the corner on Saratoga Road, so I thought it best to check things out. Although black-tailed deer are slightly smaller than their cousins, the bucks can sometimes tip the scales at two hundred pounds, and even a dead one can cause problems if a small car plows into it.

I acknowledged the call and swung a left on Lone Lake, thinking about the chore ahead of me—muscling a literal dead weight off to the side of the road. The dispatcher had told me the call was anonymous, so I didn't expect the driver to be around to help.

As I neared the center of the curved section of the otherwise laser-straight two-lane road, I saw a pile of guts and entrails lying dead in the middle of the blacktop surface. It had been only ten minutes since I'd taken the call, and the pile of viscera was still steaming in the damp forty-six-degree late March afternoon.

It wasn't unheard of for some locals to harvest recent roadkill for food, but the speed at which this had happened was shocking. Still trying to understand the scenario, I shoveled the mess aside with the scoop I always kept in the back of my Explorer police cruiser.

After finishing up, I checked with dispatch to see if the anonymous call might have been delayed after the accident, but Bruce—the operator—was adamant that it wasn't. "The guy was upset, Roger. I tried to get him to pull over and take some deep breaths, but he wouldn't listen. He kept saying, 'I gotta get home, I gotta get home.'"

"Okay, I believe you, but how do you explain a deer being field-dressed and removed less than fifteen minutes after it happened?"

"Hey, you're the famous detective; you figure it out."

Until the Hogan episode, my history with the LAPD had been under the radar. Still, the resulting press, nationally and locally, had dug up my past, and now I was a reluctant celebrity. Bruce wasn't all that impressed.

With the mess off to the side, I tried to figure out what had happened. Since no laws had been broken, it was more a matter of satisfying my curiosity than anything else, but the feeling of the whole thing was disconcerting. At four p.m. on an overcast day, the light on this mile-long stretch of road was dusky at best. I drove south to the straight-away portion of the road and then turned back north past the scene of the deer accident and to the north straight-away section. Four driveways led away from the road, all gravel, and all but two led to multiple residences.

I was sure whoever had harvested the dead animal had to live nearby, so I drove to the closest driveway. The three mailboxes at the street indicated the same number of residences to this famous detective, and my skills were confirmed when I reached the cul-de-sac a quarter mile away.

The clearing in the dense woods revealed three homes of modest construction, probably built by the same contractor, but only one seemed occupied. A young woman who looked in her early thirties answered my knock at the door.

"You startled me, officer; we don't get many visitors out here."

"Sorry, ma'am. It's not anything important or urgent; I was curious about a recent deer accident just down the road from your drive."

"Oh no. Was anyone hurt?"

"No, no, it appears whoever hit the deer is fine. It happened very recently, though, and the deer is missing, so I'm wondering how that happened."

"I'm not sure how much help I can be. My husband is a builder, and he thought it would be nice to live on a few acres, you know, away from it all. He built these three houses, and we took the smallest. The other two are owned by folks who spend the winters in Arizona, so I'm alone here with our daughter while he's up in Coupeville working on a project."

I felt for the woman but could see that she wouldn't be much help, so I did my best to soften my retreat. "Sorry to have bothered you, ma'am. I'm sure the peace and quiet of living here is wonderful."

"I guess ... but sometimes it's a little creepy, especially in the winter."

Not wanting to make her feel any worse, I thought it best not to share my feelings about this stretch of road. Instead, the detective in me pressed for a further amplification of her comments. "What do you mean, creepy?"

"We hear weird noises late at night sometimes and weird smells. Paul—that's my husband—says it's just that little guy who lives on the other side of Lone Lake Road and that he's sure he's harmless. But whatever's causing them still gives me the creeps."

"I'm sure you've got nothing to worry about, ma'am, but just in case, I'll check out that guy's place. Here's my card in case you need anything." I felt bad leaving the young mother alone in the cold, dark woods, but surely she was letting her imagination run wild.

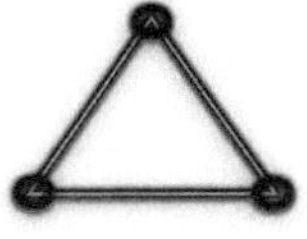

Two

The narrow gravel road snapped and crunched as I made my way back to Lone Lake Road. I hung a left and drove another quarter mile to the next driveway—this one displaying only one decrepit, seldom-used mailbox.

This private road, on the downhill opposite side of Lone Lake, was narrower than the previous one and deeply rutted and puddled from the constant winter rains. The firs and cedars brushed the sides of my cruiser as I slowly made my way down to a small clearing where the remaining feeble light from the overcast sky could barely penetrate the forest canopy. Off to the side, a crudely painted sign warned trespassers to KEEP OUT. Even though the weather and moss had done their best to obscure the thing, the blood-red lettering still spoke loudly.

With no structure yet in sight, I cautiously proceeded up a gentle rise where the forest closed in on me again. My ride began to feel stuffy, and a bead of sweat trickled down my spine. Now, almost a half mile from the main road, I rolled down the window and let the damp chill invade my space. Only late afternoon and my headlights were needed to penetrate the gloom. After another tense, tedious ten minutes, they illuminated a crudely built gate blocking the way, with another sign suggesting I stay away.

After ensuring my service weapon was firmly attached and ready, I stepped out of the vehicle, my foot landing squarely in an ankle-deep puddle. With the car running and the headlights illuminating the persistent drizzle, I lifted one end of the barrier and pushed it to the side.

I continued for another few hundred yards, where the road turned sharply to the right. When I had the car straightened out, my headlights revealed the recently killed deer carcass, still steaming and hanging from an ancient cedar.

Just beyond the cedar was a tiny structure built from stumps, branches, slabs of lumber, and various sizes of deadfall, woven together and seemingly at one with the forest. The door and single window appeared to have been salvaged from a landfill somewhere, while a rusting sheet of corrugated metal covered the entire mess. A moss-covered '74 Ford Courier pickup parked to the side displayed over fifty years of bad driving, and if there were plates on the thing, they weren't visible through the mud.

Leaving the cruiser running with the lights on, I had just opened the door to approach the structure when I heard a shotgun shell being racked into the chamber. I froze.

"Help you there, buddy? Did you happen to see the no trespassing signs?"

I turned to see what I'm sure was a human being standing in the glare of the headlights, but he more resembled a giant garden gnome. The man couldn't have been more than five feet tall, was chunky around the middle, and sported a beard worthy of Rip Van Winkle. He was dressed in dreadfully stained overalls, partially covered with at least a hundred-year-old Carhartt jacket, also suitably blemished. What I could make out of his face was dirty and pock-marked, and I guessed it was a thirty- or forty-year-old under the ratty John Deere ball cap.

His high-pitched voice gave the impression of someone who had never reached puberty, but his comfort in his surroundings and confidence in holding the weapon suggested otherwise.

"My name is Roger Wilkie. I'm the deputy sheriff in charge of this part of the island. I wondered who harvested that buck you've got hanging over there."

"Didn't break no laws."

"I'm not saying you did, but pointing that shotgun at me could be."

The chubby figure lowered his weapon but continued to assert his position. "Still doesn't give you the right to trespass."

"You're wrong; I can. I was concerned that whoever took that deer made sure it was dressed properly and wasn't carrying any disease." I was making that up, of course, but explaining the Fourth Amendment nuances to this fellow seemed unproductive.

"I know what I'm doing. You think that's the first animal I've pulled from that road?"

"What's your name, sir?"

"Name's Buzz ... Buzz Aldrin."

"Like the astronaut?"

"I'm not the astronaut."

"Okay, yes, I can see that. How long have you lived here, Buzz?"

"This property's been in the family for as long as I can remember. When my daddy died, he left it to me, and I've been here for over twenty-five years. I built the house myself."

From what I could see, the little hermit could have benefited from some YouTube videos on the art of construction.

"I see ... well, I'll be on my way. Make sure you cook that venison properly." It wasn't my best exit by any means, but this guy was a strange one, and I could learn more about him by doing some research than I could by talking to him.

I climbed back in my vehicle, made a ten-point turnaround in the confined space, and headed back down the bumpy two-track. I didn't bother to close the gate on my way out.

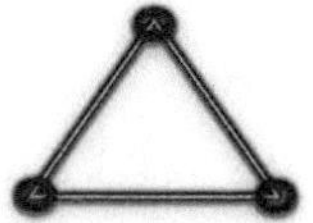

Three

"How was the day, Rog?"

I had just walked in the door, and Andie had the fireplace glowing, Jimmy Buffett in the background, the smell of something delicious in the oven, and a warm hug for yours truly before I could answer. Our home, oddly enough at the *opposite* end of Lone Lake Road, was a remodeled farmhouse perched on a slight rise on the west side of Lone Lake.

"A little strange … until now, that is."

"Talk to me."

"I got a call from Bruce about a dead deer on Lone Lake Road, up by the curves."

"So?"

"The guy usually responsible for that section is off for a few days, so I went there to clear the road. The only thing left was a pile of guts."

"Weird …"

"Not as weird as the guy who lives in the woods over there."

"Huh?"

I told her about Buzz Aldrin and his peculiarities while she pulled what looked like baked ziti from the oven and placed it on the stovetop.

"So he's not the astronaut, I take it?"

"A million comedians out of work, and you're taking their place—geez. Actually, I asked him about that, and he pretended he had no idea what I was talking about."

"Why did you bother investigating? It's not like he was breaking the law."

"I was curious; besides, one of the other folks who live nearby told me about strange noises and smells."

Andie started plating the delicious-looking pasta while I found a suitable Brunello to accompany the dish. As we sat to eat, she asked me if I thought Aldrin was the source of the odd noises and smells.

"I don't know … maybe. How about we put this topic aside while we enjoy the fruits of your labor?"

She laughed loudly, a sound that was music to my ears. We had been married less than a year, but it felt like we had been friends forever. Andie was almost ten years my junior, in her early forties. She was tenured at the University of Washington and is famous for her research on bacteria.

Her dedication to running and nurturing her pet pygmy goats kept her in peak physical condition, and every time I gazed into those ice-blue eyes, my heart melted. Thinking I had come close to losing her to Harry Hogan still bothered me.

"Only if you promise to fill me in later."

"Deal. Did you get things squared away in the barn?" We had just finished adding a room to the barn where the goats lived, just behind the house. Since Andie only traveled to UDub a couple of days a week, she needed a home office and lab, and at her insistence, we'd added it to the building shared by her three pets.

"Yup, all squared away. Got a VPN directly with the U and can even conduct lectures remotely if I have to."

We made small talk for the remainder of our dinner. I cleaned up the dishes while Andie went to the barn to say goodnight to her three pals. I was still in awe of the three little goats that had caused all the troubles the previous year—and now they were ours.

When she returned, we fell into the routine of getting ready for bed, and I marveled at my good fortune in finding this woman. As we turned the lights off, I promised to tell her about the non-astronaut in the morning since I thought it was less than appealing as a bedtime story.

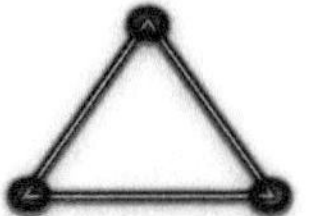

Four

I got to the Freeland sheriff's office a little before eight the following day and was greeted by Wally Turpin, who had recently transferred to Whidbey from Camano Island. He'd been with the department for a few years and had helped immeasurably with previous events.

The office was a converted single-family home that had been reconfigured to allow a private office for the senior deputy and an open squad room with four workstations for the deputies. There was a small conference room with a kitchenette in the back.

Bruce Strickland, the dispatcher, was sitting at his desk—a former dining nook—nursing a paper cup of some questionable brown liquid. "You track down that dead deer yesterday?" he asked.

"I did. Have you ever heard of a guy named Buzz Aldrin?"

"The astronaut?" Both chimed in at the same time.

"No ... not the astronaut." This was getting a little tiresome. "He's this little chubby guy who lives deep in the woods off the Lone Lake curves. Guy looks like a goddamn garden ornament."

"What about him?" Wally asked.

"He's what happened to the deer; the guy sorta lives off the land. He had that thing dressed and hanging in less than half an hour."

"So? Saves us having to clean up after the car–animal accidents out there, right?"

"Yeah, but if you'd seen his place, you'd be more concerned. Lady out there says strange noises and smells are coming from his place."

Bruce was engrossed in something on his phone, but Wally was still engaged. "You want I should do something?"

"Let's see what we can find in the county records first, and let's check out the internet; maybe we'll get lucky. You start with the county, and I'll see what I can find online. You too, Bruce, and get off the damn phone."

"What?"

"Wally, you tell him. I'm gonna get to work."

***

As I suspected, there was a tremendous amount of information about Buzz Aldrin online. Of course, that was for the astronaut, not the little troll off Lone Lake Road. I was surprised to see that most of it dealt with conspiracy theorists who, to this day, were convinced the whole moon landing thing was a hoax.

I got sidetracked for a while, marveling at the gullibility of some of my fellow human beings, before resuming my search for any other Buzz Aldrin than the famous astronaut. After twenty minutes, I threw in the towel and went to Wally's cubicle to see if he had any luck.

"Anything, Wally?"

"Yeah ... let me just get through this for a sec."

I stood by while he scrolled through the Island County database one more time.

"That property has some interesting history."

"Talk to me."

"As far as I can tell, a hundred-acre parcel there has been in the same family since the early nineteen hundreds. It seems a woman came here from San Francisco, struck a deal with the folks who owned it, and it's been in the same family ever since. Her name was Angela Morgan, but she changed it to Aldrin for some reason. That's where your friend, the astronaut, lives."

"Anything else?"

"Before I checked the county database, I did a little research on the number of accidents on that stretch of road."

"And …?"

"Before you moved here, that one-mile section of Lone Lake Road was known as the *bloody mile*. Lotsa stories in the papers back then."

"Huh?"

Warming to the narrative, Wally continued his report. "During the three years from 1997 to 2000, twenty-eight accidents occurred on those curves."

"What?"

"No lie. Now, they weren't all deer–vehicle accidents—some were just drunks running off the road—but that's an astronomical number for such a lightly traveled road. Hey, astronomical … like Buzz Aldrin, get it?"

"Yeah, good one, Wally. That can't be right, though."

"It is. I can show you the reports."

"How about in the twenty-plus years since then?"

"Three."

"What the …?"

"I know. Weird, huh? Also, of those accidents in the late nineties, four were fatalities."

"Jesus."

"Yep, my sentiments exactly."

"Who was the sheriff or the deputy in charge back then?"

"I don't know; I've been on the force fewer years than you. Maybe check with the *South Whidbey Record* in Oak Harbor. That's where the name came from. Some writer probably thought it would be cool to call it the *bloody mile*."

"Thanks, Wally; maybe I will. Meanwhile, see if you can find anything more on that astronaut."

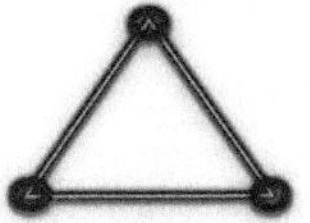

FIVE

Sound Publishing owns the *South Whidbey Record* and has since 2013. The forty-minute drive to Oak Harbor under overcast skies and constant drizzle gave me time to consider what I was doing and why I was concerned about a spate of accidents over twenty years ago.

I chalked it up to trusting my gut, which had served me well in LA and in my current position. I supposed if I hadn't had that run-in with Aldrin, I wouldn't be visiting the newsroom of the *Record*.

I entered the small one-story building that housed the Island County branch of the *Record* and found a three-desk office behind a vacant reception counter. A woman in her early sixties looked up from her computer screen and held up a finger, suggesting she'd be with me in a minute.

Wearing jeans and a sweatshirt declaring she was a Whidbey Island Gal, the wire-rimmed-spectacled woman eventually approached the counter. "What can I do for you, Sheriff?"

"Just a deputy, ma'am. I'm looking for some information from twenty-three years ago."

"I realize my youthful appearance would suggest otherwise, but maybe I can help you. I've been with the paper since '83 when I graduated from WSU."

I appreciated her self-deprecating and direct approach and told her why I was there.

"Yeah, I remember those accidents. It was like any car or pickup that drove on that road crashed. We ran pools in the office trying to guess the over-under on crashes for the month."

"Was there any investigative work done?"

"Deputy, we're a small paper and lucky to get the damn thing out twice a week. I remember writing about it and how weird it was, but that was it. Did you check with Bobby Waldron? I think he was a deputy at the Freeland office then."

"I've only been on Whidbey for six years, so I don't know the name."

"You should look him up. If he's still alive, he'll be on the south end, but he's gotta be well into his eighties by now."

"Good idea, and thanks for the help. Can I get back in touch if I have any more questions?"

"Sure. Name's Betty and I'm the only Betty here."

I began the drive back to Freeland and called Wally on the way.

"You know a guy named Bobby Waldron?"

"I've heard the name. I think he's an old-timer who hangs out in the bar at Mutiny Bay. That's the place O'Malley plays golf."

"He was a deputy, right?"

"Pretty sure ... yeah. Always telling stories to anyone who'll listen is what I hear."

"You wouldn't have an address or phone number?"

"Nah, but I think if you stop in the bar there, he'll be around, or at least someone will know where he is."

I promised myself I would let this thing go after I found Waldron. I had enough on my plate for the present, never mind events that had happened thirty years ago.

***

I drove straight to the golf club, where the skies were a little brighter and the drizzle had abated. As I approached the bar, I could see a smattering of diehards hitting range balls and practicing their putting through the large picture windows, and it looked like Kevin O'Malley was one of them.

I tried to stay out of sight lest he get his nosy little fingers into this. He always seemed to be around when something strange happened.

"Help you, Sheriff?"

"Deputy, Miss. I'm looking for a guy named Bobby Waldron. Is he around?"

"Yup. That's him near the fireplace telling stories to those folks doin' their best to act interested."

Looking in the indicated direction, I saw a white-haired older gentleman trying but failing to remain within the confines of his chair. He had to be fifty pounds overweight, hadn't shaved in a month, and I'd bet he'd be well over six feet if he stood. Two other men, possibly a few years younger, were nursing beers while glancing at their watches every ten seconds.

"Excuse me, are you Bobby Waldron?"

While my quarry looked up, his two captives quickly moved to another table. "That would be me."

I introduced myself and asked if he'd mind answering a few questions about his tenure as a deputy in the Freeland area.

"Course not. What can I do you for?"

"It's about all those accidents in the late nineties."

"You talkin' about those ones on Lone Lake? Out by the curves?"

"Those very ones."

He was quiet for a few seconds, either trying to recall events or maybe only revisiting them. "You know, we never had much crime here on Whidbey when I was on the force. It was mostly drunks here and there, maybe a break-in occasionally or an occasional traffic accident. But those damn things on the curves were like the plague. No matter what we did, we couldn't stop 'em."

"What do you mean?"

"Hell, after the first few, we lowered the speed limit to thirty-five, but no difference; they just kept happening. Then we put some of those electric signs out with the flashing yellow lights. All that did was cause folks to crash into *them*.

"We thought about puttin' flaggers out there, but I was afraid they'd get run over, so we canned that one."

I worked hard to erase the visions of orange-vested flaggers tossed into the ditch by speeding vehicles. "So how did you get them to stop eventually?"

"I dunno. Sometime in late '99, they just stopped. After a few months, we put the speed limit back to where it was, and no difference. I think there might have been a few deer accidents since, but that's it. It was strange shit if you ask me."

"Ever hear anything about an odd guy living on some property off that road?"

"Hell, son, it's Whidbey. There's lotsa odd folks around."

"Yeah, but this guy's odder than most. Little short fellow, looks like a gnome."

"A nome? What's that?

"No, gnome ... like guh-nome."

"Oh, you mean one of them garden thingys?"

"Yes, one of those. His name is Buzz Aldrin."

"The astronaut? He still around? What's he doin' on Whidbey?"

"No, not the astronaut; just the same name."

"Huh ... no, can't say I've heard of him. Strange, though, him having the astronaut's name."

I agreed, bought the old deputy a beer, and headed to my cruiser. As I unlocked the door, I heard a familiar voice.

"Hey, Rog, you taking up the game?"

"Kevin, good to see you, I think. And no, not even considering it."

"What do you mean you think? After all the help I've given you."

Not wanting to relive the events of the Hogan case almost a year ago and certainly not wanting his meddling in my current musings, I chose to go on the offensive.

"I thought I saw you putting. Aren't you playing today?"

"Nah, just a little practice. Got a big match coming up. Did I see you talking to Bobby Waldron in the bar? What's that all about?"

Man, this guy was a burr under the saddle—nothing got by him. "Just talking about some old stuff when he was on patrol. Nothing much."

"You came out here to talk to the former deputy about nothing? You sure you don't want to share?"

"Um ... yes, Kevin. I'm one hundred percent certain I don't want to share. Have a nice day now."

I quickly hopped behind the wheel, leaving my buddy standing there, and proceeded to vacate the premises.

Six

The next few days were filled with a myriad of minor crimes that were common occurrences on my patch. A series of break-ins in Clinton, an elderly gentleman with dementia walking away from his caregiver in Freeland, and a shoplifter in Langley were on the top of the list.

After more than a decade with the LAPD, the tamer, more genteel crimes on the island were a welcome, if occasionally dull, diversion. In my tenure on Whidbey, though, there had been enough national attention for a lifetime, and somehow, O'Malley had been a central figure in all of those crimes.

The history of the accidents on the Lone Lake curves and the strange fellow who lived in the woods were in a comfortably forgotten corner of my mind when Bruce's call jolted it awake.

"Hey, Rog, another deer collision on Lone Lake. The driver said he pulled it to the side and left it there. You want me to get Dwayne to pick it up, or do you want to have a look?"

Dwayne was the person who usually disposed of the animals, but because of its location and my recent dealings, I thought it worth a look. "I'm on it, Bruce. Tell Dwayne he may not have to bother if our friend, the astronaut, takes care of things." It took fifteen minutes to get to the location—enough time for Aldrin to attend to the situation if he was as efficient as before.

The dead animal was as described—pulled to the shoulder and, interestingly, just to the north of the rutted road leading to Aldrin's shack. I put a few flares in the road just in case and drove into the woods to see if my little pal wanted to partake of the free venison.

In the daylight, the disgusting excuse for a shelter appeared as I turned right into the clearing. The ancient Ford pickup was still parked to the side as before, but no one showed up to greet me.

I got out and called loudly for Buzz. Knowing the man's propensity for showing up shotgun in hand, I thought it prudent to announce myself. "It's Deputy Wilkie, Buzz ... you here? There's a dead deer if you're interested."

Nothing ... just the sound of raindrops hitting the forest floor.

"*Buzz ... Buzz ...* you here?"

I waited a few minutes, then walked to the structural masterpiece he called home. It was a miracle the thing was still standing.

The moss on the metal roof was an inch thick in places, softening the raindrops as they filtered through it and then dripped to the ground. Only about five feet high, the entry door appeared made from a three-inch slab of teak. Because of the many openings in the roots and branches that made up the exterior walls, it was impossible for the man not to have heard me. It was clear the door had been selected more for availability than design.

I walked to it, offering a perfunctory knock that could barely be heard, and managed to push it open a crack. I pushed it wider, ducked under the header, and entered the tiny dark interior. I still regret it, even today.

The ceiling of the single-room hovel was barely six inches higher than the door and was the underside of the corrugated metal roof. At a smidge over six feet, my hunching over only added to the claustrophobic feeling I suffered. Several kerosene lanterns sat on a crude table fashioned from two slabs of timber supported by two mismatched stumps, and one was still lit. Its feeble glow displayed a pine needle floor and two other stumps, apparently for sitting at the table.

In one corner was a thin mattress of questionable material supported by a stack of crisscrossed limbs. At least the thing was ventilated from underneath. Crude shelves held mismatched cups and plates, which had surely been procured from yard sales or nearby trash bins, as well as several other indeterminate objects.

Stunned as I was by the filth of the place, the smell was debilitating. The combination of poor venting from the ancient wood stove and the owner's sour body odor was overpowering. With no obvious source of electricity or running water or repository for bodily waste, it was clear those necessary human needs had to be located elsewhere on the property.

No longer able to hold my breath, I rushed into the damp forest and inhaled several gulps of wonderfully cool, moist Pacific Northwest air. Turning away from my vehicle, I walked through the heavily wooded area on the far side of the dwelling, where a worn path led deeper into the forest.

The woods were thicker here, and sure enough, a rudimentary privy was sitting in a slight depression surrounded by a thicket of blackberries. Opening the door, I saw a bench seat positioned over a hole in the ground. The entire structure appeared portable enough to move occasionally when the level of waste in the hole crept too close to the surface. About twenty feet to the toilet's right was an old-fashioned hand pump with a galvanized bucket next to it for priming and carrying water back to the little house. Without electricity, it made sense that a manual pump was the only solution. The proximity of the well to the outdoor crapper was questionable, but I doubted if any inspector had ever seen the place.

Calling out his name a few more times was met with no response, so I retraced my steps, got back into the cruiser, and gladly left the premises. It appeared Buzz Aldrin was missing, but he might be off on foot somewhere. I'd come back another time before I was willing to consider alerting anyone. Hell, nobody knew the

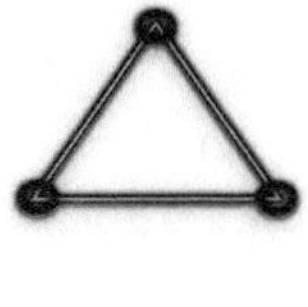

SEVEN

I waited two more days before visiting the little astronaut's property, and this time, I brought Wally with me. I wasn't all that comfortable at the location, and I wanted to see if it was just me or if there was truly something odd about the place. Well ... *odder* than it was, which was really fucking odd.

We arrived at the turnoff to the rutted drive shortly before noon. Once again, it was overcast and in the forties, but there was no rain, at least for the time being. One look at Wally told me it wasn't only me who was uneasy on the journey.

"How come I never knew this place existed?" he asked.

"I don't know. It's enough off the road so no one would know it's there, and the tall trees on these curves don't let much light in, so maybe that has something to do with it. Plus ... well, you'll see. It's not like there's a mansion in here."

When we arrived at Aldrin's shack, Wally's eyes popped out of his head. "Holy shit, you weren't kidding. Look at this place."

"Preaching to the choir, dude. Wait till you get a look inside—go ahead; I'm waiting out here."

Wally was built like a fireplug. In his mid-thirties, he served a several years with Uncle Sam as an MP before becoming a deputy for Island County. A smidge under five-ten, his barrel chest, and Popeye-like arms confirmed he could hold his own in an altercation, but his tough-guy presentation was a convenient disguise for the kind, caring soul I was pleased to have on my team. Carrying his tactical flashlight, he gingerly stepped through the heavy door that was still open a crack as I had left it. I figured the over-under on time spent in the dump at thirty seconds, and I was over by fifteen. Wally came out, gasping and coughing.

"Jesus, Rog, that's awful in there."

"Told ya."

"Whew—how does anyone live like that?"

"You've got me. Let's walk out back."

We covered the same ground as during my previous visit, and this time, I tried to do it with a more discerning eye. We walked to the pump and started turning around when Wally muttered something.

"What is it?"

"Over there ... it looks like a clearing. Let's check it out."

We made our way through and around the thick brush and found an overgrown meadow, roughly sixty feet by sixty feet.

"Kinda strange, huh, Rog, this clearing in the middle of the woods? You can see where they cut the trees and cleared the stumps."

"Yeah ... strange. If we ever find the little guy, we can ask him about it."

I had done enough exploring, so we returned to where we were parked.

"It's hard to imagine anyone living here," Wally said as we made our way to the cruiser. I nodded distractedly as something caught my eye.

"Wally, tell me what this looks like," I said as I pointed to some tire tracks in the mud.

"It looks like these aren't the tires on your vehicle, and they sure as hell aren't the tires on that heap over there," he noted, pointing toward the old Courier. "They can't be too old because of all the rain we've had. Could they have been here the other day?"

"Maybe, probably ... after being inside that shithole, though, my observational skills were not particularly keen."

"So someone else has been here?"

"Looks like it. Take some pictures, and at least we'll have a record of it. Right now, all we know is that Buzz Aldrin has been missing for a few days."

We had plenty to do with our usual level of policing, and there was no report of a missing person. Still, it was clear Aldrin hadn't been around. He might be a little weird, but if he had nobody to worry about him, then I'd have to do it.

"When we get back to the station, Wally, let's see if we can dig deeper into this guy. There's got to be a relative or some trail to someone somewhere."

It was mid-afternoon when we returned, and Bruce had given me a handful of phone calls to return. I told Wally to get back to the computer and try again to find something.

By four, I had managed to dispatch my messages and went to check on my associate. He was clacking away at his keyboard and appeared to be studying lists of things on some official-looking website.

"Any luck?"

"I can't get past all the astronaut stuff when I search for this guy. It's like no one else in the world ever had the same name."

"Yeah, I discovered that too."

"I found something on the county website, though, that surprised the shit out of me."

"Enlighten me."

"Some trust owns the property, and the contact is listed as Sable Aldrin. While looking at the property records, I found a filing for a clearing and grading permit around 1999. It was filed and granted, but no one ever picked it up, so it expired."

"Why is that interesting?"

"Two things: it was definitely for this property, and the other thing was the name on the filing paperwork."

"Aldrin?"

"Uh-uh ... it was Kevin

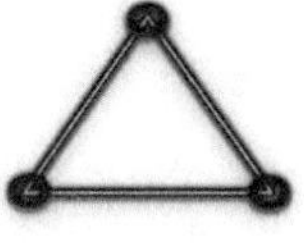

EIGHT

I met Andie at the Braeburn in Langley for an early dinner. After she'd rescued the city's water supply from lethal contamination by a psychopathic killer, she had become somewhat of a celebrity. As always, the town residents respected her privacy, preferring a smile and a hat tip to any outright intrusion.

We had just begun sipping one of the local IPAs when Kevin and Jenne O'Malley walked into the restaurant. I was thankful our two-top was small enough that an invitation for them to join us would have been silly. They were close friends, but I looked forward to spending the evening alone with my wife. Besides, there was still that permit thing I needed to ask him about, which was business—not allowed on our date night.

"Hey, Rog, Andie, fancy meeting you here."

"Yes," I said. "Fancy that."

"You know, Roger, a less confident person might detect a note of sarcasm in that greeting."

"Shut up, Kevin. Andie, Roger, good to see you. We're going to sit over in that corner and leave you two alone. Right, Kev?" I could always count on Jenne to be the voice of reason.

Andie laughed out loud at the banter and stood to give the O'Malleys a hug. "Great seeing you. Jenne, let's catch up later when the two alphas begin sparring again."

They grabbed the corner table where, if I happened to look over, Kevin could make juvenile faces at me. The guy was a pain in the ass but a great friend, always fun, and, based on the last several years, strangely effective in solving some dangerous cases. Right now, though, I preferred our quiet time.

"Hey, remember our first dinner at the University Grill[? You know, when you pretended you had to deliver those contaminated samples personally."

"Yes ... yes, I do. I also remember a university professor who balked at first at the invitation but then was glad she succumbed to my charms."

I loved it when she smiled—not with her mouth but her whole face. "Well ... she sorta did, but you're right, she was really, really glad she succumbed. And she loves you very much."

She reached for my hand when she said this, and the feeling made me thankful for the cosmic forces that had blessed me with this woman. Damn, was I lucky or what?

After a quiet moment when the only noise in the restaurant was the hum of activity, we resumed eating a terrific golden beet and goat cheese salad.

"Anything on that little guy in the woods? You know, the astronaut?"

I thought it funny the gnome-like recluse was now known internally as "the astronaut."

"He's disappeared. We're having trouble finding out much about him, but Wally stumbled on something before we left today."

"Do tell."

I related the discovery of the permit from '99 and the name on the filing.

"Are you telling me that guy in the corner making faces at you is involved in *this*, too?"

"I don't know what to say, Andie. It's like whenever there's a shitstorm, O'Malley can't be far away ... it's uncanny."

"When were you going to ask him?"

"I think I'll wait until morning—you know, after we enjoy the evening."

"That's a smart move, Deputy. You never know what's in store for you when we get home."

***

I waited until after my first cup of coffee the following morning to call O'Malley and ask him if he'd mind stopping by the station. He told me he'd do it on the way to the golf course and to expect him before noon.

I thought he was nuts to be playing golf in the drizzle and cold, and when he arrived, I told him so.

"If I waited until it was warm and sunny, it would be June before I played. You've gotta tough it out."

"No, Kev, *you* do. How about having a seat in the conference room?"

"Sounds serious, yes?"

"Nah, just a few questions about something we're working on."

"Okay, shoot; I've got a one o'clock tee time."

I produced a copy of the Island County permit report he signed and inquired about it. He looked blank but then seemed to remember something.

"Yeah, I think I remember this. It *was* sorta odd, though."

"Tell me about it."

"Well, most of the time, our design firm was hired by the owners of the project or home or whatever."

"Okay ..."

"And, sometimes, but not often, we'd work for the architect."

"I'm listening ..."

"And then, other times, when the owner wanted us to manage the entire project, we would take the lead and hire the other consultants."

"Kev, this is fun to hear about your previous business life and all, but please tell me about the goddamn permit."

"This was one of those times when we were the prime manager. These people—four of them, which we thought was a little strange—wanted to build a complex out in the middle of the woods.

"They had seen some of our work in one of the design publications and liked it, so they contacted us. At the time, our office was in Bellevue, so it was a pain in the ass getting up here. But once we saw how beautiful the island was, we said, 'What the hell?' and decided to take the job.

"We met with them a few times—they *were* a little odd now that I recall—and developed a floor plan for the project. One of the women seemed to be in charge, and the other three never said much. Because of the site, a bunch of civil engineering work was needed, as well as critical area delineations."

I nodded, trying to encourage O'Malley to get to the point.

"Okay ..."

"Anyway, I submitted the application for the clearing and grading permit so they could start the site work. As I recall, I drove out to the site about a week later to see if they'd made any progress—sometimes the county lets them begin work without the permit if an inspector visits the site.

"When I got there, I saw they'd done some clearing but not much. I tried to follow up with them but was never able to connect. I chalked it up to the project coming in over budget and them giving up. They even stiffened us for a couple of grand, too."

"You never heard from them again?"

"Nope. We'd get an occasional call from the county that the permit was ready, but that was about it. I remember what a pain in the ass it was getting to the site on that crappy road they carved through there."

"Tell me about the clients."

"It was two men and two women. They were pretty granola, as I recall, and one time when we met, there was a kid hanging around. Wasn't very tall and a little tubby, maybe young teens or something like that. I remember how they treated him; it was like you'd treat a stray dog or a cat. Looking back, it was all a little weird."

"Did you often have clients like that? I mean, two couples?"

"No, but some folks dance to a different tune. Thinking back on it, they didn't seem like couples—more like brothers and sisters."

"What were their names?"

"The main contact was Sable Aldrin. I remember that because of the astronaut Buzz Aldrin. I had just seen a movie about the moon landing, and then we got this client with the same last name. Uncanny, huh?"

"You have no idea ..."

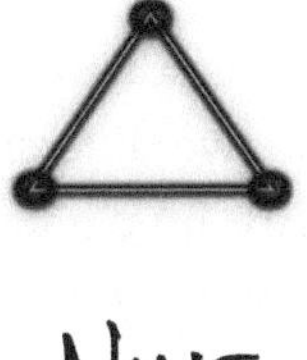

NINE

O'Malley's description of his clients and the possibility that Buzz Aldrin was with them as a teenager was only a little helpful. We wouldn't get anywhere unless we could find someone who knew more about the Aldrin clan. I didn't expect anyone to file a missing person report on Buzz, but the guy *was* missing.

O'Malley left for his tee time, and I asked Wally into my office to report on my meeting.

"This thing—hell, we don't even know if he's missing or gone or if there's even been a crime—is bothering me. Do you have any thoughts about it?"

"I don't know. I suppose he could have gone off willingly with someone."

"Yeah ... but it's not like he has many friends. You've seen his place; it's awful."

"Agreed. Seems like we should find out a little more about those clients of O'Malley's. They couldn't have just disappeared."

***

With no idea where to gather information about the mysterious foursome who hired O'Malley, I reluctantly returned to the Mutiny Bay Golf Club bar. At least

Waldron was old enough to remember something about Sable Aldrin and the others; whether he did or not was another question.

I walked past the dedicated winter golfers exiting their cars while donning rain jackets and waterproof golf shoes. It was nonsensical to me why they chose to slog through soggy fairways and chase a tiny ball over a six-mile hike in forty-degree weather.

Sure enough, Bobby Waldron was seated where I'd last seen him. This time, though, he had managed to corral two different members, who, by their furtive glances, wanted any excuse to escape his clutches. As I approached the table and greeted the storyteller, they scurried away much like the little bunnies did when O'Malley's dog happened upon them.

"Hi, Bobby. Got a minute?"

"Uh ... sure. Tommy, is it?"

"It's Roger—Roger Wilkie."

"Right, right, now I remember. You asked me about all those accidents."

"Yes, I did, and I have a few more questions about that time. I thought maybe you could help me."

"Shoot ... I'll do my best, Deputy."

"Do you remember anything about some folks looking to build a place in the woods near those curves on Lone Lake Road?"

He turned his puffy, whiskered, ruddy-complexioned head to the side and closed his eyes for enough time that I wondered if he'd dozed off. After several more seconds, I gently touched his arm, and he opened his eyes.

"I'm thinkin' here, Deputy."

"Sorry ... just wasn't sure if, well ... you know."

"Ya mean if I had a stroke or maybe just fell asleep?"

"No ... just, I wasn't sure if ..."

"Folks see a fat old man tellin' stories and they think he's senile or maybe just goin' over the edge, that it?"

I wasn't sure if my touch had flipped a switch or if this was normal behavior for him, so I did my best to make amends. "Sorry, Bobby, my bad. I didn't mean to startle you."

He seemed to settle down a bit and then offered a response I didn't expect.

"Nah, relax, I'm just venting here. I know I bore the shit out of people, but I get goin' and can't help myself. My wife's gone, and my kids and their kids live in California, so this bar here is my only social life. I'm too fat to play golf and too old to do anything else. I'm eighty-five ... and still alive, but that's about it.

"I can still remember some things, though, so what about them folks?"

"Anything you can tell me would help. I'm pretty sure the guy who lives there now is missing, and maybe it's got something to do with those four people who almost built a compound there."

"I was so tied up with all those accidents that I didn't give 'em much thought, but now that I think back on it, they *were* a little peculiar."

"How so?"

"Well, we were out there a lot because of all the accidents. Naturally, some of the folks who live out that way would call when one of 'em happened, and sometimes others would show up, you know—sorta looky-loos."

"Okay ... so?"

"There were four of them, kinda hippie-like, and sometimes they'd have a kid with them. Whenever there was a deer accident, they'd show up and offer to take the carcass. Hell, we didn't care; it was nice just to get the damn thing off the road. I never knew where they lived exactly, but it was somewhere in the woods near those curves."

"So you never went to their residence?"

"Nope. Never wanted to either; for all I know, they lived in tents. Every once in a while, someone would complain about smells, but that was mostly if they saw one of 'em in the grocery or something. We sorta let it go because they weren't there all that much and ... you know, it's not easy to tell somebody they stink and to get a shower."

"Yes, I can imagine. What about the kid?"

"Don't remember much. He was a chubby little thing, and I don't think he ever went to school ... course, it's Whidbey, lots of homeschooling here."

"Did they ever get into trouble with the law? Ever any crimes?"

Waldron closed his eyes again, but this time, I left him alone and waited. Eventually, he opened them, returning from wherever he'd been.

"Nothing we went after them for, as I recall. Come to think of it, of the four of them, the only one who ever said anything was one of the women. Not a great looker, if you catch my drift; kinda tall with a big nose and tiny thin lips. She couldn't have been much over thirty, but that's just a guess. I never wanted to get close enough to know for sure."

"Anything else you can remember?"

He was quiet again, his eyes closed ... thinking. Finally, he said, "What I remember is whenever they were around, other folks would leave in a hurry. It was like they gave off some kinda negative vibe. Sorta gave me the chills, now that I think back to it … Are we done now? I'm thinkin' I need another beer."

I nodded to the young woman behind the bar, who knew exactly what to bring Bobby. I thanked him, paid the tab, and headed for the door when he yelled at me, "Hey, Tommy … I mean Robbie … nah … Roger, yeah, that's it. Hey, Roger …"

I turned and answered, "Yes, Bobby?"

"You come across those folks, keep your distance. Somethin' fuckin' weird about 'em."

It seemed a little out of character for the guy to warn me, so I chalked it up to the number of beers he'd already consumed. I nodded, tipped my hat, and muttered, "Thanks … I think," and headed out into the drizzle.

I drove back to the office, hoping some other work would distract me from the strange events at the curves on Lone Lake Road.

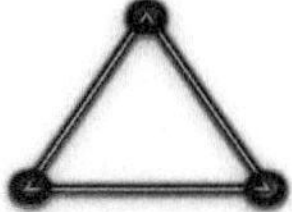

TEN

In the summer of 1851, Colonel Isaac Neff Ebey filed donation claims on much of the fertile land on central Whidbey Island. By agreeing to homestead the land for four years, the government awarded early settlers the property, oblivious to the fact that Indigenous people had occupied the land for thousands of years.

The territorial government somehow considered unimportant the fact that Whidbey Island was inhabited by as many as 1,500 American Indians as late as 1790. Shortly after Ebey's arrival, Isaac Stevens, Washington's first territorial governor, got tribal representatives from the region to agree to treaties granting their lands to the US Government.

Although unhappy with the terms of the treaties, the tribal leaders felt it was necessary for their survival. After all, the government promised money, tools, food, and education for their children. The Duwamish, Suquamish, Snoqualmie, Snohomish, Lummi, and Swinomish were also represented in the negotiations, joined by the Lower Skagit, Samish, and Kikiallus Tribes. The Point Elliot Treaty was signed on January 22, 1855, at Point Elliot—now Mukilteo.

Over the following decades, the remaining Indian villages were either burned or destroyed as white settlers eventually claimed the land as their own.

Ebey became a prominent political figure while farming over 600 of the island's most fertile acres. Under constant threat from the disgruntled natives, he built a blockhouse to be used as a sanctuary when the inevitable attacks occurred. On August 11, 1857, a party of Haida natives traveled by canoe to the base of Ebey's Landing and scaled the high cliffs on the western shore of Whidbey Island.

While Ebey's wife and children sought refuge in the blockhouse, Colonel Ebey was shot and beheaded. His body was eventually interred in the family cemetery on the bluff overlooking the sound, although it remained headless.

The blockhouse is still standing today, and the spectacular meeting of land and sea is now a National Historical Reserve—the first such reserve in the United States.

In a perfect world, we would have learned from past errors of judgment, the tragic chapter of Isaac Ebey, and the terrible plight of the Native Americans of the time and even of the present. Alas, the human race plods along with only an occasional uptick in consciousness of past and present mistakes and prejudices.

A further study of those times would reveal the odd journey of Ebey's head—or, more importantly, his scalp. Two captains from the Hudson's Bay Company sought to return the item to Ebey's family but were unsuccessful in attempting to purchase it from a local tribe. It was thought they refused to sell the scalp because of its significance in their annual celebrations of defeated enemies.

A few years later, one of the captains successfully obtained the scalp and returned it to Isaac's brother, Winfield. From this point on, the journey of the scalp becomes somewhat muddled. Some think Winfield buried it in the grave with his brother; others say his sister, Mary Bozarth, inherited the nasty thing. Those of that school of thought reported that it was passed on to Isaac's niece, Almira Enos, who eventually kept the item at her house in San Francisco.

As time passed, the saga of Isaac Ebey's scalp and its whereabouts became lost in the cobwebs of history. It may have been buried on Whidbey Island with its former owner, or perhaps it made the trip to the City by the Bay. In any case, the resting place of the disgusting item remains a mystery.

Unlike traditional scalping methods, the one used on the head of Isaac Ebey included the ears and forehead. Whether this anomaly was accidental or simply the act of an enthusiastic craftsman is uncertain, or maybe the unattached head was a bit too unstable to manage. Whatever the reason, the withered mess of hair and flesh eventually became so desiccated that one of the ears detached from the gruesome assembly and soon began its own journey.

Freed from its companions of hair, forehead, and opposite ear, the leather-like disfigured lump of dried-up cartilage somehow found its way to a shop catering to practitioners of witchcraft and those dabbling in the occult.

Located on Carl Street, The Raven's Nest's shabby exterior dissuaded all but serious seekers of the paranormal. The interior was claustrophobic and dark—even for the fading months of the nineteenth century. Tables and rickety shelves were crowded with potions, animal parts, tonics, herbs, and spices. An entire corner was dedicated to scrolls and parchments offering curses and promises of eternal damnation to those they were directed at.

***

Sarah Morgan, formerly Gyaaxa Gwang, was in her late twenties and had recently moved into her own apartment. Her tutelage under the three sisters had given her powers unlike those of ordinary folks and, with them, the confidence and judgment to use them wisely. Although many years had passed, her resentment toward the white men who had taken her people's lands remained steadfast.

Her idyllic life on Whidbey Island was a distant memory, and she still missed her father. She had been taken from her home at a very young age and forced to live at the Indian School, where she was punished, physically and emotionally, for doing or saying anything that referred to her native heritage.

After spending years at the school, being taught the white man's ways and language, she managed to escape. Distrustful of those outside her tribe, she was terrified when they came for her in the early morning before her schoolmates were awake. She went with them only when they gave her a note in her native language. They took her through the woods to the dock and put her on a ferry bound for Tacoma, where they told her to look for a boat going to San Francisco.

After several days of hiding on the waterfront, she was able to stow away on a logging boat bound for the Bay Area. With her hair cut short and stuffed under a cap, she easily passed for a young boy, and when discovered, she worked as a deckhand. The crews on the logging boats worked constantly; if a young kid could help, that was fine with them.

Upon her arrival in San Francisco, she managed to sneak away and spent the next few weeks on the streets. Although the frenzy of the Gold Rush had passed, the event had managed to populate the city with immigrants from every country. There were more languages spoken here than anywhere in the world. The fact that most of the populace couldn't understand one another seemed to make little difference to folks, most finding a way to get along.

She learned how to salvage food from the waste of many restaurants and steal from the outdoor markets. One day, as she snatched an apple from an open-air display, a strong hand grasped her wrist. Looking down at it, she saw long nails painted black and numerous age spots on the back of the hand.

"Ouch! You're hurting me ... leave me alone," she said, loudly enough to be heard by those around her.

"You think it's okay to steal from hard-working people?" The voice was precise and conveyed authority.

Gyaaxa twisted her hand to escape the vise-like grip without success, and worse, those around her resumed their shopping, now ignoring the scene. She looked up at a pale-faced woman, her gray hair in a tight bun, who seemed three times her age.

Unlike the other women she had seen in San Francisco, this one did not wear a skirt or a dress but was clothed in something with puffy legs. She would later learn they were "bloomers," and the few women wearing them were doing so to protest those trying to dictate their choice of attire.

"Who are you, and where did you come from? It certainly isn't here."

Always taught to respect her elders, Gyaaxa stopped fighting and told her the truth in heavily accented and halting English. After her first few sentences, the woman took her by the hand, gently this time, and went to sit at a nearby table. She ordered food and drinks and watched as the young girl devoured the meal without a word.

Once Gyaaxa had finished and caught her breath, she told the woman about how she was schooled and the stories of the white men driving her tribe from their lands. She told her about the revenge her tribe had taken on the invaders and how, today, they are only taught the way of the white man.

"It sounds like you've come a long way. Why did you?"

"I was told to come here. I couldn't stand how we were treated and wanted to start over. They told me to come to San Francisco."

The woman's eyes were gentle but haunting and intelligent. Her green eyes were an oasis in the palest face the youngster had ever seen, and her thin lips did their best to hide an understanding smile.

"Come with me, Sarah."

"That's not my name."

"Yes ... well it is now. The best way to start over is by fitting in, and you need a name that folks can pronounce and spell. I'll make sure to get the paperwork filed with the courts."

"What about you? What should I call you?"

"Call me Angela. Let's get you cleaned up and find a bed for you. We can talk more later."

***

A twenty-minute carriage ride took them to a strange-looking house at the corner of Fulton and Scott Streets. The building—only a few years old at the time—was pure Gothic, with multiple metal finials and an odd-looking tower protruding from the rooftop.

Little conversation took place on the journey, but when they had disembarked from their carriage and were on their way to the house's door, Angela stopped and turned to Sarah. "When we go inside, you'll find other girls—mostly older—living here. Many are from the streets, but a few were sent to us because their families couldn't handle them. My sisters, Agnes and Allegra, and I bought this place as a safe refuge for women and girls like us."

Sarah seemed uncertain of the woman's meaning and hesitated. "What do you mean, 'like you'?"

"We are independent thinkers, and many would prefer we didn't exist. Some are afraid of us, but most ignore us and leave us alone. Sarah, you're very young, but I also think you're very wise. Stay here for a few nights, and if it works, fine; if not, you can leave whenever you'd like."

She had never been spoken to like an adult before, and she liked it. *How bad can it be?* she thought. *At least I'll have a place to sleep for a while.*

A few days turned into weeks, then months and years. During that time, some women left, and new ones came, but she became part of a core group of five that hung out together, and the three sisters began calling them the Coven. They homeschooled the group and taught them the world's ways, sparing nothing.

There was some discipline, of course, but because the girls were treated and respected as equals, there was little need for it. The residents knew what was expected of them, and since misbehaving would reflect poorly on the others, it rarely occurred.

Most meals were informal, and the girls learned to cook for themselves. The exception to this was a once-a-month dinner. The three sisters prepared these special meals, which were only attended by the members of the Coven.

At first, it was like any other dinner, but it began with a strange prayer. The girls were exposed to different religions through their studies, but none seemed to relate to the words the three sisters recited.

After Angela, Agnes, and Allegra had completed the short verse with bowed heads, they looked up at the girls, and Angela spoke: "You've been invited to join these special meals we share when the moon is full. Some outsiders shun and fear us because they say we have special powers. They call us witches."

The girls looked at each other, unsure of the direction of the conversation, while Angela continued, "I'm not certain that we're witches, but it appears we *do* have abilities that others do not. We study the writings of Margaret Murray, an independent thinker of British and Indian descent. She has explored some unconventional approaches to the metaphysical world, and we have combined those theories with some we have garnered from other sources."

The members of the Coven were transfixed by what they heard, still not understanding the endgame.

"There are times when we can right a wrong. There are also times when we can punish an evildoer or reward those who deserve it. You five have been chosen because we think you are ready to take the next step. If any of this makes you uncomfortable or you want to leave for any reason, now is the time. From this day forward, on the evening of the full moon, we will show you what we have learned and teach you our ways."

Not one of the girls chose to leave; such was the magnetism of their hosts and the bond of their group. Sarah and her friends attended the monthly dinners, which went well into the night. They learned about mystics in other parts of the world, their methods and spells, and their mastery over the physical world. They learned of talismans and other magical items and potions.

As the members of the Coven grew older, they left their sanctuary one by one until Sarah was the last. The three sisters, now well into their seventies, were no longer accepting any boarders and were content to live out their days in the strange-looking house on Fulton and Scott. On Sarah's last day, there were tears, hugs, and promises to stay in touch.

She knew the city well and found an apartment nearby where she could begin her work. The sisters gave each girl a monthly stipend in perpetuity to carry out their duties without worrying about funds for food, clothing, and lodging. The Coven members had been taught well, and the sisters harbored no doubts about their abilities or dedication to the cause. Sarah would do her best not to let them down.

Now, as she ambled down the cramped aisles of The Raven's Nest, she took note of the so-called objects of the spirit world. Most were fakes and dried-up animal body parts with no powers whatsoever, regardless of the talents of the person executing the spell. Some of the potions and herbs were useful; however, the collection of scrolls and ancient spells was harmless and ineffectual.

Upon turning back to the entrance, a small reddish-brown object caught her attention. It sat between a wolf's paw and an urn full of magic dirt from somewhere. When she touched it, a tingle traveled up her arm, and she immediately pulled back.

She hailed the ancient shopkeeper, who shuffled over to her. "What is this item?" she asked.

"It's an ear."

"That's what I thought, but why here, in this shop?"

"I buy things from lots of folks. Some say the items are haunted or powerful, or sometimes they have a story that travels with them. Some of the stuff here is so old, I've forgotten why I bought it in the first place."

"Yes ... that's interesting, but what can you tell me about this ear?"

The old man closed his eyes, bent his head, and stroked his chin, obviously inspecting corners of his brain not recently visited.

"I think the woman who sold it said it had fallen from a man's scalp from Washington. She said the Indians up there cut off his head and then scalped him. Of course, that confused me some, you know, because if the guy's head wasn't attached, then why bother with the scalp? Right?"

"Maybe they used it in ceremonies."

"I suppose. Seems barbaric, though, doesn't it?"

"You mean like stealing land that my ancestors owned for hundreds of years and forcing them to live on tiny parcels? Like giving them deadly diseases and forcing their children to forget their heritage? You mean barbaric like that?"

"Um ... sure, yeah, like that." Shocked by the woman's outburst, the proprietor turned to go back behind the counter.

"How much do you want for this thing?" Sarah asked.

"Nothing. It's yours; you can have it." The proprietor appeared more intent on showing the customer the exit than making a sale.

"Thank you, sir," she said, placing the dried-up dusty item in her purse as she left the premises.

***

As time passed, Sarah's skills improved to a level surpassing that of her mentors. At first, she kept in touch with the other members of the Coven, but eventually, they went their separate ways, and she lost contact. She had vague recollections of her father and their life on Whidbey Island before she was taken from him. She understood now why he did what he did, and she hoped he found peace in knowing his daughter had managed to escape her forced confinement.

Her life as a witch left little time for romance, but that didn't stop her desire for an occasional dalliance with the opposite sex as long as it was a one-and-done thing. While she took extraordinary measures to ensure she wasn't saddled with a child, the inevitable finally happened.

She gave birth to a baby girl in the fall of 1902 and called her Angela in honor of her tutor, who had recently passed away. Although she hadn't wanted or planned to have a child, the event proved a blessing to Sarah. While exhausting, the day-to-day necessities of raising a daughter as a single parent were rewarding and eye-opening to the young witch.

Before the blessed event, she was consumed with devising spells, causing disease and natural disasters to befall the Pacific Northwest descendants of those who had stolen her people's lands. Now, with her hands full, she had little time to create mayhem. Strangely, her love for her daughter also softened some of the resentment she harbored for the white man.

She began to realize that just because the early settlers had decimated the Indian way of life, their offspring might not be as guilty. As Angela grew up, she was taught the magic and power bestowed upon her mother by the three witches from Fulton and Scott. She was encouraged to use her gifts for good, and when an opportunity for revenge arose, she brushed it aside.

Although Sarah had used the ear from Isaac Ebey's scalp to initiate a severe outbreak of cholera among Northwesterners shortly before her daughter's arrival, it now sat in a dusty jar on the top shelf of her bedroom closet.

As the years passed, Angela grew more powerful yet remained steadfast in her commitment to choosing good over evil. When her mother died, she packed away everything in her apartment and moved to Whidbey Island, the place she had heard so much about growing up.

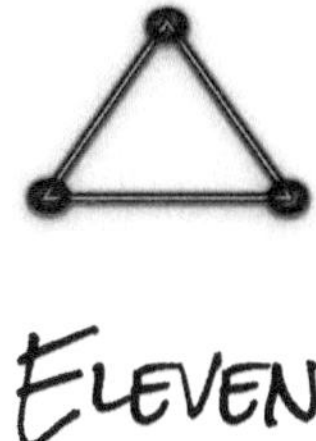

ELEVEN

Compared to San Francisco, Whidbey Island was a step backward in evolution. Angela Morgan was at first shocked at the beautiful weather. Her mother had told her about endless days of rain and dark skies, but surely she had been mistaken.

It was July. The skies were deep blue, the days long and sunny, and the air fresh and free from the exhausts of noisy cars and trucks. However, there was no electricity, running water, or sewer system.

The property she purchased was heavily forested and only accessed by a primitive road that branched off Lone Lake Road. She hired two men from a bulletin board at the Langley Post Office to help clear enough land to plant a garden and rebuild the dilapidated cabin once used by the former owners.

When winter arrived, along with its blustery winds, rain, and storms, Angela began to see the truth about her mother's stories. The first year was difficult. Her cabin was only half finished, and the temporary roof of fir boughs was constantly blown away. The river rock fireplace was restored, though, and the land clearing had provided enough firewood for a lifetime.

With little time for studying and practicing her craft, she wondered if moving to this island had been wise. Eventually, however, the nasty winter turned to spring and summer, and the glorious weather returned.

Her two helpers—brothers—returned to complete the cabin and build the necessary outhouse. Robert and Steven Aldrin were a bit rough around the edges but were excellent carpenters. Whether it was the absence of other men or perhaps Robert was a charmer, Angela and he eventually hooked up, and she became pregnant.

Possibly because of her mother's independence, Angela chose not to marry Robert, but for some unknown reason, she changed her last name to Aldrin. After the brothers moved off the island to greener pastures in Seattle, she focused on raising her daughter and living off the land in her hundred-acre forest.

As the years passed and more people came to Whidbey Island, Angela did her best to shield her daughter, Eve, from outside influences. Although a somewhat slow learner, she eventually mastered most of the lessons passed on through two generations through constant repetition and encouragement.

While her mother tried to keep Eve on their property, it became impossible as she progressed into her teenage years. Occasionally, she ventured into the town of Langley and developed a circle of like-minded friends. They weren't witches, of course, but they *were* teenagers, and experimentation was essential for their development.

Angela became ill when Eve was just shy of her twentieth birthday. She could no longer keep up with the garden, and the cabin began to fall into disrepair. Eve was more interested in her friends and considered her mother an eccentric. She wasn't even sure about all the silly witch stuff.

After becoming infatuated with John Walker, a man ten years her senior, she moved to Bellingham to be with him in the fall of 1955. She rarely made contact with her sick mother and wasn't aware Angela had passed away until months after the event. She hated the Whidbey property and was glad she had moved away.

Eve gave birth to two daughters and a son while living with Walker and was unsurprised when her man left her and the three kids to go to Alaska on a fishing boat. Her mother had set up a fund to provide for her, but she was unsuccessful when she attempted to discover where and how it was funded and disbursed. The only information provided was that the account was set up years ago to be passed on to the eldest daughter born to the eldest daughter.

The next fifteen years were a lesson in humility for Eve. With three children to raise by herself, she soon understood her mother's challenges and was remorseful at how she had treated her. When the kids were at school, she revisited the lessons her mother had tried so hard to teach her.

While digging through the unopened boxes of junk she had stashed away upon relocating to Bellingham years ago, she discovered the ancient scrolls and their spells. Strange objects were also tucked away, including a shriveled-up ear stuffed in an old wooden box.

She started with simple spells and curses and eventually progressed to voodoo and more sophisticated forms of witchcraft. She traced her family history back to its origins in a house in San Francisco and finally understood the provenance of the dried-up ear.

Eve understood why her mother and grandmother had attached such significance to the revolting object, but she could see no sense in retribution to Ebey's descendants. She tucked it away without giving it another thought.

She began working with Sable when her eldest daughter turned thirteen, hoping to pass on the family business. At first, her siblings, Orla and Thorn, were envious of the attention their older sister was receiving, but when they saw how Sable resisted the training, they were happy not to be a part of it.

As time went on and the three offspring of Eve Aldrin reached their late teens and early twenties, their lives appeared unremarkable when observed from afar. To those involved, however, it was an unfortunate story. Sable's attitude to witchcraft was indifferent to the point where her mother gave up all attempts to educate her. Instead, Orla and her older sister hung out at the local Burger King looking for boys while Thorn and his new friend, Alan, did the same for girls.

Because most of the local kids thought there was something strange about the Aldrins and their buddy, Alan, they often hung out together. It wasn't long before Sable and Alan started sleeping together, much to Orla's jealousy and Thorn's disgust.

The offspring now had little to do with their mother and lived together in a two-bedroom apartment in the Fairhaven District. Although some mild resentment existed about Alan and Sable, the four patched things up. The residual grumpiness had more to do with sleeping arrangements than anything else. Thorn and Orla were sharing a room, and they were unhappy about it.

A flu outbreak of near-epidemic proportions broke out in the early nineties, and Eve developed pneumonia, a complication caused by the infection. Her children heard she was ill but couldn't be bothered visiting and didn't return to their childhood home on Wilson Street until weeks after their mother died.

By this time, Sable was pregnant and was pissed at Alan for causing the situation, unmindful that perhaps she had also played a part in the unfortunate occurrence. They abandoned their apartment and moved into their childhood home.

Now that Sable had begun to receive the stipend from the fund set up many years ago, they gave up their menial jobs and looked for other ways to fritter away their time. The attorney who executed Eve Aldrin's will mentioned some property on Whidbey Island that was part of the estate as well. The four discussed how exciting it would be to build a reclusive estate on the island after the baby was born.

With nothing else to do, they began exploring the documents Eve had left behind. After a few days, with papers strewn about the dining room table, Alan asked Sable, "Did you know your mother thought she was a witch?"

"I know. She was—and she tried to teach me the trade."

"You're fucking crazy."

"No, she's not," Orla said. "She *was* a witch. You should have seen the things she could do. She was scary sometimes."

"You mean all this shit, these scrolls and spells and stuff ... they're real?"

"Yup." Thorn smiled as he replied.

"Can we learn to do the same things?"

"*You* can't; it has to be the eldest daughter. That would be me." Sable seemed to take delight in being the chosen one.

"Show me something ... a spell or something."

"It doesn't work like that, and it takes years of study to be good at it."

"Why didn't you learn how?"

"I didn't care about that stuff. I still don't."

Alan wouldn't let the issue go. "If you can get to the point where you can cast spells, then maybe we can get more money, you know, and take care of people who piss us off."

"I'm not sure, Alan ..."

"C'mon, we'll all help. Right, you two?"

Orla and Thorn nodded vigorously, happy to encourage their sister now that there might be something in it for them.

"Okay, it's settled; starting tomorrow, we start teaching Sable how to do witch-craft." Alan couldn't wait to start, but Sable seemed uncomfortable with the proposal.

***

Buzz Aldrin was born on Halloween. That the son of a witch was born on such a day didn't escape the foursome, and they celebrated the blessed event. All but Sable; she was exhausted from the ordeal and slept the night away while her three compadres toasted the birth of Buzz.

There was plenty of discussion about the name, but Sable had thought about it for nine months. If the kid were a boy, she would name him after the guy who landed on the moon. She was his mother and didn't care what the others thought.

The foursome became so focused on Sable's development as a witch that the Whidbey property became an afterthought ... and so did the unfortunate Buzz. The constant attention and urging by the others left little time for mothering, and the kid was never a priority. Because his presence was inconsequential to the group's singular purpose, he was left to spend his formative years watching mindless television, eating, and wondering what made his mother so important.

Sable's development was initially slow, mostly because her teachers knew little about witchcraft. She wished she had listened more when her mother had attempted to show her the ropes. Eventually, though, through trial and error, she began to understand things and eight years into her studies, she finally succeeded in casting a spell.

Their closest neighbors were older folks who mostly tolerated their bohemian lifestyle. However, the group became highly suspicious of them after several visits by Child Protective Services, who questioned their parenting of young Buzz.

At her tutors' urging, Sable attempted to cast a spell on the octogenarians, ordering the spirits to punish them for their actions. Whether the spell or the unseasonal summer windstorm felled the giant fir in their yard wasn't certain. The bizarre accuracy of its landing place—directly into the bedroom and onto the queen bed the couple shared—left little doubt in the foursome's minds that success had been achieved.

There was no remorse for the demise of their neighbors—they were old anyway—and the accomplishment was cause for celebration. Finally there was a witch in the house.

While Buzz watched the latest episode of *The Simpsons* with little understanding of the underlying satire, his four housemates celebrated their triumph. The noisy adults bothered him, but he knew better than to say anything.

In the succeeding years, Sable became more powerful. Several spells brought them more riches than they could spend, and their search for a challenge led them back to the property on Whidbey Island.

"This place looks cool. We can build a bunch of buildings here away from pesky neighbors and do whatever we want. We've got plenty of money; we only need some plans and a builder." Alan was the group's de facto head, either because he *wasn't* one of the siblings or because he was partnered with Sable. The others looked to him for direction, regardless of how imprudent it might have been.

The foursome, with young Buzz in tow, traveled to Whidbey Island to check out the hundred-acre parcel. Although they lived only an hour from the island, none had ever set foot on it. When they reached South Whidbey, they were impressed by its quiet beauty and sparse population.

Using the maps and paperwork found in Eve's stored boxes, they located the overgrown two-track leading from Lone Lake Road. The healthy spring burst of foliage made the primitive road seem even smaller, and the lethal blackberry bushes constantly scraped the sides of their SUV.

"I think this is it," Alan announced as they arrived at a broken-down split-rail gate. "Let's walk from here."

The four adults made their way through the light undergrowth through tall firs and cedars while the youngster trailed behind. Buzz was astonished at what he saw and felt more at peace in this place than ever in his life.

After forty minutes of hiking, they came upon what was left of a small cabin. Nature and the sometimes violent winter storms had forced the structure to cave in on itself, leaving only the stone fireplace intact.

"This must be my grandmother's place," Sable said as the group stopped to inspect the fallen structure.

"It has to be. I can't believe how quiet and private this place is," Alan agreed. "Let's start looking for someone to come up with a plan for a compound. I'll bet we can build it in a year or two."

The others agreed and began looking for the best site to build on while Buzz was occupied watching a black-tailed doe and her fawn trot by less than fifty feet away. He seemed hypnotized by their ability to tiptoe so quietly that only he noticed them. He felt better about it, too.

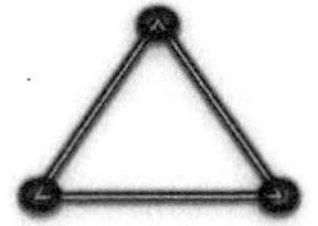

TWELVE

By the time Sable Aldrin and company arrived on Whidbey Island, her powers had reached a level of competency, at least when compared to others who practiced witchcraft.

She contacted a design firm whose past she found appealing, and they met at a small café in Langley. She chose the obscure little place because some of her spells had attracted more attention than desired from the Bellingham Police, and she felt it necessary to keep her and her companions' presence low profile.

O'Malley and Associates were a husband-and-wife team who seemed to know what they were doing, so she hired them to develop some ideas for their compound. According to the designers, the project would take considerable time, especially with the septic and land-clearing permit process.

Alan convinced the three Aldrins that it would be possible to live on the property in yurts during the design and building phases of the operation. Buzz was given little thought. The kid was homeschooled only in the broadest sense and seemed a little slow on the uptake.

Alan and Sable would live in one, and Thorn and Orla would take another. Alan said they could bunk with Buzz in the smaller unit if either of them complained. Neither complained.

They moved to the island in June, drilled a well, and spent the summer building the yurts and preparing for the dark rainy season.

Most days were spent clearing the site the designers had suggested for their compound. It was hard work, but the foursome was dedicated. Buzz picked up sticks every once in a while but mostly wandered about the property, observing nature and thinking about things. Sable continued her studies when she wasn't too tired but found few targets to practice on.

The dense population of deer on the island provided an endless source of protein for the group, with trips to the grocery store only necessary twice a month. In time, both the men and the women became skilled at butchering the game and finding numerous ways to cook the venison.

Little heed was paid to the hunting policies of Island County. Still, eventually, it became necessary to find a method of killing the animals without the noise of gunshots during the off-season. On a return trip from the grocery store, Alan saw a small doe lying on the side of Lone Lake Road. He stopped, noticed that the blood was fresh, and put the carcass in the back of his pickup.

While he drove down the dirt road to their settlement, he had an epiphany. When he pitched the idea to Sable and the others that evening, all were excited about the proposal. Sable would concentrate her efforts on spells, making motorists do the work for them.

At first, there were many miscues, and people, instead of deer, became casualties. As her proficiency improved, however, the supply of venison for their tiny community was never in doubt.

There were even times when a deer–car collision occurred without any effort on her part. The local sheriff's deputy encouraged them to dispose of the animals on such occasions, and word began to spread about the strange folks living in the woods off Lone Lake Road. That was fine with them; they preferred the seclusion.

***

For three years, the foursome—and Buzz—lived in the little circle of yurts on the property purchased by Angela Morgan. Their occasional disagreements and disputes began to surface more regularly and got to the point where they were arising almost daily.

At first, there were complaints about the living arrangements. Then, it was about whose turn it was to fetch the water and who spent too much time in the outhouse.

Initially, Alan and Sable always sided with each other, but over time, even their relationship became strained. Early on, Sable admired Alan's independence and his authoritarian personality. Ultimately, however, those attributes wore thin. He began to resent the time she spent on her witchcraft and how those activities intruded on their sex life, while she resented his efforts to control her.

The plans for their compound seemed to be taking forever to develop, with a new hurdle from the county at every turn. The O'Malleys tried to explain the complexity of the issues to them—something about critical area designations, property line adjustments and setbacks, and so on—but that didn't assuage their impatience.

Buzz seemed to stick to the sidelines, mostly observing and hanging out on the property, but as far from the group as possible. The constant bickering made him anxious, and although she paid him little attention, he was worried about his mother and that asshole she was living with. He had never cared much for Alan; lately, he had begun to detest the man and fear for his mother's well-being.

One evening, after a communal offering in the courtyard circles, a particularly nasty argument broke out among the four adults while Buzz huddled in his junior-sized yurt.

It began with Alan telling Thorn to get off his ass and get the outhouse cleaned up. Then, a strange thing happened. Perhaps it was the close quarters or the hard work, or maybe it was the culmination of those hours enduring the obnoxious aura that surrounded Alan. Still, whatever the tipping point, Sable joined her brother and sister in an all-out verbal assault on their de facto leader.

After things quieted down, Alan chose to sleep under the stars while Sable slept in their yurt. Thorn and Orla retired to their shelter, Thorn still mumbling about what a dick Alan was.

Buzz stayed in his bed but couldn't sleep; he was so disturbed by the vehemence of the fight. He must have dozed off because he was awakened by the pickup starting sometime after midnight. The others must have been tired because no one else came out, and he eventually went back to sleep.

The following day he awoke to shouts from Thorn. "That fucker took the truck and left us," he screamed.

Sable and Orla came out of their yurts to see what all the noise was about. "Alan took off?" Sable asked.

"Looks that way, the son of a bitch." Thorn was pissed.

"Maybe he went to the store?" Orla asked.

"No, he didn't. He left in the middle of the night." The three looked over at Buzz, who had just entered the clearing.

"How do you know?"

Clothed in a ratty T-shirt and sweat shorts, Buzz looked at the ground, uncomfortable with the attention. "I saw him leave."

"Why didn't you say anything or wake us, Buzz?"

Thorn's accusation didn't help Buzz's confidence. "I dunno ... I fell back asleep."

"Jesus ... Sable, he's your kid. Can't you do anything with him?"

"Leave him alone, Thorn. Buzz, help us get ready for breakfast."

Little was said as they ate breakfast, all seemingly trying to understand where this left them.

"Let's ditch this whole thing and head back to Bellingham." Orla left no doubt as to her preference.

"How about you, Thorn?" Sable assumed the director's duties in Alan's absence.

"I'm with Orla. Screw this woodsy crap; let's get back to civilization and real food and bathrooms."

"Okay, if you two feel that way, I'll go along with you. I like this place, but Alan has soured it for all of us. I can focus on my work there just as well. We'll head out in the morning; I'm sure I can conjure up a sympathetic driver for us by then."

Buzz listened to his mother's plans to abandon their island home but was experiencing the birth of an independent streak that would alter his life's journey.

***

The following morning, on a sparkling, sunny August day, the three siblings packed whatever they could carry and prepared to leave their home, deep in the woods off Lone Lake Road. Always an afterthought even to his mother, Buzz had yet to appear.

"Where's the kid?" Orla asked.

"I'll get him; he's probably still sleeping." Sable crossed the courtyard and opened the door to the half-sized yurt where her son had spent the last three years. She came out holding a piece of paper and shouted her son's name. "*Buzz ... Buzz ...* where are you? Get over here!"

"Sable? What is it?" Orla asked.

"Goddammit ... he left this note. Says he doesn't want to leave with us, and he's staying here. He says not to bother looking for him."

Orla and Thorn, loaded down with their packs, stood silently for several seconds, just looking at Sable. Then Orla asked her sister, "What do you want to do?"

Sable lowered her pack and said, "We've got to try to find him. He's only fifteen years old."

Thorn said, "He knows these woods better than any of us, Sable. If he doesn't want to be found, we won't be able to find him."

"I don't care. He's my son. We can't just leave him." The years of ignoring her son to focus on her witchcraft studies and her relationship with Alan appeared to be replaced by a sudden motherly concern.

They spent most of the morning shouting his name and roaming aimlessly throughout the property before they came to the same conclusion as Thorn: the boy would not be found.

Telling herself that she would return every week to try and find her son, Sable joined the others and walked down the rutted dirt road leading to Lone Lake Road. It may have been possible for her to use her supernatural talents to locate her son, but either by omission or intention, it did not happen. Buzz, at least for the foreseeable future, was on his own.

The three reached the main road, where a somewhat befuddled older gentleman waited in his SUV. He would drive them to Bellingham, then return to his home on South Whidbey without remembering where he'd been or why.

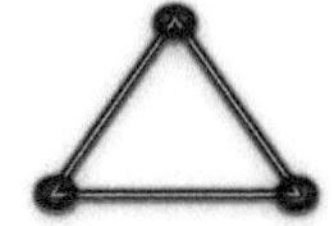

Thirteen

I made it home just before dark, just after five in the Pacific Northwest in February. I couldn't wait to share Wally's research and his suggestion that perhaps witchcraft was a reason for the strangeness surrounding Buzz Aldrin.

Andie hadn't yet returned from her weekly meeting at the University of Washington, so it was up to yours truly to get dinner going. Tonight was easy: heat the frozen Bolognese, put the water on for the pasta, and tear the romaine into pieces for the Caesar salad.

She texted me after driving onto the ferry from Mukilteo, so I knew it would be less than half an hour before she arrived. I built a fire in the river rock fireplace, the only untouched item in the century-old farmhouse I had restored upon my arrival on Whidbey Island.

When I heard her on the porch, I opened the door and hugged her despite her protests about me getting raindrops on the wide-plank fir floors.

"What's all this about? I've only been gone for the day, and you miss me this much?"

"You bet. If you had to spend the day investigating creepy places with Wally Turpin, you'd be happy to see *me* as well."

"What creepy places? The Lone Lake Road thing?"

"Yup; let's get you comfortable and settled in. Then we can talk about the witches."

"The *what?*"

An hour later, we sat at the table sipping the last of the Brunello, feeling stuffed from our Italian indulgence. I told Andie about the history of the Aldrin property and Wally's suspicion that elements of the occult were a possible factor.

"Let me see if I've got this straight. There's a possible missing person, and this odd little fellow lives alone in the woods."

"Correct."

"And this potential missing person is descended from a great-great-grand-mother who was maybe raised by three witches living in a haunted house in San Francisco. Does that sound about right?"

"I suppose so, but it seems a bit far-fetched when you say it like that."

"Hmmm ... it does? Really?"

"All I can say is if you were with us out there, you might see things differently."

"I'm not so sure ..."

"Okay, it's settled. You're coming out there with me tomorrow to show me how my concerns are misplaced."

"Nuh ... unh ..."

"Oh yeah. You've convinced me I need fresh eyes on things, so how about it?"

"Will you stop this nonsense if I go?"

"Sure thing."

"You're on then, Buster. Let's clean this mess up."

***

Because it was a Saturday and we both had the day off, we didn't get things moving until after eight. Andie suggested a breakfast sandwich at the Whidbey Donut Shop, where we bumped into several locals.

Wally was there but in uniform since he was on duty. After telling him our plans, he turned to Andie, wearing his mischievous grin, and said, "You think we're nuts, don't you?"

"Maybe not nuts, just disillusioned. A woman of science such as myself won't be swayed by odd bits of information from the internet, especially those not well-sourced." She loved giving Wally a hard time.

My deputy turned to me and said, "I'll bet your lovely wife will change her tune once she visits the property. Maybe she should spend the night in the astronaut's house."

I enjoyed the friendly rivalry but was interested to see what Andie thought of the strange place, so we took our sandwiches to go and headed into the misty, foggy, forty-degree Whidbey morning.

It was only a fifteen-minute trip to Aldrin's drive leading from Lone Lake Road, and we had barely finished our breakfast by the time we arrived.

"I've driven by here plenty of times and never noticed this road."

"Told you it was a weird place."

"Just because it's hard to see doesn't mean there's something funny going on."

"Mm-hmm ... we'll see."

We turned onto the bumpy, muddy access road and jostled for half a mile, past the KEEP OUT sign, and up to the derelict gate. I looked over at my wife, whose bravado seemed to have dampened ever so slightly.

"It's pretty dark in here, isn't it?"

"Um, yes ... yes, it is." I put the cruiser in park and started to get out to swing the gate aside.

"Where are you going?" Andie's confidence seemed less apparent now.

"Gotta open the gate, hon. Be right back."

After shoving it as far as I could, there was barely enough room to squeak by. Mother Nature's relentless restoration of this forest had already begun to alter the traces of human activity.

We pulled ahead, seeing nothing but trees until we turned right into the small clearing. The headlights suddenly illuminated the pile of stumps and rotting lumber that Buzz Aldrin had called home. The ancient pickup seemed oddly comfortable by the side of the structure.

"Holy shit, what the hell *is* that?"

"That's my buddy Buzz's home."

"You never told me it looked like this."

"I remember trying to, dear, but you said something about me exaggerating." I couldn't help myself. "C'mon, I'll show you around the place."

I went around to her side of the SUV and opened her door, but she seemed reluctant to leave the warmth of the vehicle. "Maybe I should just experience it from here."

"Of course not. If you don't go inside, you won't have all the data you need. Right?"

She unenthusiastically joined me, and we ventured into the claustrophobic little dwelling. I made sure to bring along my Maglite to illuminate the cave-like dump.

Andie stepped gingerly across the pine needle floor and reached for my flashlight. "As long as you got me in here, let's see what's on the shelves."

She looked at the meager display of filthy dishes and utensils and shook her head. "This is disgusting." She saw a small box on one of the shelves and reached for it.

"Maybe we should leave his stuff alone, hon, you know … in case he comes back."

"I thought we were investigating—seeing if there are any clues as to where the little guy might be. No worries, though; the smell is driving me out of here … just wondered what this was." She lifted the top, looked inside, then dropped it and shrieked, "Goddamn, what the fuck *is* this?"

I picked the item up from the floor where it had tumbled out of the little wooden box. Then *I* dropped it, this time on the counter, where I asked my wife to shine the light on it.

"What the hell is this?" I asked her.

"If I'm not mistaken, it's an ear … but a very old one. We used to work on cadavers when I was working on my doctorate, and while none were as old as this, sometimes we'd lose a body part, and it would eventually turn up. When they did, they'd be shriveled up like this—well, not quite like this one, but it's an ear anyway. I'm sure of it."

"Why do you think it's here?"

"No idea; you're the cop. Isn't that your job … you know, detecting?"

I considered it for a moment before making a decision: "Let's put that thing back in the box and take it with us. Maybe someone can figure out who it belongs to."

"Works for me. Now, can we get out of here? The smell is killing me."

I took the little wooden box with the ear in it and allowed Andie to proceed ahead of me out of the smelly dump. When we made it outside, we inhaled deeply, only slightly succeeding in ridding our sinuses of the foul odor.

"Whew, nice place your friend has here."

"Isn't it? I tried to tell you."

"What now?"

"Let's walk that way." I pointed deeper into the forest in the direction Wally and I had traveled. "There's more to see."

Looking hesitant but curious, she followed me past the outhouse and deeper into the woods until we reached the former yurt settlement with the stone circle courtyard.

"This is where Buzz and the others lived?"

"It's what we think, yes."

"You said there were three children from this Eve Aldrin, right?"

"I did … yes, that's what he said." I could see where she was headed and was glad she'd come along. Apparently, world-famous microbiologists were pretty good at sleuthing. At some level, I supposed that was the nature of their job.

"So who was the fourth person? Had to be a guy, right? You know, cuz the kids were two girls and a boy."

"Good catch, Andie. You're right, I'm sure of it."

We walked around the decaying campsite, Andie noticing the three circles and their charred interiors. "Everything looks abandoned except for these circles. It looks as though they've been used recently."

"Yup."

She walked to where the remains of the smallest yurt were and nudged a stick of the collapsed wooden frame with her boot. "You think maybe Buzz lived in this one?"

"We think so. Remember, this was twenty-some years ago. He would have been a youngster then."

She considered this briefly before announcing, "Okay … can we get out of here now?"

I thought it seemed sudden, but I had no objection to leaving this strange property. "You bet. Let's go."

We were quiet until we returned to Lone Lake Road and headed home. "Well … what are your thoughts?"

"I think I'm glad we're not back there."

"And?"

"I have no idea about witches or witchcraft, but I'll admit that is one strange place. It gives me the creeps."

"Mm-hmm, told ya."

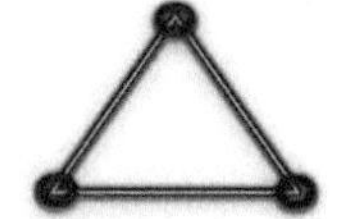

FOURTEEN

After his mother, aunt, and uncle had departed, Buzz exited his hiding place. One of the nearby giant firs had been toppled during a recent winter storm, its roots pulling up tons of earth, creating a cave-like space beneath it.

Because the group always ignored him, he spent most of his days wandering the forest ... observing. He became aware of the wildlife, the trees and plants, and the changing seasons. He watched Alan and the others butcher the deer and how they cooked and preserved it.

Early on, he became aware that his mother was a witch, and he saw the power of her spells. When he asked her about it one day, she told him not to pay any mind, and it was only for the Aldrin women anyway. Still, he *did* pay attention—to her words, offerings to the higher powers in the stone circles, and the talismans she used.

The accidents on Lone Lake Road were her fault, he knew, and when the innocent people stopped dying—just the deer now—he was relieved.

Before they moved to Whidbey Island, he sat at home and watched television with little curiosity about anything beyond it. Now that he had spent three years in the natural world, he had an entirely different outlook.

He saw predators kill, not for pleasure but for sustenance. He understood which plants and berries were edible and which were not. He felt rather than consciously understood when his mother and Alan were at odds and did his best to keep a low profile during those times.

As the months passed, the forest and all that it held became his teacher, quickly replacing the humans he lived with. When he saw Alan leave and then the decision made by his mother and the others, he knew he would not join them. This was his home.

Ten days after he was abandoned, he heard a vehicle coming down the access road. He once again hid under the enormous fallen tree and listened as his mother and aunt called for him.

Buzz had removed his mother's scrolls and incantations from her yurt and several other items he considered important, placed them in his pack and carried them with him until he could find a more permanent place. The two sisters looked through his mother's yurt for several minutes and then through his.

"Maybe he's not here anymore," he heard Orla say.

"Where would he go? Besides, it looks like he's removed some of my things."

"I don't know. Maybe someone found him and gave him a home."

"Don't be silly. Who would give that fat little kid a home?"

When he heard his mother say *that*, he was crushed. He knew he'd always been an afterthought but preferred not to think about it. He waited until they left, confident they wouldn't be back any time soon and this would be his home.

Since it was summer, there were plenty of berries and vegetables from the garden to eat. Some venison jerky was still left behind, but he knew he would have to find a way to get his own meat.

Ultimately, the jerky ran out. He walked the access road until it hit Lone Lake. He walked a half mile south, turned around, retraced his steps, and then walked north until he came upon a recently killed raccoon. He took it back to the yurt camp, butchered it the way he'd seen Alan do with the mule deer, and cooked it for dinner.

It tasted awful. He suspected the damn things lived on other nourishment besides the grass and berries and fruit that the deer seemed to like. He threw what was left away and stood on the step of the yurt, gazing at the circles in the courtyard and thinking back to his mother's incantations.

He recalled her saying her powers were passed on to the eldest daughter in their lineage, but what about after his mother died? *He* was the only child, and based on her attitude toward children, he doubted she would have another. *Maybe I could do it if I practiced*, he thought. He remembered much of what he'd seen and heard her do, and the materials she'd burned in the rings were easily obtained from the forest. Now that he had her scrolls and incantations, was it possible?

Gathering various plants, he scavenged for bird feathers and animal parts and built each circle as he'd seen his mother do. He ignited the fires and recited the verses precisely as his mother had done, then continued until the fires smoldered and died.

After repeating the ceremony every day for almost a week, he began to doubt his success. Then, on the fifth day, he heard the screech of brakes from far-away Lone Lake Road. He ran as fast as his short little legs could carry him and finally reached the end of the access road.

A small SUV was pulled to the side, its front quarter panel smashed in and bloody. As he peered out from the foliage, it pulled away. No deer was in sight, but he felt sure one must have been hit. Cursing his bad luck and lack of witching prowess, he turned to go back to his camp. There, lying in the middle of *his* road, was a tiny fawn, bloody and unbreathing. The poor thing must have returned to the woods and died while he observed the driver's car.

Still in his early teens, the last several years had taught him what he needed to know to survive in the wild. The animal was small, but even after he field-dressed it, it was still heavy. By the time he got it back to camp, he was beat. He hoisted the animal up in a tree to keep it from other wildlife looking for a free meal, then collapsed in his yurt.

When he awoke, it was nearly dark. He visited the outhouse and the well with the hand pump, filling a bucket with water. He would use it for his soup and later for washing up and brushing his teeth. His mother had told him these things were important.

That day, he learned two things. First, either his spell had worked, or he was very fortunate. Second, to survive, he would need some form of transportation. There was no way he could carry anything larger than a raccoon back to his camp, and he was positive *that* wouldn't be on the menu again.

He remembered his mother's final incantation and how she had conjured up a ride back to Bellingham. He wasn't sure how it went, but he tried it anyway. This time, instead of animal parts with the herbs, he threw in a tiny toy truck he'd had since he was a tyke. He spent ten minutes reciting her words repeatedly, then waited until the fire died and the little truck was nothing but a lump of plastic.

Lying in his bed that night, he marveled at the quiet and the peace he felt without the others around him.

When he awoke the following day, he noticed the lump of plastic was missing, and in its place was a miniature toy truck, but different from the one he'd burned. This one was much older and was scratched and dented. He considered it briefly before tossing it aside, convinced that his spell had succeeded only if he were an insect.

He went to the outhouse, did his business, and exited the little shanty. As he was about to return to camp, he glimpsed an unnatural color in a tiny space between the trees. He carefully approached the rusted green object, and his heart skipped a beat. It was a decrepit old pickup wedged into a bramble of blackberries just to the side of the rutted road. And it was a duplicate of the little one he'd found in the circle.

There were no plates on the vehicle. He supposed someone could have ditched it, but he couldn't figure out why. The forest was quiet—he'd know if someone was around.

He inspected the truck's interior and found tattered seats, probably destroyed by rodents. He'd never driven before, but it seemed almost everyone did, so it couldn't be that tough to learn. The door squeaked as he opened it and sat behind the wheel, the exposed springs digging into his backside. There was a key in the ignition on the column. He turned it: Blue smoke and sputtering droplets shot from the exhaust as the little engine fired to life.

Unlike the truck Alan drove, this truck had three pedals and a shifter stick on the floor. He randomly stepped on each one and tried pushing and pulling the stick, grinding the gears, and stalling the vehicle each time.

Eventually, Buzz figured out the machine. He backed it out of the blackberries and moved it to the small clearing near the gate where Alan had parked his truck. The path to the yurt camp was much too narrow to accommodate any vehicle, but he wasn't worried; nobody ever ventured into these woods.

Now that he could move roadkill from Lone Lake Road in his truck, things would be easier. There was still the matter of gasoline and money for the fuel, though. It took him several weeks of trial and error with hundreds of combinations of spells, talismans, and herbs, but finally, he managed to find one that would keep the truck's fuel tank full.

After he had loaded a mature buck who'd been smashed by a minivan into his truck one day, he had an epiphany. Over the summer, he'd bring the carcasses into the clearing inside the gate, quarter them, and lug the pieces to the yurt camp. He'd done so without considering any alternatives.

What if I had my house here, he thought? *The yurts were slowly deteriorating anyway, and I could build my own house.* And so Buzz Aldrin, amateur warlock and contractor, began building a structure that would take years to complete and would never grace the pages of *Architectural Digest*.

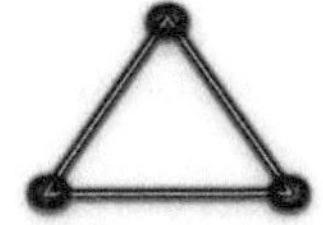

Fifteen

It was Monday morning, and I was back in the office with Wally and Bruce, who was glued to something on his phone. We always started the week with a meeting to ensure we were all on the same page.

With the sheriff of Island County located in Oak Harbor, our team on the island's south end was pretty independent, and both he and I liked it that way. He was a good guy, but politics and optics intruded on his time more than he would have liked. I knew he'd be there, though, if we needed support.

The little conference room was crowded with the three of us and two other deputies. Bruce was responsible for the donuts this week, and everyone appreciated his score from Whidbey Donuts.

Each deputy summarized their activity for the previous week and discussed upcoming events requiring policing. When it was my turn, I covered most of the items Wally had reported and then filled the team in on my visit to the site with Andie.

It seemed Wally had told the others enough about the oddities of the Aldrin place that they appeared to be listening more than usual. I reached into the small paper bag I'd been holding and pulled out the little wooden box. "Also, while investigating the dwelling, we found this."

I placed the item on the table and saw four pairs of eyes glued to the object. "What is it?"

"Why don't you open it and see, Wally?" I couldn't help myself. My deputy was a stocky, muscular fellow with the courage of a lion. He was my best friend, but that didn't mean we didn't take pleasure in seeing the other's discomfort on occasion.

He lifted the cracked wooden cover, peered inside, then jumped up, shouting, "Jesus fucking Christ ... what *is* that?"

The others had backed their chairs away from the table, and even Bruce had abandoned his phone to look at what had spilled from the box as Wally dropped it.

"Why ... it's an ear. Andie found it in Buzz's place. We were wondering why it was there."

"I'm telling you, Rog, that is some weird shit out there. Why are you so interested in the guy?"

I thought for a moment, not exactly sure what to say. "I don't know. Maybe it's because Buzz is a nobody with no one to care about him. It seems he's disappeared, but we're the only people aware of it. I think there *might* have been an abduction, and I'd like to find out if there was. When I met him, sure, he was odd and distrustful, but I think that was because he liked his solitary existence. I think anyone that independent wouldn't willingly give it up."

"Okay, Boss, what's the plan?"

I placed the shriveled appendage back in its box, then left it on the desk. "Since you've got a head start on this, Wally, see what else you can find out about the four others who lived there. See if you can locate them and find out who the guy was who wasn't a member of the Aldrin family. Maybe I'll try Waldron and O'Malley again to see if they remember anything else."

***

Most of the morning was spent filing reports and returning emails and phone calls. I figured my best chance of catching Waldron at the golf club would be early afternoon, and I wasn't mistaken.

"Well, if it isn't my old friend Robbie," he yelled across the bar at me as I walked in the door.

"It's Roger, Bobby ... Roger."

"Yeah, that's what I said ... Roger. You come to buy me another beer?"

"Sure did." I raised my hand to the woman behind the bar, who must have been psychic because she was already topping off a fresh draft.

Waldron was like a kid on Christmas morning as she placed it on a napkin in front of the old-timer. He raised it in thanks, took a big slurp, and gently placed it back on the little white square. "So, what can I do you for, lawman?"

"You remember when we talked about those folks who lived in the woods out on Lone Lake?"

"Course I did; I'm not senile, you know."

"No, of course not. Could you tell me anything else about the four of them? Whatever you remember about how they acted—maybe what the chemistry was like in the group."

The big man closed his eyes and leaned his head back. I knew the routine now, so I let him have all the time he needed. My watch said it had been three minutes, which seemed like thirty, and I was just about to say something when he returned to Earth.

"Like I said before, they gave off some weird vibe, so no one—including me—wanted much to do with them. What I remember is mostly the kid. He was sorta on his own, like the others could've cared less about him."

"Okay ... how about the adults? You said the woman did most of the talking, but what about the guys?"

He closed his eyes again, but this time only briefly. "One of them—he was tall and well-built, I think—seemed to be the leader."

"You said one of the women did the talking, though."

"Right, she did. But she was always looking at this guy like she needed his approval or something."

"Do you remember his name?"

"Nah ... wait a minute ... something short. I remember some astronaut had the same name."

Jesus, again with the goddamn astronauts. "Not Buzz ... like Buzz Aldrin?"

"Nah. I think they called the kid that, though. It was somebody else ... that's it, it was the shepherd."

"The shepherd?" I was beginning to think I'd lost him.

"Don't be obtuse, Roger."

"Obtuse?" *Where the fuck did that come from?*

"Obtuse, you know—slow to understand or dull-witted."

I knew when I was on shaky ground, so I attempted another parry. "You thought it was an astronaut's name?"

He was quiet again, then shouted, "*That's it—Alan.* Alan Shepard."

"His name was Alan Shepard?"

"Arrgh ... no, stupid ... just Alan. I only heard him called Alan."

Stupid? I let it go and was grateful for the additional information. I stood to leave and said, "Thanks a lot, Bobby. You've been a big help."

"You're not leaving because I said you were being obtuse and stupid, I hope?"

This guy was full of surprises; if anyone thought him a fool, it would be at their peril. I could see how clever he might have been as a policeman. "Nope, Bobby. That's just pleasant kibitzing between friends. We're good."

"Friends, huh?" He stood deliberately, with great effort, and offered his hand as he spoke.

"Yeah ... friends." I shook it, tipped my hat to him, and left the club, wondering how much fun it might have been to have Bobby Waldron as a partner.

My next call was one I was hesitant to make. It was to Kevin O'Malley, and although he was my friend, there was no denying that bad things seemed to happen wherever he and his wife went, and he was always in the middle of it. I needed to be very careful about how much I disclosed.

***

We met for coffee at the Crabby Coffee in Freeland and grabbed a table in the courtyard.

"So, to what do I owe the pleasure of this free latte, Roger?"

I knew it would be difficult to keep his nose out of things once I opened this can of worms with O'Malley. "Remember when I asked you about your project off Lone Lake Road?"

"Right. The folks who stiffed us."

"Yes, those. You told me there were four of them and a kid. Two men and two women, correct?"

"Yes."

"Thinking back to them, what can you tell me about the men? You know, your impressions of them."

"You want to tell me what this is all about?"

"Actually, no ... no, I don't. I *can* tell you that as far as I know, there has been no crime. It's just something I'm looking into."

Displaying that grin on his ruddy Irish face that said *I know something is going on*, he surprised me by not badgering me for information. "As I said before, the main contact was the woman, Sable; she always took the lead."

"Yes, I know, but what about the two men? What did they look like? How did they act?"

He looked up to his right, likely trying to picture his former clients. "One of the guys was slightly built and seemed always to be next to the women. Thinking back, his features were similar to those of the two women."

"The other guy?"

"He was much taller and bigger—not fat, just muscular. When I picture them, I remember Sable always watching him, wanting his blessing."

"You remember his name?"

"Nope—don't think I ever heard it. There *was* one thing, though, thinking back to then ..."

"What?"

"I remember that pudgy kid playing with bugs or crickets or something once, and the big guy went over and swatted him and told him to beat it. I remember thinking he was a real asshole. Funny thing, though, none of the others seemed to care or console the poor kid."

Kevin's recollection confirmed my developing picture of Buzz Aldrin's life as a youngster. It was no wonder the kid had ended up living by himself.

"Does that help?"

"It does, Kev, thanks."

"You sure you don't want to confide in your old buddy?"

"Um, yes. I'm sure."

"Okay, but if you need help, you know where to find me."

I laughed and thanked him, and we spent the next half hour sharing recollections of our past escapades. When it was time for me to get going, he gave it another try. "You sure I can't help?"

"Tell you what, Kev, if I find I'm in over my head, and all my deputies and the rest of the law officers on Whidbey Island are confounded, maybe *then—and only then*—I'll come looking for you."

"Cool ... so maybe, right?"

"Bye, Kev."

***

When I returned to the station, I found Wally writing things on a yellow legal pad at his workstation. "You know they have computers that do those things, Wally."

Startled, he looked up and replied, "Yeah, I know, but this helps me think better. Any luck with Waldron and your buddy?"

"Bobby is pretty sure the guy named Alan isn't the brother. He said he was tall and beefy, and O'Malley confirmed it. They both felt that even though Sable Aldrin did the talking, Alan was calling the shots."

"What about you? Find out anything?"

"I found out three incidences of folks named Aldrin in Bellingham. One is a ninety-year-old man living in an assisted living facility. Another is Bernice Aldrin, seventy-five, a former professor at Western Washington University."

"Wally, just tell me ... did you find the ones we're looking for?"

He loved it when he had information he knew I was looking for. "Thirdly, there are three others, but they're all at the same address—there's a Sable, an Orla, and a Thorn Aldrin living in Fairhaven. According to what I've found, they're in their mid-to-late fifties."

"Gotta be them, right?"

"I'd bet on it, Rog. What do we do now?"

Before he could answer, Bruce barged in. "Rog, got a call from some lady off Lone Lake Road. She says there's lots of smoke and bad smells coming from the property across from her. She says you'd know who lives there."

"Shit ... come on, Wally, let's see what's happening."

***

We radioed the fire department en route, just in case they were needed; as it turned out, they were. Arriving at the entrance to Aldrin's drive, we saw plumes of black, stinking smoke boiling out of the forest.

We drove down the access road as fast as we dared and reached the clearing, where Buzz's bizarre dwelling was engulfed in flames. The ratty little truck was nothing but a charred cinder, and it appeared the forest house would soon follow.

Within minutes, the South Whidbey Fire/EMS SUV pulled in behind us, and two officers joined us. Lieutenant Holly Gould stepped forward. "Hey, Roger, is this your doing?" she said with a half smile.

I'd met her at a few functions and appreciated her no-nonsense approach to her job. Her reputation was stellar, and the entire Sheriff's Department knew there would be no loose ends if she were on the job. I dodged her question for a minute and asked, "Hi, Holly. Anything you can do here?"

"Road's too shitty to get our rig in here, but judging by what I'm seeing, it won't make any difference. Whatever this was, it's gone. I'll get some crew in here to mop up and make sure nothing spreads. Hell, everything's so wet, we won't have any trouble. Talk to me ..."

I told her what we knew about the place until her eyes glazed over and she abandoned us to direct her team members. Wally and I looked around as the flames died, unsure what we were looking for.

"Roger ... over here."

We dodged the smoke and walked to where Lieutenant Gould held a five-gallon gas can. "Think we know what started this."

"For sure?"

"I'd bet on it. I smelled it as soon as we arrived. Someone wanted this place burned to the ground. I'm not saying the world isn't better off without it, but it's arson."

"Thanks, Holly. We'll keep at it and see what we can find. Otherwise, we'll catch you later. I'll let you know if we get anywhere."

We walked around the burning structure and headed toward the outhouse and the former yurt encampment. Only a few paces into our trek, Wally grabbed my arm. "Rog, take a look." He pointed to a tire track in the mud only a few yards from the smoldering pickup. "This looks fresh, right?"

I agreed and wondered what they were doing on this side of the burning mess. "You took some shots of those tracks we saw here last week, didn't you?"

"Yup."

"Let's get some of these and see if they're identical. The tread looks similar, but we'll need the state lab's help to identify them."

Wally spent a few minutes getting pictures from various angles before we continued to the yurt settlement. Except for the stone circles, it appeared undisturbed from the last time we'd been here.

"Looks like someone's been doing a little cooking."

"I don't think so, Wally; these fire pits are more than places to cook. Why three of them, and why in a perfect triangle? If it were cooking, they'd only need one. No, I'm guessing they're for some ritual or spell or something."

"So you're buying the witch thing?"

"I'm not sure if I am, but something strange is going on, and I bet if we find Buzz, we'll get some answers."

"You mean if he's still alive."

"Yeah ... if he is. Bag some of that ash from the circles and we'll have the lab look at it. Maybe we'll get lucky."

Retracing our steps, we found Buzz's former home was now a smoking pile of debris with several firefighters surrounding it, daring any sparks to escape into the forest. We said our goodbyes and thanks to Holly and returned to the office. This case—or whatever it was—had my attention, and I had a feeling it wasn't going away quietly.

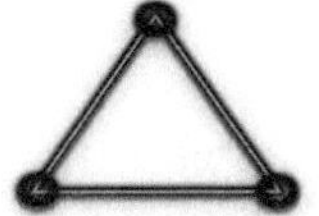

Sixteen

I t always seemed more effective to pay a visit to folks I wanted to interview rather than attempt to get them on the phone. Most people are without landlines, and too often, a call to their cell phone could be misinterpreted as someone selling something.

I left the office early the following morning and headed north for the ninety-minute trek to Bellingham. Wally had a couple of burglaries to follow up on, so I was solo on this trip. The weather was cold but sunny, a rarity during February, and the drive was exhilarating. Wisps of fog dotted the landscape as I wound through Deception Pass and skirted Pass Lake on my way across Fidalgo Island.

The rest of the drive was uneventful, and I arrived in Bellingham a little before noon. The village of Fairhaven, on the city's southwest side, boasts century-old structures turned into chic eateries and coffee shops. Throughout the years, it has been known for its bohemian lifestyle, but more recently, its charm and livability have made it one of the most desirable places to live in this upper northwest corner of the state.

Arriving at the address Wally had given me, I was surprised to see a large two-story Victorian home at the end of Wilson Street. Surprised because it was the only one of that style on the street, and although it appeared well cared for, the shrubs and trees practically obscured the lower level. Their concern for maintaining their landscaping appeared near the bottom of their priority list.

I went through piles of leaves and fallen branches from the winter storms, climbed the six steps to the front landing, and engaged the brass knocker on the eight-foot, jet-black, six-panel door. The sound seemed to echo from the other side of the entrance.

Thirty seconds later, I gave the ring in the lion's mouth another whack against its back plate and waited again. After a full minute, I heard the faint sounds of footsteps clicking against a hardwood floor, increasing in volume until they stopped on what I presumed was the other side of the door.

"What do you want?" The reedy, high-pitched reply left little doubt that my visit was neither expected nor desired.

I briefly held my credentials to the tiny peephole and said, "My name is Deputy Roger Wilkie from Island County. I'd like to ask you a few questions."

"About what?"

"You own some property on Whidbey Island that I'd like to talk to you about."

"What about it?"

Yelling through the thick door wasn't what I had in mind, so I tried another tack. "It's about Buzz; something may have happened to him."

I heard several bolts sliding, and the imposing door opened about a foot; it was enough for me to see who was on the other side. The woman was tall. I was just under six feet; she was at least three inches taller and had to be considerably older than my fifty years. If she *were* a witch, she was perfectly cast. Her parchment-like skin and hawkish nose would have been a severe shortcoming in her Match.com photos.

"Are you Sable Aldrin?"

"Yes."

"Is Buzz Aldrin your son?"

A look of regret seemed to pass as quickly as it appeared. "He is, yes."

"Have you seen him lately?"

Her sunken eyes looked down for several seconds. She tucked a lock of shoulder-length gray hair behind her substantial ear and answered, "No. I haven't seen him for a very long time."

"Would you mind if I came in for a few minutes? I have some other questions that I think you can help with."

"Follow me." She turned and headed down a dark hallway, leaving me to close the door, which I did—very slowly.

The interior of the house was unpleasant for a multitude of reasons. With dark, stained, intricate millwork, wood floors best described as chocolate, and lighting that only bats would approve of, my discomfort meter was red lining. As if this weren't enough, a cloying odor of decaying organic matter amplified by a temperature above eighty made me wish I had stayed on the porch.

She led me to a high-ceilinged parlor furnished with a lumpy sofa and two Queen Anne chairs facing. She took one of the chairs, leaving me the other, since another woman and a man occupied the sofa.

"This is my sister, Orla, and my brother, Thorn." I stayed where I was and nodded at the two seated across from me. The woman seemed much shorter than her sister and several years younger. She had the same skin tone but was more fortunate in the facial feature department. Her nose was unremarkable, and her wide-set eyes might have made her reasonably attractive in her younger years.

Thorn, on the other hand, was a dead ringer for Bela Lugosi, assuming the vampire had worn jeans, a flannel shirt, and a Mariners baseball cap. Neither of the siblings said a word, although I did get a slight nod and a hint of a smile from Orla.

"We've been together all our lives, and even though it's my name on the tax rolls, we share ownership. Now, tell me about Buzz." Sable got right down to business.

I told her about meeting Buzz and our suspicions that he was missing. When I got to the part about the fire at Buzz's home, she appeared surprised that he even *had* a house on the property. She only interrupted my narrative when I mentioned that Buzz had told me he'd inherited the property from his *daddy*.

"First," she said, "he did *not* inherit the property from his *daddy*; it's still in my name. When we're gone, he will inherit it, but that asshole he calls a daddy will never be in the picture."

The disgust in her tone was mirrored by a grunt of affirmation from her brother. Her distaste for the father of her son seemed a more powerful emotion than her concern for Buzz.

I paused momentarily to catch my breath in the fetid, sweltering room before asking, "What can you tell me about his father? Is it Alan?"

"It is. We lived together until we left Whidbey Island." She told me what I mostly knew about the yurts and their attempts to build a private compound. She related the events that led to their breaking up and how they couldn't find Buzz when it came time to leave.

"So you just left a teenage kid in the woods? On his *own*?" It wasn't a proper interviewing technique to raise my voice, but I lost control for a minute.

Sable looked at me with fierce eyes. "Do not judge us. You have no idea about this family or who we are. Buzz was young, but he knew the forest and was happy there. He was never happier than in those woods."

I resisted the temptation to tell her who I *suspected* they were or that if she had been a better mother, maybe Buzz wouldn't have had to retreat to the forest. But she was right; it wasn't my place to pass judgment—unless, of course, someone broke the law.

I decided to go in another direction. "What can you tell me about Alan? Where he is? When did you last see or hear from him? Do you think he could have something to do with Buzz's disappearance?"

Before answering, Sable looked first at her brother and then at Orla. Thorn nodded to her as if granting permission.

"Buzz is the only first-born descendant from his great-great-grandmother who hasn't been a girl."

"Okay?"

"Unlike most families, ours has ... traditions, let's call them ... that are unique. They are passed on to the eldest daughter at a certain age, but it is not a simple thing. The daughter must study and practice her craft and, like anything else, eventually she becomes proficient at it."

"Um ... okay." I was beginning to feel uncomfortable, but maybe it was just the smell and the temperature.

"When Alan lived with us, he saw the possibilities my ... uh, craft ... might provide. He encouraged me to use my talents in a way that enriched him and, I guess, us too. Sometimes unplanned things happened that were unfortunate while I was, um ... studying and learning.

"Anyway, when we moved back here, I stopped practicing after a while. We're comfortable with my trust and the inheritance we got from our mother. People leave us alone, and we keep to ourselves, reading and growing old together."

"I think I understand, but what about Alan? And what's his last name, if you don't mind?"

"Alan Becker is an opportunist and a prick. About a year after we moved back, he attempted to reconcile. I told him I wanted nothing to do with him and to leave us alone. He threatened to expose some things that happened on Whidbey Island unless I supplied him with the trappings of luxury that he thought he deserved.

When I told him to go ahead, that nobody would believe him anyway, he said he would tell the world about my family and our ... skills.

"I did as he asked for a long time—he only came around a few times a year. After a while, I found it more difficult to, um ... procure what he wanted. Finally—and this was a few months ago—nothing I tried would work anymore. It was as if I no longer had the gift.

"He came by and told me he'd researched our family and traced it back to some Haida Indian girl. Then he started asking about Buzz. Alan insisted that since I could no longer give him what he wanted, maybe Buzz might have learned how to do ... things."

Could these people be descended from witches? Maybe the heat is making me delirious. "Is that possible? I mean about Buzz; could he have learned your ... uh ... craft?"

Sable took her time, carefully choosing her words. "I don't know. If so, he would be the first male to do so—of course, he's the first male born in the family." She looked at Thorn and corrected herself. "Sorry, Thorn, I meant the *first-born* male."

Her brother just smiled, obviously taking no offense. Then *he* spoke. "Alan only cares about himself and will do anything to get what he wants."

"Which is what?"

"Money ... money and land. He was always after us to give him the Whidbey property, but there's a caveat in our inheritance that forbids it leaving the family as long as there is a living member," Thorn replied.

"Any idea where he could be?"

Sable answered. "No idea. He could be anywhere in the Northwest. Is Buzz really missing?"

I sensed a hint of motherly concern poking through. "Yes—yes, he is."

"Will you let us know if you find him?"

I wasn't sure how to answer, so I said, "If and when I see him, I'll say we spoke and that you were wondering about him. It'll be his call to let you know, okay?"

Sable took a deep breath, probably thinking things I'd have no clue about. She said that would be fine and stood to show me out. I said goodbye to Orla and Thorn and then to Sable at the door.

When I finally reached the porch and the door closed, I grasped the rail and breathed huge swallows of fresh air. February in Washington had never tasted so good. Then I remembered something I had forgotten to ask.

I hated to go back into the house, so, hoping I could get an answer from on the porch, I once again used the brass knocker. This time, Sable opened the door after only a few seconds.

"Something you forgot?"

"Yes—the three stone rings outside the yurts. What were they used for?"

"Cooking, of course."

"Um ... no, I don't think so. You wouldn't need three for cooking; they're laid out in a perfect triangle. If you tell me the truth, it may help my investigation."

Sable took a few seconds and seemed to reach a decision. "I used those circles when I was practicing. After I became more proficient, they were only used once in a while, when we ... uh ... when we needed something."

I'd come to the brink once more, so I thought, *Screw it, I'm gonna ask the question.* "Sable, are you a witch?"

She looked through me rather than at me with coal-black eyes that would make Genghis Khan weep. "What do you *think*, Deputy?"

Then she turned and closed the door, leaving me wishing I had chosen another line of work.

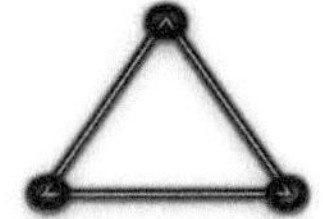

Seventeen

I spent a few more hours in Bellingham at the local police department trying to locate Alan Becker without success. They were aware of him, however. His reputation as a philanderer and an opportunist was well documented, and the detective I spoke to referred to him as a serial douchebag.

The afternoon drive back to Freeland was as lovely as the morning's, but my meeting with the Aldrins had me preoccupied and slightly unsettled. I spoke with Wally during the trip but was hesitant to tell him everything I had learned. I knew he could tell something was bothering me, and I appreciated that he would let me get to it when I was ready.

I arrived home as the sun was setting over Lone Lake and remembered that this day was one of Andie's UDub days, so it would be another hour before she arrived.

Throwing my hat onto the hall tree just off the entrance, I glanced at the mirror over the console table and was surprised at what I saw. My shortish hair seemed to be grayer than when I'd left this morning, and my usually tanned but slightly weathered complexion seemed to have paled. Even my handsome green eyes—Andie's words, not mine—appeared dimmer and hooded.

I convinced myself it was just because I was tired from the trip and had nothing to do with the strangeness of the participants. I showered and shaved and felt a little better. We'd made a large pot of chicken chili several days before, so I put the leftovers on a simmer, wrapped some cornbread in foil, and put it in the oven to warm, then turned on the local news.

I must have dozed off, because the next thing I heard was the door closing and then Doctor Andie Saunders embracing me.

"How's the famous Whidbey Island Deputy?" she asked, still holding on to me.

"He's happy you're home."

As I spoke, she pulled back to look at me, a look of concern crossing her face. "Roger ... you okay?"

"Sure ... of course I am."

"You look ... I don't know, like something's bothering you."

If she thought something was bothering me, then maybe it was. "Let me get you a glass of wine, Andie. I want to tell you about a very strange day."

I poured each of us a glass. Then we sat on the sofa facing the fireplace while the aromas of cumin and cornbread invading the space brought a measure of comfort I sorely needed. I told her where I'd been and who I'd met with. I did my best to describe the meeting at the Aldrins', but my portrayal sounded wooden, even to me.

"This bothered you, yes?"

"Very much so. I mean, they were cordial folks but odd in a way I've never experienced. The house smelled funky and had to be a thousand degrees in there." I shivered at the thought.

"Tell you what, big boy, let's grab some food and come back in front of the fire and relax. You can put the hockey game on, and if that doesn't distract you, nothing will."

I'm not sure what I ever did to deserve this woman who always seemed to know the right things to do and say. By the time the game ended—Kraken won in overtime—I had forgotten about the day's activities and felt much more myself. We called it a night, and I slept fitfully, with Sable's penetrating eyes waking me, it seemed every thirty minutes.

I rose earlier than usual and left Andie sleeping. I told Wally to meet me at the office at seven to talk and promised I'd bring him a breakfast sandwich from Whidbey Donuts.

"Food first, Boss." Wally got right to business as soon as I walked into the office.

We were quiet as we wolfed down the delicious combination of eggs, cheese, and sausage on the soft brioche bun. He finished first, went into the kitchenette to fetch coffee for both of us and returned, placing mine in front of me and looking expectant.

"Talk to me, my sensei."

I related the events of the previous day and my impressions of the Aldrin family. To his credit, interruptions were limited to burps and slurps of coffee, Wally choosing to wait until I had finished before saying anything. I ended my report by telling him what I'd learned from the BPD.

"We got us a coven of witches then, right?" Leave it to Wally to cut to the chase.

"I didn't say that."

"Sounds like it to me. I told you so, Boss."

"I don't know whether I believe in that stuff, Wally, but they sure were strange. Now we know that this Becker is Buzz's father, and his reputation is, let's say, less than admirable. Let's do a deep dive on this guy and see if we can locate him."

The mission now clearly defined, Wally couldn't wait to sink his teeth into it. "I'll see what I can find; there's gotta be a trail somewhere."

As he stood to get to work, I thought of something. "Hey, Wally?"

"Yeah?"

"Anything back yet on that ash we collected from those stone rings at the yurt site?"

"Nope. Supposed to be this afternoon, though. I'll let you know as soon as. Kay?"

I said yes and headed to my office to clear the pile of routine reports that had accumulated in my absence. By the time I came up for air, the overcast day had disappeared, and it was once again dark. With less than ten hours of daylight, there were times when I longed for the sunny days of Southern California, but they were fleeting. The life I now lived on this sliver of land in the middle of Puget Sound was one I cherished and would never give up.

Wally popped in just as I was tidying things up on my desk. "Hey, Boss, got the report back from the lab on that stuff we bagged from the yurt site."

"And?"

"A bunch of stuff you'd expect and a few things you wouldn't."

"Wally ... just tell me."

"There was the usual stuff—leaves, twigs, and such—but there were traces of a number of herbs and spices and a few animal parts. Based on the highest concentration, the list goes like this: nettles, parsley, yarrow, mugwort, ginger, cinnamon, sage, and a few others. The animal residue was mostly deer hooves and ears."

I wasn't sure what to make of the results, but I knew they were beyond my understanding. "Hey, Wally?"

He looked up from his report. "Yes?"

"You know any witches on the island?"

"Seriously?"

"Yeah ... it seems like we're in over our heads. I've heard groups of Wiccans are on the island, and some consider themselves witches. Maybe we should talk to them and see if they can shed some light on our problem."

"Well ... yes, I've heard there are."

"Good. Tomorrow you can find out who they are and pay a few of them a visit."

"Me?"

"Yup."

"I don't know. I've got a bunch of month-end reports to finish."

"No problem, I'll get Bruce to help you with that."

He looked around as if there were a lifeline somewhere. "Really, Rog?"

"Yeah. I'm getting a bad feeling about this whole thing, and we need to know what we don't know."

He was quiet for a few seconds, then looked up at me. "You know how sometimes you get excited and look forward to the next day? You know ... you have trouble sleeping and everything ..."

"I do, yes."

"Well ... I'm gonna have trouble sleeping tonight, but it's not because I'm looking forward to tomorrow."

I laughed as I stood to leave and said, "It'll be fine, Wally; I'm sure they're people like you and me. Well ... maybe not *just* like us, but probably normal in most ways."

"Yeah, sure they are, Rog; see you tomorrow ... no, wait ..."

"What is it?"

"Remember those photos we took of the tire tracks at the astronaut's place?"

"I do."

"We got something back on those. The tread is from a Cooper off-road tire used on pickups and SUVs. They're popular with serious off-roaders but don't sell tons of them because they're expensive. They go for almost six hundred bucks a pop."

"Geez, I can see why. Anything unique about them?"

"There's wear on the outside of one of the tires that's abnormal, so maybe an alignment issue with the vehicle."

"This helps, Wally; go home and get some rest so you'll be ready for a fun day tomorrow."

He flipped me the bird on his way out the door.

Eighteen

Buzz had no idea where he was ...

When Alan—he had never thought of him as his father—had shown up almost a week ago, he didn't know what to make of it. It had been twenty years since he'd last seen him, but he hadn't changed much. Even though he was pushing sixty, his six-three muscular frame showed little deterioration. His hair was mostly gray, no longer shoulder length, and now somewhat receding. The arrogant smirk was just as he remembered it and still made Buzz a little queasy whenever he was around the man.

He heard the rumble of the F-250 Super Duty King Ranch Edition pickup before it reached his gate. Grabbing his shotgun, he stood to the side and waited until the driver dismounted. He knew immediately who it was.

"Hey, Buzz, is that you? Last time I was here, you were just a snotty little kid."

"What do you want, Alan?"

"Is that any way to greet your old man? I was in the neighborhood and thought I'd stop by and see how you're doing." As he spoke, he walked to where Buzz, who had lowered his weapon, stood.

It was as if the twenty-plus years had vanished as Buzz's confidence was shattered in the man's presence. While he stared at the ground, he felt Alan move closer, then the click of a revolver cocking as a hand grabbed the barrel of his shotgun.

"Let's put this away, shall we?"

He let go of the gun while Alan steered him back to his home.

"Goddamn, would you look at *this*. You build this all by yourself?"

Buzz offered no answer.

It looked as though Alan wanted to see what the inside held, but his height didn't allow him to enter, even if he stooped over. He appeared upset at this development, then seemed to accept it.

"Turn around, hands behind you," he said to Buzz, who did as he was told. He felt the zip-tie tighten around his wrists.

"We're going on a little trip. Your mother isn't much help anymore, and I have a sneaking suspicion you might be able to help me."

He hadn't heard the word "mother" for over twenty years. He thought about her infrequently, but she was his mother, and a tiny place in his heart still wondered about her. If she no longer had to deal with *this* asshole, then all the better.

"Where are you taking me?"

"You'll see ... or maybe you won't. We've got a long ride ahead of us, and I'd rather not have you stinking up my ride. Let's put you in the bed under that camper top. There's an old mattress in there, and the tinted windows will keep you hidden—not that anyone will care."

Alan helped Buzz climb inside—not an easy task with his hands behind his back—then closed the tailgate and locked it from the outside. With the camper's rear window still open, he tossed in a water bottle and started to close it. "How am I gonna drink that with my hands tied?"

"We'll be on the road for a few hours. If you can't get those ties off by then, well ... you don't deserve a drink." With that, he slammed the window down and locked it as well.

Buzz had driven the old Courier once in a while but hadn't been in a confined space for over two decades. The rugged suspension of the truck jostled him mercilessly as Alan made his way to Lone Lake Road. It was better once he was on the paved surface, but the heavy-duty pickup wasn't designed for passenger comfort—at least when lying in its bed.

He had lived alone in the forest for so long that he'd never considered how he looked or smelled. Now, enclosed in the truck bed, he began to see why the few people he'd come across—the deputy for one, and sometimes folks on the road when he confiscated a dead or wounded deer—turned away or even held their breath. Without a shower or indoor water, his grooming habits were negligible. Once a week he would heat water from his well and perform a sort of sponge bath. It was enough to keep his weathered skin free of insects and minor infections, but judging by the reactions of others, there was still the issue of body odor. And now, confined in the small enclosure, he was beginning to see why.

His wardrobe was limited to tattered jeans, flannel shirts, work boots, and filthy but warm fleece jackets. He'd wear them until they were no longer useable, then throw them away and procure another set. Although his skills in witchcraft were considerable, he never considered conjuring up anything new. Instead he was content to find a package of used clothing by the side of the road, sometimes alongside a deer carcass recently deposited by a surprised driver doing fifty miles per hour down Lone Lake Road.

Soon they were on a freeway, and the drone of the off-road tires made him drowsy. He'd managed to saw off the zip-tie by rubbing it against a tie-down anchor; then he'd polished off half the water in the bottle. Now, exhausted from stress and fear, he stretched out on the old mattress, his wrists no longer tied behind him. He fell asleep instantly and dreamed of his tiny home in the forest.

When he awoke, there was only silence. The truck was no longer moving, and it was dark. He heard the crunch of boots along the side of the truck, then a key being inserted in the lever on the camper window. As it rose, he saw Alan's grin, and once again, his gut clenched.

"Rise and shine, stinky. *Goddamn*, it smells in here. Gonna take me forever to fumigate this thing. So you got the ties off, too, huh?"

Buzz said nothing as the tailgate was lowered and he climbed down from the truck. The only sound was the faint whistling of fir boughs as a light north wind chilled the air. He knew the sounds of the forest and was sure they were far from the echoes of civilization.

"Get in front of me and follow the trail," Alan directed as he illuminated the path with a powerful LED flashlight.

"You're gonna scare the animals with that thing."

"Like I give a shit. How about you shut up and keep walking until I tell you to stop?"

It seemed they were walking uphill most of the time, and after twenty minutes, the spill of light revealed a decaying log cabin emerging from the shadows.

"Okay, Buzz, inside now."

He climbed onto the porch with Alan close behind and pushed the door open, the hinges squealing in protest. The flashlight revealed the unexpected.

The interior was a large room with a two-story vaulted cedar ceiling. Half the room was comfortably furnished, with a small kitchenette off to the side. The other half was partitioned off by a newly framed eight-foot wall accessed by a narrow steel door secured by two large sliding bolts. Plywood covered both sides of the wall to a height of four feet, with the remaining four feet secured by galvanized hog wire and capped with a four-by-four wrapped with razor wire.

Becker slid the bolts aside, shoved Buzz inside, and then bolted the door again. "I'll be back in a few minutes."

He heard his captor go outside and wondered what was happening. Without warning, the cabin's interior was bathed in light, and ten minutes later, Alan returned.

"Just because we're in the middle of the woods doesn't mean we can't have electricity, right, Buzz? I put that generator in an insulated building way out back so you couldn't hear it. Wasn't that thoughtful of me?"

Buzz said nothing, still trying to process what was going on. He took in his surroundings and was surprised at what he saw. There was a comfortable-looking bed against the wall, a toilet and sink on the other side of the room, and a small refrigerator next to a wall cabinet.

"You have no idea how long it took me to find and modify this place. I hope you appreciate my efforts."

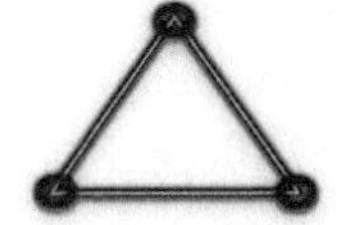

Nineteen

Wally walked into the office, as animated as I'd ever seen him. I'd arrived early to try to do a little more research into Alan Becker but had had no luck so far.

"Hey, Roger, guess what."

"I give up; what?"

"I spent yesterday afternoon with a bunch of witches."

"Oh, and how did that work out for you?"

"They were pretty normal folks in most ways. I kinda liked them."

"But ..."

"They were gentle folks. They view religion and spirituality differently; otherwise, they raise kids, have jobs, and live peacefully. They reminded me a little about how Native Americans feel about the Earth and the afterlife. They feel the Divine is present in nature, and the flora and fauna are sacred. Most of 'em are environmentalists, too."

"You did say *witches*, didn't you?"

"Well ... that's where there's some disagreement among the group. These folks get along wonderfully, but there are as many flavors as Ben and Jerry's. Some believe in the afterlife, and some don't. Some consider themselves witches and warlocks, and some Wiccans. Some have seances, say they connect with those passed on, and others don't buy it. The witches say they can cast spells and practice their craft constantly, but I sensed some doubt from others."

"Bottom line?"

"No fucking idea."

"Not helpful."

Wally fidgeted for a few seconds, playing with the coffee cup he'd walked in with. "I'd say mostly it's a group that believes in a different kind of religion, and there are some fringe players that believe in witchcraft. Can these fringe players cast spells and do magic? I can't answer that, but some believe they can if they work at it hard enough."

"Did you ask if anyone knew anything about Buzz or the group from twenty years ago?"

"I did. A couple said they'd heard some scuttlebutt about it, but that was all. When I asked one of the witches if it was possible to cause accidents and have deer killed on demand, she said it was conceivable if the magic was strong enough."

I shook my head, trying to erase the image of the three witches from *Macbeth* and wondering what the hell I'd gotten myself into. "So there's a possibility that Buzz *is* a witch or warlock or whatever, at least according to your new friends."

"Yes, and from what you told me about your meeting with his mother, it sounds like he might be."

"Do you agree there's a good chance this Becker kidnapped Buzz?"

"I do, Roger; I think it's more than a chance. He's either taken him or done something with him."

"According to Buzz's mother, Becker wondered if the little guy could provide the same services she had. Let's assume he's got him tucked away somewhere."

"What do you want me to do?"

"Find Becker. Start with where he's been and go from there. The Bellingham Police might be able to help, so check there first. Take what they've got on him and dig deeper into it. Buzz might be a little weird and eccentric, but if he's been taken against his will, we need to find him."

***

Wally spent the next eight hours alternating between his computer and his phone. Just when he thought he'd found something, his follow-up proved otherwise. At four-thirty he received a callback from a detective with the BPD.

"Deputy Turpin?"

"Speaking."

"This is Detective Kate Mahoney from BPD. You were trying to locate an Alan Becker?"

"I am, yes."

"Well ... I don't know where he is now, but I know where he was living."

"Please ... tell me."

"He was renting a house on Lake Whatcom up until last week. I'll text you the address. The realtor says he packed up and left. She also said he left the place a mess, and there was no way he was getting his deposit back."

"Did he leave a forwarding address—you know, for his deposit?"

"No, he didn't. I guess that's another reason he won't be getting it. What are you looking at this guy for?"

Wally wasn't sure about sharing, but the detective had done the legwork, so he told her. "We think he kidnapped someone—his kid."

"Damn, we knew he was dodgy, but kidnapping? How old was his kid?"

"We think late thirties."

"Huh? Why would he kidnap his adult kid? Is he disabled, or does his wife have money or something?"

"The kid isn't married and has no money. It's something else."

"You're sounding a little evasive, Deputy. You know, if you share, maybe I can help." Mahoney almost sounded as if she was teasing him. He liked it.

He made a decision. "I'll tell you what, Detective, I'll be in Bellingham tomorrow, and if you're around, I'll fill you in. It's a strange story, believe me."

"I'll take you up on that, and it's Kate. What time?"

"I should be there by eleven. We can interview the property manager and take a look at the house. I'll see you then, and it's Wally."

He arrived in uniform at the Bellingham police station at 10:45 the following day and asked the desk sergeant for Detective Mahoney.

"Take a seat, Deputy, and I'll get her for you."

He busied himself with his phone for ten minutes before he heard the lobby door open. "Deputy Turpin? I mean, Wally?"

The woman speaking wore jeans, sneakers, and a windbreaker with BPD on the right sleeve. Her brown hair was cut in a short bob, which highlighted the smattering of freckles across her cheeks. Intelligent green eyes, a slightly upturned nose, and porcelain skin confirmed her Irish heritage. Her slender yet well-toned physique made it clear that she spent some serious gym time, and for the first time since he could remember, Deputy Turpin was speechless.

"Wally ... it *is* you, right?"

He bolted upright, extended his hand, and answered, "Yes ... yes, that's me ... Wally. And ... you're ... Kate?"

"You seem surprised."

"I, uh ... wasn't expecting, um ..."

"You weren't expecting what?"

"I just thought ... ah, shit. You surprised me, that's all."

Mahoney smiled from ear to ear. Her looks were often a disadvantage when her superiors—mostly men—thought she was just a pretty face. Now, though, the embarrassment she saw on Turpin's face was endearing. She had liked his voice on the phone and was glad he'd turned out to be something other than the mansplaining cops she frequently ran into.

"Come on, Wally, let's go talk to some folks. I'll drive."

***

The drive to the northeast shore of Lake Whatcom took a half hour, but rather than take a police cruiser, the Bellingham detective took her vehicle, a yellow 1969 Mustang GT. Wally had seen a few of them at classic auto shows but had never ridden in one and was still mesmerized by the rumble of the 351-cubic-inch engine as they pulled into the winding driveway of a lakefront mansion.

The homes along this section of the lake were perched on generous lots, most exceeding an acre, and none went for less than three million. Pulling under the porte-cochère, a nattily attired fortyish woman exited the ten-foot entry door to greet them. She looked curiously at the couple arriving in the celebrated American sports car.

"Detective Mahoney?" she asked as they climbed from the Mustang.

"Yes—thanks for meeting us here. This is Deputy Turpin from Island County; he's working with me on this, or I should say *I'm* working with *him*."

"I'm Terri Johnson. My company has managed this property for over ten years, and this is the first time we've ever had any problems with renters."

Mahoney joined Wally as they shook hands with the realtor. "You said the tenant was Alan Becker?"

"Yes. He's lived here for five years.. He was late with the rent occasionally, but other than that, no problems. Well ... we did receive a few calls from the neighbors about loud music once or twice, but most of these homes are empty during winter. Please come inside and I'll show you how he left it."

They entered the mid-century mansion and were staggered by the smell of rotting garbage and rodent feces.

"Jesus," Mahoney said, holding her arm up to her nose. "What the fuck is that smell?"

The realtor seemed a little surprised by the detective's language, but Wally knew how cops communicated and, frankly, appreciated the honest appraisal.

"It seems Becker became averse to taking out the garbage and trash the last month or so. He let it pile up where all the waste cans overflowed, and the mice and rats had a field day. I've hired a cleaning company *and* an exterminator to handle this mess."

The enormous great room had soaring sixteen-foot cedar ceilings and was anchored at one end by a ledge stone fireplace wall and at the other by sweeping views of Lake Whatcom. It was also the repository for dirty clothes, piles of semi-occupied pizza boxes, and enough beer cans and wine bottles to have hosted a tailgate party for the entire Seahawk fan base.

"Man, what a mess. This place is beautiful, and this asshole does this to it." Wally finally found his voice.

They hadn't moved from their observation point in the foyer and seemed reluctant to do so. "What about the rest of the place?" Wally asked.

"Just like this; the bathrooms are worse," answered the rental agent.

"What can you tell us about Becker?" Wally could tell Mahoney was anxious to vacate the premises.

"Not much. The credit check was a little sketchy, but he doubled the deposit, and his references checked out, so we thought he'd be okay. And he was for years until just recently."

Wally had a thought. "Do you remember who he used for references?"

"I've got it right here; I brought the paperwork."

She put on reading glasses, fumbled with a fistful of pages, and came up with what she was looking for: "Here … on the application … he listed Sable Aldrin and Orla Aldrin as references. We checked them out, and they said Becker was fine."

Not surprised by this revelation, Wally asked about the neighbors, especially those with complaints.

"That would be the Montgomerys; they live next door. They usually winter in Palm Springs, but they both got Covid last year, so they're staying home this winter."

"Thanks for your help, Terri," Mahoney said. "I think we'll try to talk to the neighbors. Good luck with the mess here; it looks like you'll need it."

They left the property and drove two hundred yards to the driveway to the south. The New England–style home was not as flashy as the one they'd just left, but the view was spectacular and the grounds were well manicured.

As they walked to the front door, Kate turned to Wally and said, "You seemed to recognize those references on the Becker application."

"I did. Those people are part of the story. Let's grab a coffee when we're finished here, and I'll fill you in on the rest of the details." She still looked questioning as they rang the doorbell.

It was less than ten seconds before a gentleman, likely in his mid-seventies, opened the door. "Yes?"

They introduced themselves and said they'd like to ask a few questions about the man's former neighbor. The slender, gray-haired Mr. Montgomery nodded and invited them inside. "I'm glad that guy's not living there anymore. He was an obnoxious asshole—I'm sorry, please excuse my French."

He noticed the two law officers exchanging knowing looks and nodded at the leather sofa in the great room. "Please have a seat and ask your questions."

Wally took the lead. "Maybe you can just tell us your impressions about Alan Becker. We know he lived here for several years, and we're trying to locate him. He seems to have disappeared."

Montgomery sat in an upholstered chair across from them and told them what it was like having Becker for a neighbor. "At first he stopped over and introduced himself, seemed like a nice guy. He spent lots of money on toys and cars, but when we asked what he did for a living, he muttered something about consulting and then changed the subject.

"There always seemed to be a party going on. They played loud music and left crap all over the place until the HOA made him clean it up. He heard we were the ones who complained, which only made him more annoying. He'd sit in his garage and rev up that giant pickup he even parked on the lawn wherever he felt like it; the sound was deafening. It got so bad we hated living here. We heard he left the place a mess; is that true?"

"Yes, it is. Do you have any idea where he might have gone?" Kate steered the conversation in another direction.

"No, but I don't care either, as long as we never see him again."

They thanked him, left the house, and were quiet until inside the car. "I guess it's safe to say the Montgomerys won't be missing Becker anytime soon," said Kate as she got behind the wheel.

"Yeah, seems like the neighbor from hell. His description of Becker fits with what we know, too."

"Which you're going tell me about, right?"

"I am. Let's stop at that Starbucks we passed on the way here."

After picking up their lattes, they chose a table near the window, and Wally told the Bellingham detective the entire story. When he started with Buzz Aldrin, his home in the woods, and his possible abduction, she first appeared amused, then skeptical.

"Come on ... you're telling me a guy named after an astronaut lives off the land alone in the woods?"

"Hold on, Kate, there's more. He's from a long lineage of witches."

She halted her cup only inches from her lips after Wally's last words. "What the fuck, Wally? Don't tell me you believe in that stuff."

He held both hands up and said, "Not so fast. Wait until I'm finished before you come to any conclusions."

He continued with the story, telling her about the accidents on Lone Lake Road, the fire in the woods, and the yurt encampment with its stone circles. He concluded with Wilkie's meeting with the Aldrins and, finally, his interviews with the Wiccans and witches of Whidbey Island.

"So that's why we're looking for Becker; we're pretty sure he kidnapped his son. Based on his mother's comments, it seems Buzz has become a full-fledged warlock, and his old man wants to use his son's talents for his selfish ends."

Kate looked at him now, still skeptical but with a hefty dose of intrigue and a hint of humor in her crinkled eyes. "You folks from Whidbey Island can sure come up with some doozies. Hell, last year, you had that guy trying to poison everyone, and a couple of years before that, there was that woman who invented that vanadium battery thing. Now we've got a family of witches, a warlock, and a kidnapping."

"*We've* got?"

"You don't think I'm leaving you alone, do you? If Becker is somewhere around here, it's still my jurisdiction. If you behave yourself, I'll let you come along for the ride on this." This last was delivered with a smile that caused a minor flutter in Wally's gut or heart; he couldn't tell which.

"Does this mean I can drive your car?"

"No, it does not. C'mon, let's see if we can figure out where Becker and the astronaut are."

Standing, she grabbed Wally's hand and pulled him out of his chair. He made a note not to engage in any arm wrestling with this woman.

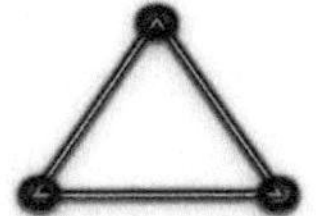

TWENTY

Buzz couldn't sleep. The years spent in the forest had shaped him. Now, confined to a twenty-by-thirty-foot room, his anxiety level had exceeded anything he'd ever experienced.

Instead of starlit nights and the sounds of the animals and insects of the forest, there was only the hum of the small refrigerator and the glow from a lamp somewhere on the other side of his walled prison. Alan had yet to tell him what he wanted. He'd left early and had spent most of the day away from the cabin.

Buzz longed for his home in the woods off Lone Lake Road. His days there were filled with the simple tasks of gathering food and firewood, building and repairing his house, and any remaining hours were spent studying and observing nature. When necessary, he used the stone circles in the yurt camp to address the few other needs the forest could not provide.

He would occasionally revisit the scrolls and documents his mother had left behind, but his proficiency in the craft had evolved to the point where there was little he didn't know. Among those few things, though, was the enigma of the shriveled-up ear his mother had left behind.

She'd treated the artifact as if she were afraid of it but suspected its power was such that getting rid of it was not an option. When she left with her sister and brother, the revolting body part had remained in her yurt, and Buzz had claimed it along with the rest of her incantations and spells.

"You've got one more night of sulking before we get to work," announced Becker when he entered the cabin just as the daylight was disappearing. "You'll need to keep your strength up, so we're having chicken pot pie for dinner."

Buzz said nothing as he watched Becker place the grocery bag, along with some others, on the counter. Since his diet had been venison, berries, mushrooms, and kale for a long, long time, he wasn't sure about this pot pie thing.

"Why do I need to keep my strength up? What do you want with me?"

"You're gonna help me get what I want—what's owed to me."

"What are you talking about?"

"Your mom thinks maybe you can do what she used to do."

"Huh?"

"You know, the witchy stuff, the magic—how you can make things happen."

Buzz had no idea where this was headed, so he asked again, "What are you talking about?"

"Your mother has taken care of my financial needs for a long time. It's selfish for her, since her failure to do so would result in me divulging all your family's secrets—and I mean *all* of them."

All this was news to Buzz, who had no formal education and had spent twenty years away from civilization. What he did have going for him was a high IQ, thanks to his ancestry and a keen understanding of the natural order of things. The difficulty was in imagining why someone—his father in this case—would try to hurt his mother.

"Do you get it now, Buzz? Did it get through to that imbecilic brain of yours?"

"I ... I think so."

"So there's no confusion, let me be crystal fucking clear. I want the property on Lone Lake Road and enough money to build my own place there. Understand now?"

Buzz was petrified. The property was his, and it was all he knew. Now, his father wanted it for himself. *Where will I go? What will happen to me?* He nodded absentmindedly and sat on the bed, trying to grasp what he'd heard.

"What's the problem, Buzz? Cat got your tongue?"

"Um ... no ... I understand, I guess. I don't know if I can do what you want."

"Well, we're gonna see about that. First, though, if you're going to be in this house with me—which you are—then we've got to do something about the smell. I'm going to let you out, and you're going through that door in the corner, where there's a shower. Get in there and clean yourself up. When you're finished, put these on." He threw a plastic bag full of clothes at his captive. "I don't care if they fit or not; I'm throwing all your old shit out."

Buzz caught the bag and did as he was told. He'd taken sponge baths in the woods but hadn't been in a shower since he was a kid. The warm water splashed over him, and he watched the rivulets of grime trickle into the drain as he tried to process what was happening.

Alan had never treated him well, but he also had never abused him, nor had he hurt his mother or those in her family. Still, the air of hostility around him was enough to cause him to fear for his safety and, for the time being, he would surrender to the man's demands.

He dried himself off, donned the jeans, sweatshirt, and sneakers from the bag, and combed out his beard with the brush on the sink. Looking in the mirror, he saw a bearded, long-haired, chubby-faced man with a hawk-like nose staring back. It had been so long since he'd seen a mirror that he was shocked.

Living in the forest, he'd never given much thought to his appearance and did only the bare minimum to keep disease and infections away. Now, after washing off years of dirt, his beard felt claustrophobic. He found a pair of scissors in a drawer and hacked off all but an inch. He scraped the heap of hair from the sink and threw it into the wastebasket. Then he walked out to face his father.

"Well ... look at you, Buzzer. I see you got yourself all cleaned up and a beard trim. At least you smell better. Get back on your side of that wall while I make dinner."

Becker locked the door to the prison-like room, then went into the bathroom and spoke from there. "Just checking, sonny-boy, to make sure you didn't take any sharp instruments with you. Glad to see you left the scissors here."

He heated the pot pies in the oven, and when they were done, he passed a tray with the food and utensils under the door. Buzz was told the small refrigerator had water bottles in it. Because the hog wire allowed the two cabin occupants to see each other, it was almost as if they were roommates. Of course, one was secured inside a room topped with razor wire to prevent *that* roommate from escaping.

The dinner was bland compared to the venison he usually ate, but it wasn't awful and relieved his hunger. He had little to say to his father, and when he'd finished, he passed the tray back under the door, then quietly stretched out on his bed. Maybe he would sleep tonight.

***

The first thing he heard was rain pelting on the roof. It took several seconds before the cobwebs cleared, and he remembered where he was. Then he heard his father's voice: "Up and at 'em, Buzzer. We've got work to do—or rather, you have."

Buzz had never thought of what he was capable of as magic. He considered it more of a ritual that he performed when he needed something the forest couldn't provide, and mostly, it came true. He copied what he'd seen his mother do and used the scrolls she had left behind to perform the incantations. There were talismans, too, that she'd abandoned that he used in his ceremonies, although the shriveled-up ear was one he was reluctant to explore.

Now, his father expected him to do something he was ill-equipped to handle, but with no other options available, he began to think through the process.

"What should we do first? What do you need from me?" Becker asked.

Even though he pretended otherwise, Buzz knew the land he lived on was his mother's, which had been in her family for generations. He remembered her talking to her sister about his great-great-grandmother, who had initially settled there, and the difficulties she must have faced. If his well-being and that of his mother and her family hung in the balance, he had no choice but to give in to his father's demands.

"I need some things from my home." He felt the only way to undo the property's provenance was to use a talisman from long ago, and he had just the item in mind.

"What things? Tell me, and I'll get them for you."

Buzz tried to imagine this giant of a man hunched over, looking for the shriveled ear somewhere on the shelves of his woodsy hovel. "You won't be able to do that; I need to go there."

Becker looked pissed at the delay, but he recalled how tiny his kid's house was and nodded in understanding. "Okay, let's go, but don't try anything. Remember what happens if this doesn't go according to plan ... *my* plan."

This time, Buzz was allowed to sit in the cab with his father driving. He marveled at the truck's luxury and was mesmerized by the sheer number of dials, screens, and lights on the dashboard. With his only experience being the ancient Ford Courier, he was stunned at the advances that had been made.

They arrived at the Lummi Island ferry dock in fifteen minutes and boarded the twenty-car boat. Since Buzz had slept the entire trip when he was abducted, he was unaware they had been on an island. He said nothing during the short five-minute journey to the mainland, content to absorb the many new sounds, smells, and sights.

Noticing his son's look of wonder, Becker couldn't help himself. "I guess you don't get out much, eh, Buzz?"

"No."

"Just think, once I take over the property, you'll be able to live in the civilized world and experience all these things daily. How does that sit with you?"

"I don't think I like it."

Becker laughed loudly and said, "You'll get used to it. Maybe you can visit me once I move in. Hah!"

Buzz offered no reply. He sat there wondering what would become of him.

The three-hour drive to his home off Lone Lake Road passed without conversation, although it would have been difficult with the noisy country music blasting on the radio. When they finally pulled up to his architectural abomination, he climbed down from the big truck and walked toward the tiny structure, wondering if it were the last time he'd see it.

He pushed the door open and entered, already sensing that someone had been inside. A faint smell of jasmine still lingered in the air. The overcast skies combined with the towering fir canopy made it necessary, even though it was midday, for him to light the oil lamp on the table.

He could see smudges in the dust on the shelves where things had been moved and saw the small square imprint of the spot that formerly held what he was looking for. He turned to the shelf over his bed that held the scrolls he'd taken many years ago from his mother's yurt and took them down.

When he emerged, he saw his father standing in front of him, holding a five-gallon gas can. "Get in the truck."

"What are you doing?"

"Since you've got what you need and I'm gonna be the new owner of this property, I don't want some shithole cave ruining the place. I'm taking care of that right now."

"No ... you can't," Buzz screamed in his high voice.

"I said ... *get* in the fucking truck. I'll do whatever I want." Then he grabbed Buzz by the arm and shoved him toward the pickup. He opened the door and pushed him inside.

After slamming the door, Becker splashed gasoline over as much of the structure as he could, including the wretched old Courier. With what was left in the gas can, he poured a trail twenty feet away, struck a match, and watched the astronaut's home burst into flames while its former occupant wiped tears from his eyes.

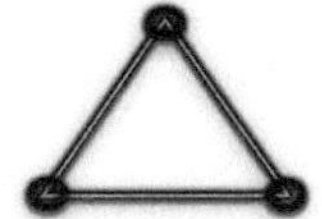

TWENTY-ONE

It was Wednesday morning, and I was looking forward to hearing Wally's report on the previous day's trip to Bellingham. He was usually in before me, so I was mildly surprised when he had still not arrived at nine o'clock.

"Hey, Rog, you're missing a deputy." Of *course* Bruce had to point out the obvious.

"Yes ... I am aware, but thanks for the heads up. Don't you have something to do?"

Whenever Bruce got snarky with me, I found it helpful to remind him of the dispatch reports he was routinely late with. Luckily, Wally walked—or rather floated—into the squad room at that very moment.

"Hey guys, how's it going?" he asked with a smiling face.

Bruce and I exchanged glances, wondering what had happened to produce a side of Wally Turpin we hadn't seen before. The combination of late *and* cheerful was disturbing.

I purposefully looked at my watch and invited him into the conference room for a chat.

Before I could say anything, he seemed to realize he needed to explain his tardiness. "Sorry I'm late, Boss; I ended up spending the night in Bellingham and came here directly from there."

"Wow, you must have gotten into something up there." The words were barely out of my mouth when a fleeting look of something—maybe bliss—flashed across his face.

"Yeah, Rog, about that ..."

"I'm listening."

"I met with a detective from the BPD, and we interviewed the rental agent from Becker's house and the neighbors." His words were rushed.

"And?"

"It's clear the guy's an asshole. Left the rental place a mess, and the neighbors are thrilled he's gone."

"Okay ..."

"Well ... I had to fill this detective in on what we're working on ... so I did. Then, we went back to the station and started digging through Becker's past interactions with their department. Anyway ... this detective and I ended up having dinner, and, well ... it got late, so I spent the night there."

"Wally?"

"Yes?"

"This detective wouldn't be a woman, would she?"

"Um ... yes, she, uh ... would."

"And you like her? Not in a police officer kinda way, but in another kind of way?"

"Uh ... yeah, I think I do."

"You think? You spent the night with her, and you *think*?"

"Okay, okay ... yes, I do, very much."

We'd become acquaintances when Wally joined the force and close friends since he'd moved to Whidbey and become my right-hand guy. He was as dependable as anyone I'd ever served with, and now it was apparent he was smitten in a way he'd never been before.

"Tell me about her."

"She's Irish, and she's got this face that's ... I don't know. Whenever I think of her ... man, I don't know, Rog ... I've never met anyone like her."

"Is she any good at detecting?"

"You should see her interviewing people ... she's incredible. She's a gym rat, too, and strong as an ox. Honest, Rog ... she's really cool."

"That's terrific, Wally. Tell me, what else did you learn about Becker?"

When I told Kate—that's her name, Kate Mahoney—about all this witch stuff, she thought I was nuts. But then I told her about the Wiccans and witches I'd met, and then all the weird things with the Aldrins and Buzz, and the deer and the accidents, and she committed to keeping an open mind. She's really cool, Rog."

"Um, yes ... yes, you said that."

"Sorry."

"Nah, don't worry about it ... Becker?"

"No forwarding address and no relatives. We've got a description out on his truck—one of those big Ford Super Duty things—and we posted his tags."

"Anything else?"

"Yes. This morning, over breakfast, I told Kate about the tire tracks from Buzz's place and how the tires weren't all that common. She said we should go back to Becker's rental—the neighbor said he parked off the driveway on the grass half the time—and see if we could find any tracks, so we did."

"Did you?"

"There were lots of them from lots of cars and trucks. Most were old, and the rain had made them too mushed up to be of any help. There was an area to the side of the drive under what was a tent, like for an RV or something, and there we found some tracks in the mud that the rain couldn't reach. They looked the same to me. I got some good pictures that I'll get to the lab."

"That's great, Wally; if nothing else, we'll have proof that Becker's truck was at Buzz's. Maybe we'll get lucky, and someone will spot it. Any other ideas?"

"Kate thinks he's still somewhere in the Northwest. We thought you might want to revisit Sable Aldrin to see if she has any ideas about Becker's plans. You know, what he might want Buzz to do for him."

Nowhere on the list of things I wanted to do over the rest of my life was there a place for a return visit to the Aldrins, but Wally's suggestion made sense, so I put the ball back in his court. "You make a good point, Wally, but since you have such a good relationship now with the Bellingham Police, I think you and Detective Mahoney should handle this."

His face showed equal parts excitement and discomfort. "Are you sure, Boss? I mean, you've been there before, so maybe you should continue with them."

"Nah, shouldn't be a problem. I'll call her and tell her you'd like to stop by. I'm sure your new detective friend will enjoy it too."

Wally caught up on his paperwork while I called Sable Aldrin's number. She answered after only a few rings, and her calm, detached voice reminded me why I didn't want to set foot in her place again.

"Yes, Deputy, what do you want?" She got right to the point after I told her it was me.

"We have a couple more questions we'd like to ask you. Would it be okay if Deputy Turpin stopped by tomorrow?"

"Not you?"

"Well ... he's working on this too with someone from the Bellingham Police Department, so I think it's best if they do the asking."

She was quiet for a moment, perhaps thinking—correctly—that I never wanted to set foot in that place again. "That will be okay, Deputy Wilkie; please tell him ten o'clock is fine."

She disconnected abruptly, and I informed Wally of his impending appointment the next morning. "Thanks, Rog. I'll call Kate and let her know."

The sparkle in his eyes from the anticipation of talking to his new *friend* was a pleasure to see. I was pleased for him and hoped the visit to the Aldrins wouldn't be too much for the BPD detective. According to Wally, though, she was Wonder Woman and could handle anything. Hell, maybe she could.

TWENTY-TWO

The BOLO for Becker's truck did get issued, but by the time it had, Buzz and his father were back on Lummi Island. The sliver of land was just over nine square miles, with a population of under a thousand residents during the winter. What it had going for it was several large acreage parcels owned by folks from the East Coast, either for investment purposes or because they'd inherited them.

Becker had stumbled upon the cabin while looking for something isolated yet still within shouting distance of Sable and her clan. His plans were fluid and largely depended on what miracles his adult son managed to perform. When he'd first hooked up with Sable many years ago, he was skeptical of her abilities and only stayed around when he began to see her potential. While she may not have been the most attractive filly in the pasture, her enigmatic personality and the promise of future riches kept him interested and even tolerant of her siblings.

The cabin was listed as a wilderness retreat on the bulletin board at the small island post office, and that was indeed what it was. A phone call to the posted number and a Zelle transaction to an account in Connecticut were the only steps necessary for a three-month lease.

It had taken an entire month and numerous cuts and slashes from the razor wire to partition off the cabin. He felt the threat he posed to the Aldrin clan would be enough to keep his son in line, but just in case, the walled prison would provide a necessary backup plan.

The trip to the property on Lone Lake Road had instilled more confidence in Becker about his ability to control his son. Now that his home had been burned to the ground, his mother was no longer practicing, and he had no connections to the civilized world, the astronaut had limited options.

Although Buzz had been practicing witchcraft for years, it was mostly an intuitive process for him. Since time was never a factor, he'd figured out most of the stuff by trial and error. Now that his asshole father was telling him *what* to do with no clue about *how* to do it or what materials were necessary, he was doubtful of his abilities.

During their journey to Whidbey and back, Becker told his son about his family's ties to the island and the story of his great-great-grandmother and *her* ties to Ebey's Landing. Buzz suspected the shriveled-up ear that used to be in his house might have had something to do with the whole affair, but now that it was missing, he would have to look for other talismans.

He considered telling his father his concerns, but only fleetingly. The man only thought about himself, and at this point, the less he knew, the better.

When they arrived at the cabin, Buzz returned to his pen like a well-trained dog. Paying no heed to the unlocked door, Becker went to his side of the house and started preparing dinner.

"You forgot to lock the door," Buzz shouted brazenly from his side of the wall.

"No, I didn't. I figure you're not going anywhere as long as I can make trouble for your family. Am I right?"

"I guess ..."

"That's what I thought. How about you start making a list of the things you'll need? I know Sable used to use herbs and spices and things. There's paper and pencils in that drawer, so how about you get going on this?"

It had been over twenty years since Buzz had held a pencil in his hand. Even then, his homeschooling had been woefully inadequate, and his penmanship was a mixture of printing and scribbling. Now, though, it was a struggle to shape the letters and numbers.

The dinner consisted of chicken pot pies, again making Buzz long for his former diet of venison jerky and blackberries. He didn't understand how people could eat this crap. By the time the pies had been cooked, he had put most of what he thought he would need on paper and handed it to Becker.

"What is this?" he asked his son when they were seated at the kitchen table.

"The list you wanted ... you know, the stuff I'm gonna need."

"This looks like some two-year-old wrote it; I can't read this."

"Well ... that's the best I can do. If you like, I can tell you, and you can write it down."

"Jesus ... what a fucking moron," Becker said under his breath but loudly enough for Buzz to hear him.

Buzz knocked his dinner aside, ran into his walled-off space, and threw himself on his bed.

His father yelled at him, "Get your ass back in here."

"Fuck you." He had never used the word before, but he'd heard Alan and others use it when they were angry, and it seemed to impact those at whom it was directed.

"*What* did you say?"

"I said ... *fuck you.*"

Becker stormed into Buzz's room and slapped his son's leg. "Listen, you little shit, I'm gonna own that property, and you're gonna get it for me regardless of what you think of me. Got it?"

When there was no reply, he slapped his leg again. "I said, *got* it?"

"Yes," was the soft reply.

Becker stood there silently for several seconds, then said, "Okay, tell me what you need."

Having reached a truce, the son told the father what he would need to produce the magic to terminate his family's ownership of the hundred acres off Lone Lake Road. The only home he'd known for over two decades and property that had been in his family for five generations would soon be owned by the blackmailing asshole that was his father.

It took several days for Becker to accumulate all the items Buzz had requested. The warlock prepared and aligned three stone circles for the job since they wouldn't return to Whidbey Island anytime soon. Uncertain of the exact construction and positioning of the fire pits, he did his best to recall and duplicate those from the yurt settlement.

The cabin was centered in the middle of a thirty-acre parcel of land and well off the paved road, so there was little concern that other residents would bother them. It was still mid-winter and wood-burning fireplaces and stoves were the norm for heating on the sparsely inhabited island.

Referring often to his mother's scrolls and incantations, he went from one circle to the next, arranging the plants, herbs, and spices his father had collected while mumbling the sacred words he'd heard from his mother.

He waited until the witching hour—in this case, 3:30 a.m.—to ignite the fires and recite the verses that would activate the spell. During all this time, Becker watched his son, fascinated by the activity. In less than thirty minutes, the fires were nothing but embers, and Buzz was slumped on the cold, wet earth, tired as hell by the ritual. Becker ignored him, went into the cabin, and fell asleep.

It was six a.m. when Buzz awoke, shivering and wet. He limped into the cabin, stripped off his drenched clothing, and fell into bed. It was the first time he had attempted any magic beyond providing for his basic needs, and the mental energy expended both surprised and unnerved him. He'd seen his mother collapse after several of her ritual ceremonies but never understood the drain on her psyche until now.

In the few minutes before he fell asleep, he wondered if his efforts had accomplished anything, even though he knew the results might not happen immediately. He remembered how his mother had struggled for years before becoming proficient; even then, outcomes often varied. His last thoughts were those of his former home in the woods and the depressing acceptance that he'd never see it again.

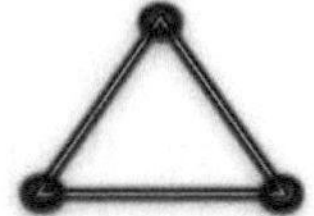

TWENTY-THREE

There was little progress I could make finding Becker until I heard from Wally after his visit to the Aldrins. I busied myself with several petty crimes of a more local nature until he returned.

There was a shoplifting episode from the Star Store in Langley and a chainsaw theft from the Ace Hardware in Freeland. Based on witness descriptions, both were suspected of being done by the same person. Since Bruce had little dispatching or paperwork to do, I sent him to apprehend the crook and bring him in for questioning. He rarely got to do real police work, so he was excited about the opportunity.

By three o'clock we had booked the thief, and Bruce was preening about the office, having collared his first criminal. His glory march was interrupted when a woman in a BPD windbreaker and jeans entered the office. Her striking Irish features and no-nonsense approach suggested her identity, which was confirmed by the appearance of Wally Turpin closely following.

She scoped the room and strode purposefully up to me. "You've got to be Roger Wilkie, right?"

Wally was right about one thing: her smile lit up the room. "That's correct, and I'm guessing you're Kate Mahoney."

"I am. Wally says you sent us to the Aldrins because you were scared to go back there." She said this with a smirk and a gleam in her eyes.

I was beginning to see what my deputy liked about this woman. "How about you and Wally step into the conference room, and we can chat about your visit?" I said sternly, hoping to regain the higher ground.

They walked into the room ahead of me, Kate looking at Wally with a look that suggested *Maybe I went too far.*

After we were seated, I turned to the Bellingham detective and said with as straight a face as I could muster, "Wally said you were a wiseass. Welcome to our little slice of heaven." Then my frown turned upside down, and I extended my hand.

She looked relieved and said, "Sorry about that; Wally told me to say it." She looked at her temporary partner, who was now red-faced.

"Hey, I did not; she's always doing shit like that."

Kate and I laughed aloud, with Wally finally getting into the act.

"Tell me how your visit to the Aldrins went."

They looked at each other, neither one wanting to go first.

"Okay, let's try this," I said. "Wally, how about you start?"

He began hesitantly, not sure how to put his recollections into words. "Well ... first of all, you were right about that place. It was like an oven in there, and there was that funky smell--not like garbage or anything, but still, something nasty. It was hard to breathe." He looked at Mahoney as he spoke, and her nod and look of disgust at the recollection confirmed his report.

Kate then picked up the narrative. "Sable introduced us to her brother and sister, but she did most of the talking. She seemed concerned about her son and asked if we'd found anything yet. We told her we were working on it and asked if she had any idea where Becker might have gone."

"And?"

"She said she didn't, but then her brother, Thorn, spoke up. He said, 'Tell them about the stuff he used to say when we were on Whidbey.' At first, Sable looked annoyed that she'd been interrupted, but then she was quiet while trying to remember.

"Then she recalled him talking about how he liked island life and the idea of having his own compound. Sable seemed to think he was enamored with the concept, and maybe he still felt that way."

The three of us were quiet. I was thinking about the more than 170 San Juan islands in Puget Sound, with over twenty of them having permanent residents. It was an impossible task even if we started with the most populated ones.

"Anything else?"

They looked at each other for a few seconds before Wally tilted his head toward me, perhaps encouraging Kate to express her thoughts.

"We both came away feeling sorry for them. They are strange, certainly, but we think Becker has been screwing them over for years, using Sable's talents, gifts, or whatever to enrich himself. We think she regrets getting involved with him and feels guilty for how she treated her son."

"You're probably right, but I think that's something she'll have to live with. Let's get a description of Becker's truck out to the DOT so they can alert the ferry terminals going to the San Juans. The lab confirmed the tire tracks at the rental on Lake Whatcom are the same as those left at Buzz's. If he *is* on one of them, and it's one not served by the ferry system, then we're screwed."

"Roger?"

"Yeah?"

"Why does he need Buzz, and if he's the one who burned down the shack on Lone Lake Road, why do that?" Kate seemed to have ideas of her own.

"Tell me what you're thinking." She had both my and Wally's attention.

"I think he wants the property where Buzz lived. I think he burned the house out of spite and then kidnapped Buzz to force him to turn over the property. That's the only thing that makes sense."

I hadn't looked at that angle before because I was more concerned about finding Buzz than the reason he'd been taken. But it now seemed a plausible theory.

"Didn't Sable say the property had been in the family for generations and that eventually Buzz would inherit it?" Wally asked.

"She did, yes."

"Then how would Becker get Buzz to turn over the property since it's not his yet?"

Kate considered this, then answered, "If they *are* witches and Buzz can cast spells and do magic—which I'm still skeptical of, by the way—maybe Buzz can undo the ownership of the property and put it in Becker's name."

"Yeah, but *how*?" Wally asked.

"If your partner here is correct, Wally, then that's the question we need to answer. Also, Kate, if you're right, it makes sense that Becker probably wouldn't be hiding out anywhere more than an hour or two from Whidbey. That leaves this island—which I doubt because we would eventually find him here—or some-place inland. The ferries to the other islands would be problematic."

"So, what's the plan?" Wally was anxious to do something besides talk.

"Right now, there's not much we can do except hope we get a sighting on that truck. Get with the county, Wally, and have them flag you if there's any title activity on the Aldrin property. Kate, I think there's still a good chance that Becker is somewhere in the Bellingham area. Why don't you do a little more digging into his background—past acquaintances, old school chums, girlfriends, maybe—and see if you can get any leads?"

The disappointment on their faces reflected that they would be operating independently for a little while. They were both adults, though, and they understood that the Whidbey Sheriff's Department wasn't there to facilitate their dating activities. Nevertheless, I was confident they would find a way to stay in touch.

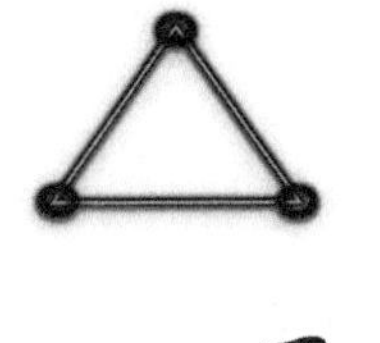

TWENTY-FOUR

After four consecutive days of three- to four-hour sessions and now with exhaustion getting the better of him, Buzz Aldrin had serious doubts about whether he could accomplish what his father wanted.

It wasn't helpful to be reminded daily what would happen if he failed. After every session, Becker would log on to the Island County website to verify the ownership of the Aldrin property on Whidbey Island. When he saw no change in the property's registration, he would threaten Buzz anew, causing him even more angst.

Because his capabilities were limited to what he'd observed of his mother, Buzz was unaware of the depth of his power. He was convinced that what he was doing wasn't working and told his father this.

"Then find a way to make it happen; do something different," Becker shouted.

Buzz tried to think of something. He knew the talismans used in casting a spell were critical to its success, but, unschooled as he was in the black arts, what he could accomplish was only through trial and error.

"I think I need something with ties to the property and the original owner. If you want me to erase any trace of my family's connection, I need something from before it was in our name."

"Shit, that's over a hundred years ago; you'll have to do something else."

"I don't think anything else will work. It *has* to be something from back then." Buzz seemed to be more assured the more he thought about it.

"Wait a minute. Whatever this is has to be old, right?"

"Yup."

"Did you know the person who bought the parcel was an Indian?"

Buzz looked like his father was speaking another language. "Um ... no."

"Yeah, I did some research on it before I picked you up. She was your great-great-grandmother and had this Indian name that was changed to Sarah."

"Okay ... so?"

"I found out she had some connection to Ebey's Landing on Whidbey. Maybe we should go there and see if we can find something that could work."

Buzz was quiet. His confidence was ebbing, and he felt at his father's mercy. With nowhere to go, no home and no future, he silently nodded his acquiescence and surrendered to his captor's wishes.

***

Overcast skies and dreary conditions were the norm for late winter in the Northwest, and the trip from Lummi Island through Bellingham, Anacortes, and Oak Harbor passed without conversation. For almost two decades, Buzz had lived in harmony with nature and the sounds of the forest's birds, animals, and insects. Now, exposed to the twanging country music that blasted from the truck radio, he longed for the peaceful existence he feared he would never see again.

His thoughts were interrupted by the ringing of a phone, strangely but thankfully dousing the volume of the whiny voices on the radio. Becker picked up the device and glanced at the screen before putting it to his ear.

"Yeah, what is it? I told you not to call me ... No, he's with me. We need something from before the Aldrin family purchased the property ... No, I *told* you I'll be in touch when I have something ... I do, no, yeah, sorry ... me too, bye."

Buzz, gazing out the window at the rugged forests of north Whidbey Island, could feel his father's stare but chose to say nothing. He was surprised someone else knew of his predicament, but whoever it was made no difference. He was fucked.

As they approached Coupeville, the Island County seat, vast fields of forage crops rose to the west. They halted abruptly at the 200-foot cliffs overlooking the waters of Puget Sound. This vista was not quickly forgotten by the million or more annual visitors to the 17,000-acre historical reserve.

As he took in the panorama, Buzz felt a slight tingle. If he had been here before, it would have been only in passing as a young teenager. Still, something about the astonishing natural majesty of the landscape triggered an awareness from deep in a dusty corner of his mind. Becker took note of the uptick in his attention.

"You see something?"

"No ... nothing; just a feeling about this place. I haven't been here before, I don't think, but it seems like I have."

"I'm gonna park by the visitor center, and we can decide where to go from there."

On the cold, rainy afternoon, he parked the big Ford in the puddled gravel parking lot, one of only four vehicles. They climbed from the high cab and began walking toward the sand cliffs the raiding party had scaled over a century and a half before.

High above the hundreds of acres of farmlands, the patchwork of greens, browns, and yellows was mesmerizing. The drizzle had turned to a fine mist, making the gauze-like scene even more hypnotic. As they approached the edge of the cliffs, they arrived at the blockhouse where Isaac Ebey's family had taken refuge so long ago and where the raiding Haida tribe had beheaded him.

The tingle Buzz felt earlier had morphed into a rumbling in his gut, and a feeling of electricity surged through his body. They stopped and read the plaque on the building, which detailed the demise of the early settler.

"Seems kinda silly, the Indians cutting the guy's head off and *then* scalping him," Becker said.

Buzz didn't respond; he was thinking. He had experienced a similar reaction when he'd handled the shriveled ear his mother had left in her yurt. He knew she wouldn't have kept it unless it was important, and he remembered her telling Orla the item had been passed down through her ancestors. It was why he had kept it yet was reluctant to do anything with it.

Even if the ear would perform as a talisman, he no longer had it. He recalled the place on his shelf where it had been and how he'd noticed its absence on his final visit just before his father had burned his home to the ground. He thought he knew its location, but for now, he wouldn't share the information with his father. Not yet.

They walked further until the trail ended at the cliff's edge, each step away from the blockhouse easing the feeling in his body. Buzz was now sure of the connection between his family and the tragedy that had befallen Isaac Ebey. What he could do about it was yet to be determined, but for now, he would do what he could to delay the inevitable.

Pausing at the trail's end, he spoke to his father. "I have an idea of what might work."

"Please tell me, O brilliant one." Buzz didn't understand what his mother had seen in this sarcastic asshole, but for now, he would string him along.

"Let's take some sand samples from the site here, and maybe we can get a splinter or two from the blockhouse. That should give me something from before Sarah bought the property."

"Will that work?"

Buzz now knew the one thing that *might* work was the shriveled-up ear likely belonging to Isaac Ebey. If his father was correct, it was a direct tie to the Natives who had killed the man and who were also the ancestors of Sarah Aldrin. He doubted whether the sand or the material from the blockhouse would be of any use, but it would buy him some time. He answered, "I can't be sure, but there's a good chance it will help."

They filled an empty water bottle with sand from the cliffs and managed to pull a three-inch strip of bark off one of the logs at the corner of the blockhouse. With their treasures in tow, the father led the way back to the pickup, followed by his reluctant son.

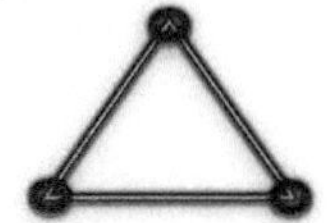

TWENTY-FIVE

The Freeland office of the Sheriff's Department was small and staffed by only a handful of deputies, of whom I was the senior. When I arrived on Friday morning, Wally was slurping coffee and looked eager to update me. Bruce, as usual, was busy scrolling through something on his phone while the two other officers—newer recruits—were leaving for patrol.

It was one of the rare days when I was the last to arrive, but one of the goats was ill, and Andie needed my help.

"Glad you could make it, Boss."

"Shut up, Wally; you look like someone who wants to tell me something."

Insults bounced off the man like bullets off Wonder Woman's bracelets. "Let me get you some coffee, Fearless Leader, so I may illuminate you with what we've learned about the Aldrin situation."

This was why everyone loved Wally. He knew how to find humor in almost anything yet was sensitive enough to know where to draw the line. I was glad he was on my team, and if past experiences were worth anything, I trusted the man with my life.

After I was seated behind my desk and he had delivered a steaming cup of Whidbey Coffee's finest, he pulled up a chair. "Remember when you told me how Becker mentioned Ebey's Landing and the Haida Indians when he spoke to the Aldrins?"

"I do, yes."

"Well ... after I was done talking to the county, they agreed to let us know if there was any change in ownership, and then I started researching the names of the registered owners on the Lone Lake property."

"And ...?"

"Remember when I told you that Angela Aldrin, who was Sarah Morgan's daughter, purchased the property?"

"Yup."

"Well ... everything I can find on her hints at her being this generous woman who was kind to everyone she met."

"So?"

"So her mother, Sarah—formerly Gyaaxa Gwang; remember, she was from the tribe that carried out the raid that killed Isaac Ebey—was sort of a dick. A few notes I found credited her with starting a plague on some folks here in the Northwest. I think her nastiness subsided somewhat as she got older, but it seems she held a grudge against the white men who kicked them off her land on Whidbey."

"Can't say as I blame her, but where are you going with all this? We've known most of it."

"Yeah, I know, I know. What I was thinking, though, was maybe, if it *is* witchcraft, it all ties back to that raid at Ebey's Landing. Maybe we need to keep our eyes on anything going on there."

I thought about Wally's hypothesis for a minute. Even if Buzz's kidnapping was somehow related to the Haida raid, there wasn't much we could do but have the local deputies from Coupeville keep their eyes open.

"I'll make sure the troops up there keep their eyes peeled. The sheriff knows about our concerns, but remember, we *still* don't have proof Buzz has been abducted. We think he was, and from what his mother says, he was, but there is a slight chance he went along voluntarily.

"Anything from your Bellingham friend?"

At the mention of Mahoney, I detected a pinkish cast rising on my sidekick's face.

"She didn't have much luck finding family members; there weren't any still around. She returned to the neighbors, though—the Montgomerys—and reinterviewed them. They said there were lots of partiers at Becker's, and they noticed one of them—a woman—had been there a lot lately. They didn't know her name, of course, but they did give Kate a description."

"Any help?"

Wally shook his head in resignation. "Not much. Average height and weight, grayish short hair, somewhere around fifty. Could be anyone."

"Is it worth having them talk to a sketch artist?"

"I don't think so. They did say they'd for sure recognize her again, though."

"I guess that's something, but this passive approach is beginning to wear on me. There's gotta be something we can do besides just waiting for Becker or his girlfriend to show up."

Wally waited a few seconds before saying anything, and when he did, I was surprised that he'd already given this some thought.

"Suppose we did something to get Becker to react."

"Like?"

"Like making a change in the ownership of the property. Becker must be checking with the county regularly if we're right about why he's got Buzz. If he noticed something had changed, he might have to revisit Sable."

"So you've thought about this, eh?"

"Well ... I was talking to Kate, and she thought it might be a good idea, you know, I mean, like, if we wanted to ..."

"Tell your friend we should talk about it. In fact, see if she can make it here for a short meeting this afternoon. I'd like to brainstorm about the best way to do this."

The look on Wally's face was that of a child receiving a trophy for their first hit in tee-ball. "Um ... sure. I'll try to get her right away."

Wally left my office on a mission. I remembered how I'd felt when I'd first met Andie, and thoughts of her had left little room for anything else. It seemed my second-in-command was smitten, and if this turned out to be anything close to my good fortune, I was thrilled for him.

***

Kate Mahoney somehow cleared her schedule so that she could meet with us at three o'clock. I entered the conference room to find Wally and Kate seated, both grinning, pleased to be in each other's company.

"Thanks for making the trip, Kate," I offered, knowing nothing short of an asteroid destroying the Earth would have kept her away.

"Wally said you wanted to talk about finding a way to get Becker to make a move."

"Yes ... yes, I do. He also told me it was your idea."

Wally was searching for lint on his trousers when Kate, appearing unsure of the direction of the conversation, glanced at him. "Oh, he did?"

I felt bad for my buddy, but only a little. If he'd had the chance to zing me, he would have done so gladly; still, a rescue was in order. "Yes, he did, and I think it's a great idea."

She looked back at me, now smiling, and Wally seemed to lose interest in his pants. I continued, "What do you think will get his attention?"

"Well ... I ... *we* were thinking if Becker saw that the land Buzz was living on had changed ownership, he might turn up at the Aldrins' place."

"How could that happen?"

"Suppose we talked Sable into selling it?"

"I'm thinking that would be difficult to accomplish."

Wally responded, "Kate thinks if we came up with some sort of contract that would guarantee it would be sold back to her at the same price after we apprehend Becker, we could pull it off."

"And whose name on the title would bring Becker out of hiding?"

"I think it would need to be someone other than the Aldrin clan. If it were one of them, he would probably keep pressuring Buzz to make something happen." Kate seemed to have given the idea more than a passing thought.

I wasn't optimistic we could convince Sable Aldrin of the ruse, but I played along. "Did you have anyone in mind?"

Wally and Kate looked at each other sheepishly, and then my deputy spoke. "We don't, Rog. There are lots of folks it shouldn't be, but we couldn't find anyone who could stir the pot enough to cause Becker to show himself."

I thought about everything we'd discussed. Most of it made sense, but it was still just conjecture. We had Sable Aldrin's account of her interaction with Becker and his truck's presence at Buzz's place. Kate's conclusions rang true, though, and maybe because she wasn't as close to the investigation as I was, I trusted them. I tried to think of someone we could use as bait to lure Becker but came up empty. And then I had a thought.

"We'd need to use someone who made sense, maybe even someone Becker might know of, right?"

I got nods from both of them.

"Suppose we could use someone who had a history with the property, wasn't a member of the Aldrin family, but was someone we could control. Would that work?"

"Ruh-roh ... I'm getting a funny feeling, Roger." Without knowing the department's history, Kate looked bewildered at Wally's interruption.

"Listen, Wally, this could work."

"Hey, it's your funeral. The guy's a walking shit magnet."

Kate was still in the dark and finally asked, "Who are you two talking about? Why is it such a big deal?"

"It's O'Malley, isn't it?" Wally asked.

I nodded.

"Who's O'Malley?" Kate wanted to know. It was clear she didn't like being in the dark.

I exhaled deeply, knowing it was up to me to educate our new teammate. "Do you remember a few years back when that white supremacist group tried to kill the members of that private golf club in Bellevue?"

"Of course; it was national news."

"How about that shootout with that drug kingpin a couple of years ago here on Whidbey?"

"I do, but so what?" Kate still couldn't fit the pieces together.

I kept talking. "How about that vanadium battery that changed the world's power grids?"

"Yes, I know that that also happened on your turf."

"Then last year the serial killer poisoning the water tanks all over Island County?"

"Okay, okay, so your island is riddled with crime. What does that have to do with O'Malley?"

Wally picked up the thread. "Kevin O'Malley and his wife have been at the center of every one of those events, and that's not even mentioning a couple more that happened away from here."

"So he's a cop or a private eye?"

Wally looked at me for help, but I let him do the honors. "Nope. He and his wife are retired interior designers in their sixties."

"*What?*"

"Wally's right," I said. "For some reason, they can't stop being in the middle of shit, so you'll understand why we have some hesitancy here. He did some work for the Aldrins when they first lived there, and Becker was with them, so it might make sense if he was the buyer."

Kate still seemed to be wrestling with the idea of a couple of old decorators being masterminds at crime-solving. "Honestly? Those two were involved in all those crimes?"

"Take our word for it, Kate, they were. I hesitate to involve them, but maybe we can use his name and ensure he keeps a low profile."

"Yeah, sure, Rog—O'Malley and low profiles don't fit in the same sentence." Wally still had doubts.

"You're saying Becker would know of this guy if he suddenly saw the property changed ownership and was now in O'Malley's name?" Kate began to see where I was going with this. The Bellingham Police Department was lucky to have someone with her instincts.

"Correct. I'd make sure he didn't get involved, and other than signing some documents, he wouldn't have to do anything."

"Think he'll go for it?" Wally still had some doubts.

"Are you kidding? He'll jump if he thinks he can get his grubby golf fingers into something. First, though, we'll need to talk to Sable Aldrin to see if she'll agree; that land has been in their family for a long time."

The three of us were quiet for a moment, possibly because we were picturing another visit to the Aldrins. I know I was.

"So ... El Jefe, looks like you'll be coming to Bellingham soon, eh?" I understood what Wally saw in Detective Mahoney. She was bright, attractive, and a real character; as far as he was concerned, she had all the bases covered.

I would have loved to delegate the meeting with Sable Aldrin to Kate and Wally, but I knew it was my place to handle the damn thing. "Sad to say you are correct, Kate. Hopefully, I'll get with Sable tomorrow and tell her what we're thinking. Wally, how about you introduce your good buddy here to O'Malley and make sure he's okay with this?"

"You think there's any chance he won't be?"

"Nah, I know better. Come up with a story that doesn't include witches or spells or kidnappings. If he suspects there's more to it than a land deal, we'll never get rid of him."

We concluded our meeting and agreed to reconvene the following afternoon after my visit to the Aldrins and the two lovebirds' visit with Kevin O'Malley. This had all the makings of a colossal shitshow now that the door was slightly ajar for O'Malley to stick his nose in.

TWENTY-SIX

Alan Becker had always been an opportunistic, conniving individual. Blessed with good looks and a physique that most found desirable, he made his way to Seattle after a short-lived effort to become a Hollywood star.

Rather than put in the time to study his craft, he relied on his charm and guile to manipulate his way into auditions that turned into disasters. After word spread of his methods, no serious studio would consider him. He briefly considered a career in the porn industry. Still, after hearing gossip attributed to several of his past sexual conquests that despite his prodigious physical presence, he was not equally blessed with a proportionately sized prerequisite, he was too embarrassed to try.

Seattle was already one of the great tech hubs of the world at the turn of the twenty-first century. With only a high school degree and no intention of expanding his education, Becker struggled to fit in with the highly educated, ambitious youngsters who made up most of the workforce.

After only a few months, he moved northward, hoping to find a smaller town where his limited talents would be more productive. When he reached Belling-ham, he stopped. He'd heard older folks were looking to retire here, and maybe he could find a way to coax some of their 401(k) funds away from them.

Looking back at his early years in Bellingham, Becker was surprised that he'd been able to put up with Sable Aldrin for as long as he had, although he knew why. He'd stumbled upon the family on his second day in town while grabbing lunch at the town's only Burger King, and, always looking for an easy score, he suspected the Aldrins were easy prey for someone with his aptitudes.

The three of them appeared to be trolling for friends with little success. Their needy demeanor and eccentric dress and mannerisms left little doubt about their chances of finding anyone with like qualities. The oldest was tall, with short brown hair framing a narrow face whose singularly prominent feature was a beak that could provide endless income for a cosmetic surgeon. However, a look at her eyes offered enough mystery to create interest and even hinted at the tiniest bit of danger.

The brother was an inch or two shorter than his older sister and had dark, brooding eyes suggesting a perpetual frown. The youngest was smaller than the other two and reasonably attractive. Becker thought her chances of meeting anyone of the opposite sex would multiply if she could find a way to ditch her older family members.

Since it was clear who the leader of the curious threesome was, Becker succeeded in getting behind them in line and managed to strike up a conversation with the tall one named Sable. Because he was new in town, talks about the area, the awful weather, and the difficulty meeting friends were easy. He learned that the brother was Thorn, and Orla was the youngest. At the time, he thought the names a bit curious, but eventually, it all made sense.

They arranged to meet again the next afternoon and began hanging out daily after Thorn and Sable finished working their menial jobs and Orla finished school. Becker knew there was something odd about the family, but something about their naïveté kept his attention. After a few months of the two boys and the two girls doing things that friends do, Becker, either because of a long period of abstention or maybe his taste in women was changing, began looking at Sable in other ways than simply friends.

She was superbly unattractive by conventional standards, but there was *something* about her that Becker found exciting and even mysteriously intoxicating. As time passed, it was clear Sable felt similarly about him, and ultimately they became a couple. Becker was no stranger to bedding members of the opposite sex, so when his time in the sack with Sable turned out to be an almost apocalyptic experience, he was hooked.

Those early years had been fun, even though her brother and sister were always around. Then when they started working with Sable, helping her understand the spells, incantations, talismans, and everything that went into the damn witchy shit, she began to change. He stayed the course because of the promise of the riches to come, and then there was the land.

When they met with the designers and moved to the yurt camp on Whidbey, the future was exciting even if—he admitted now—he was in denial about what a future with Sable and her two siblings might look like. Reality finally set in after almost three years in the woods with the Aldrins and Sable's idiot son. For some reason, he never thought of Buzz as his own.

He lived off the money he had taken from Sable for a while, and when it ran out, he returned to the trough once more. This time, though, it wasn't charm or romance he brought. It was blackmail.

At first, they were shocked to see him and wouldn't open the door. They relented when he told them he'd publicize their story and heritage. Sable had provided him with enough to live a lavish lifestyle, but even that wasn't enough. He pressed Sable for more and more, but instead of her delivering, he got less.

After one of his last visits, Orla showed him the door and slipped a note on his way out. He opened it in his truck and read: *Meet me at the Burger King; you remember where it is.*

He waited almost forty minutes before he saw Orla pull up in a red Mini Cooper. She got out immediately and climbed up into his truck.

"Hi, Alan, nice to see you."

He wasn't sure where this was going, but what the hell? She was almost coming on to him. "Um ... good to see you too. What's this all about?"

"Sable can't do much for you anymore, but I might have some ideas." As she spoke, she traced her fingers along his arm resting on the console.

Startled, he pulled away. "What are you doing, Orla?"

She reached up, turned his head to her, and looked directly at him. "You know all those years while you were screwing my sister and I was bunking with my goddamn brother? You know what I was thinking?"

"Uh ... no."

"I was thinking, why did you choose Sable and not me? It's not like she's a much of a looker."

"Um ... I don't know. We just sorta hit it off."

"Bullshit. You were in it for what she could do for you. Right?"

He thought it would be poor form to admit something about Sable aroused him, so he chose another tack: "Okay, okay, you're right. I thought if I could get close to her, there'd be something in it for me."

"Do you think I'm attractive?"

"Well, sure ... of course."

"Suppose I told you that Sable's powers have diminished. That there's very little she can do for you now."

"You're crazy."

"No, I'm not. It's as if all these years of dabbling in the spiritual world have left her depleted. There's nothing she can do for you now."

Becker grasped the steering wheel tightly, now facing straight ahead. He kept thinking about his initial euphoria at owning a private chunk of land with his compound. The partying, the toys, and the money were one thing, but having his private kingdom was another.

He faced her again, this time with a more compliant attitude and a softer expression. "What did you have in mind, Orla?"

She told him about their great-grandmother, Sarah Morgan, a Haida Indian, who had been mentored in witchcraft by the three sisters in San Francisco. She told him of the ties to Ebey's Landing and how the traditions had been passed down to the eldest daughter through generations.

"It's all interesting, Orla, but so what?"

"So Sable thinks that Buzz might be able to perform witchcraft."

"But ... how? You said ..."

"I know what I said about the eldest daughter, but Sable thinks her powers were lessening because someone else's were strengthening. She thinks that even though Buzz isn't a daughter, he might have developed his skills while living in the forest. How else can he eat? How does he get clothing? She thinks he used her old scrolls and talismans and learned by himself. She says the source of power in the family is finite, and there's only so much to go around. She thinks Buzz is taking over."

"I don't know if I believe you."

"Don't. Stop by the house and talk to Sable; see what she says. If I'm right, you promise to take me with you when you get the Whidbey property," she said with a lascivious smirk.

Becker started looking at Orla in a new light. She didn't have the mysterious aura of Sable, but she was a lot younger and infinitely better looking. *What the hell*, he thought. *I'll take her up on that visit.*

***

Alan Becker used the knocker on the front door of the house on Wilson Street the following week. He'd considered Orla's proposal but still wanted confirmation from Sable.

Orla answered and smiled coquettishly as she opened the door to let him in. She greeted him loudly enough for the others to hear: "Alan, what a surprise. What are you doing here?"

Sable appeared in the hallway, a disgusted look on her face. "What do you want?"

"You know why I'm here. I need some cash."

"I can't help you anymore, Alan. My powers have dried up."

So far, so good, he thought. "How could that be?"

"If you don't use them, you lose them. I've lost them."

"I've been doing some research, Sable. Let me tell you what I've learned."

Becker proceeded to relate the history of the Morgans/Aldrins, as Orla told him, and then asked her questions about Buzz. "How does your kid get food, and how do you know if he's even alive?"

"Firstly, he's also your kid. I know he's alive because I follow the police blotter from the Whidbey newspaper. Anytime there's a deer accident on that section of Lone Lake Road, it disappears immediately. And the few neighbors living there always complain about smoke and smells. I'm his mother, Alan; he's alive."

"Could he be a witch?"

Sable looked at her hands and took a deep breath. She stared at him, then spoke carefully. "He wouldn't be a *witch*, you idiot; he'd be a *warlock*. Secondly ... I suppose it's possible."

Now that it was confirmed, Becker glanced at an innocent-looking Orla and smiled.

Sable caught the son of a bitch's grin and screamed, "*Get out!* Don't you ever fucking come back here, and if you even think of hurting Buzz, I'll find a way to make you wish you hadn't." Becker turned quietly to the front door, now convinced Orla had been telling the truth.

Over the next few months, Orla's visits to Becker's Lake Whatcom house became more frequent. They discussed several options for getting Buzz to comply with their wishes, but Becker stressed the need for flexibility, and, in the end, it was left up to him to make the operational decisions. It was agreed that Orla would keep a low profile and stay with her brother and sister until she moved to Whidbey Island with her new squeeze.

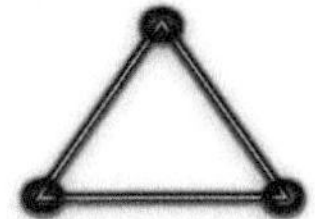

Twenty-Seven

I called Sable and asked if I could meet with her. She balked at first, but when I told her we'd come up with an idea that might cause Becker to show his face, she agreed. Wally and Kate had met with O'Malley, and, of course, the old geezer had agreed. The challenge was ensuring the retired designer and his wife kept their noses out of the caper.

When I arrived, Sable was alone. The house smelled the same, and it was still hot as hell. Without asking, she told me Thorn was at Home Depot picking up plumbing supplies for a leaky faucet in the upstairs bathroom. I had difficulty seeing the guy fixing anything, but, hey, maybe he was mechanically inclined.

She seemed a little nervous, so I made small talk by asking how her sister was doing since she wasn't there either. A look of doubt clouded her pale face, and she appeared to be searching for the right words to answer me.

"Orla's out somewhere. I'm not sure where; it's her life."

Her response suggested more was happening than she was letting on, so I asked, "Is everything okay, Sable?"

She was silent momentarily, probably deciding how much to tell me. Then, tentatively, she began. "I haven't been a very good mother. I was more concerned with myself, my magic, and my relationship with Alan than I was with my son.

I left him alone in the woods when he was a teenager. What kind of person does that? Even witches take care of their own children.

"Now my son's father has kidnapped him. Poor Buzz, all he ever wanted was to be left alone. Thorn lives in the moment and is of little help except, I guess, to fix shit around the house. I feel like I'm by myself in all this."

I hesitated to interrupt, but I was curious where this was going. "What about Orla?"

"Yes ... what *about* Orla?"

"I, uh ... I don't know."

"She's been gone a lot over the past few months, and when she's here, it's like she *isn't* here. I'm getting some odd vibes from her, and she hasn't shown much concern over Buzz being missing."

I wasn't sure what to say, so I changed the subject to why I had come. I explained our idea of putting the property in someone else's name to rile up Becker so he'd show his face. I wasn't sure how she'd react to transferring land that had been in her family's name forever, but she surprised me by asking how it would work.

"You would quit claim the deed to another person, and we'd register the transaction with the county. After this is over, he will do the same back to you."

"I don't think I can do that."

"Can't or don't want to?"

"Can't. I pay the taxes on the property because it's in my name, but the deed is part of an irrevocable trust set up by my grandmother. It has conditions that only allow transfer to the eldest daughter in each generation."

"So even if you wanted to transfer the property to Becker, you couldn't?"

"Correct. The only way would be to go back in time to undo all that Angela Morgan set up. I'm sure that's what Alan wants Buzz for."

Shit, the plan we'd come up with was good, but it looked like we were stymied. Sable looked at me expectantly, probably thinking I'd find a way out of our problem.

While I was still mulling other options, she said, "What if you could get the county to fudge it?"

"Huh?"

"You know, get them to show some other name as owner for a few days. Doesn't the sheriff's office have some clout with the county?"

"I don't know ... maybe."

"Who were you going to use?"

"The guy you worked with when you planned on building there, Kevin O'Malley. We figured Becker would think he wanted to develop it, and that would upset him even more."

"Do you know that Alan stiffed him when we decided not to build?"

"Let's not worry about that. Kevin has surely forgotten by now. Also, he's a good friend—sometimes a pain in the ass but trustworthy as hell. Plus, we can control him."

"Will we be able to keep this from my brother and sister?"

"It's just your name on the deed, so unless they see it online, it shouldn't be an issue. Why, if you don't mind me asking?"

"It's in my name, but it was always going to be for the three of us. Thorn might worry—he does that about everything—and Orla ... I'm just not sure. I'm afraid to let her know what's happening right now."

The quieter this was, the better our chance of flushing Becker, so the fewer people who knew, the better.

"That would be fine. So you're on board with this?"

"If you think it'll allow us to find Buzz, then absolutely. I might not have been much of a mother then, but at least I can try now."

I stopped in Coupeville on the way back to Freeland and asked the sheriff to meet me at the county offices. The man was a political animal, but, more often than not, his heart was in the right place. It took some persuading, but once we convinced him that a man's life could be at stake, the county assessor agreed to temporarily show the property owner as Kevin O'Malley.

If this plan was successful, my guess was things would happen soon.

TWENTY-EIGHT

He knew using the material from Ebey's Landing for talismans was futile. The bark from the blockhouse still gave him a tingle, but experience had taught him to trust his instincts. No, there would be no magic from his work anytime soon.

Buzz went through the motions. He constructed the ceremonial fires in each of the three stone circles and placed the herbs and pseudo-talismans in the center of each one. He recited the necessary verses in the proper order for the benefit of his onlooking father but was sure they would bear no fruit.

If he successfully changed the property's provenance, he would have no home. Delaying the outcome might not help in the long run, but at least he could buy some time and hope for a miracle. The shriveled ear might hold the key, but he'd keep that to himself. He believed the deputy might have taken the item for some unknown reason and was glad the fire hadn't destroyed it.

"This gonna work?" Becker asked.

"I won't know until it does or doesn't. If it does, the property will change ownership; otherwise, it will stay the same."

"I thought you said these things we brought back would do the trick."

Buzz was annoyed by this man. Yes, he *was* his father, but the only thing he had provided was the sperm. He felt no connection to him and—strangely, because he hadn't seen her in decades—he felt protective of his mother. Perhaps it was because Becker was intent on causing her loss to benefit himself, and he felt sorry for her. That the abandoned child felt anything for the mother who had done so was odd, but then again, Buzz Aldrin was a unique individual.

"I said they *might* work, Alan; it's not an exact science."

Becker said nothing and walked back into the house on Lummi Island. He'd stopped worrying about Buzz leaving since he had explained the penalty for not cooperating.

After the last fires had smoldered out, Buzz returned to his room and crashed on his bed. He was sure nothing would come of the ceremony and wondered what his father's wrath would look like when he found out.

Becker accessed the county website so often that he left their home page open on his computer. He checked daily to see if any changes to the property tax records for the parcel on Whidbey Island had occurred. When he rose the following morning, he padded out to the small kitchen table, hit the space bar to reawaken his laptop, and navigated immediately to the Island County website. He clicked on the familiar parcel, and up popped the details for its owner and taxable entity.

Goddamn, that little fucker ... he raced into the walled-off section that was Buzz's and kicked the leg hanging over the side of the bed. "*Get up* ... get up, you piece of shit." He kicked him again.

"Huh ... wh ... what do you want?"

"Who the fuck is Kevin O'Malley?" Even as he asked the question, the name was familiar to him.

"I dunno."

"Why does *my* property now show him as the owner?"

Buzz thought the timing was inappropriate to point out that the Whidbey property *wasn't* his father's, so he let the thought slide.

"I ... I don't know. I don't know how it happened or who that is."

Becker was still for a moment. Something about that name ... then it came to him. *It's the guy we talked to about designing the compound. Shit.*

Buzz was still frightened, but his father's anger had ebbed somewhat. He timidly asked, "Do *you* know who it is?"

"I do. Someone from long ago. Thing is, I don't know how he became the owner, but I'm damn sure gonna find out."

Now that the storm clouds had passed, Buzz pressed his luck. "I didn't have anything to do with it." Even to him, it sounded whiny.

"Shut up, Buzz. Even if you didn't, your goddamn magic didn't work. Now, there's someone else in the picture. I need to figure this out. You stay here and do something; there's someone I need to visit."

Buzz stayed where he was until his father had dressed and left. Somehow, he knew Alan would visit his mother and feared for her safety. His father had always been a hothead, and it seemed the years had only worsened his temper.

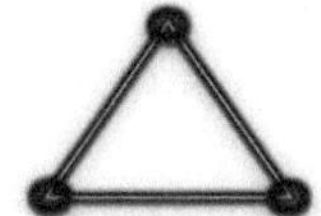

TWENTY-NINE

Kate Mahoney found herself fantasizing. She was parked in her yellow Mustang at the end of Wilson Street, hoping that the ruse they had fabricated would lure Becker into confronting Sable Aldrin. She had dated lots of guys, mostly cops, but none seriously. Wally Turpin was nothing like any of them.

He was a fireplug of a man but softer and more empathetic on the inside than anyone she'd ever met. She loved it when he blushed when he wasn't sure if his words had ruffled her feathers, yet she respected that he shared his thoughts. The thought of settling down with anyone, much less a cop from some island, had somehow crept into her thinking. Just the image of him smiling sent a shiver through her. She had seen him last night after their meeting with Wilkie when he'd explained the details of the name change on the deed, and it seemed like a long time ago. With any luck, she'd be done with her shift at three, and they could meet in LaConner for a bite.

The GT was not an innocuous-looking ride, but it was probably the last vehicle a cop would employ on a stakeout, so she chose to use it.

She'd been at it since seven and was just about to fire up the 351-cubic-inch engine to ward off the forty-degree outside temperature when a black Ford Super Duty pickup rumbled by at a pace far greater than acceptable on the quiet residential street. She instantly abandoned her daydreaming and reverted to cop mode. This *had* to be Becker.

The oversized pickup pulled into the Aldrins' driveway and rocked to and fro as the driver threw the transmission into park. Looking through her Nikon binoculars, she watched as a tall, fit-looking man climbed from the cab, vaulted the four steps to the porch, and banged on the front door. She saw the door open a few inches and held her breath as the visitor flung it open and walked purposefully inside.

"He's here, Roger; we've got him," she reported to Wilkie as soon as he answered his cell.

"Can you follow him? We need to find out where he's got Buzz stashed away."

She hadn't expected Becker to show up so soon, and her personal ride was less than ideal for tailing someone, but she'd be damned if she let this asshat get away. "I can do it, Roger. What about backup?"

"If we don't get there by the time you need it, call BPD; otherwise, I'd like for Wally and me to be it. We're in Coupeville briefing the sheriff, but we're on our way."

Kate hoped the Island County deputies could make it in time. She trusted her fellow officers in the Bellingham Police Department, but she preferred working with Roger and, of course, Wally because, after all, it was their case.

Becker had been inside for almost fifteen minutes before she saw the door open again. His large frame filled the opening while he was still facing inside. It appeared as though he was shouting at someone while emphatically pointing at them. Abruptly, he slammed the door, turned, and walked to his truck.

Shit, she thought. *The deputies are over a half hour away—that's if they use lights and sirens—and now I've gotta follow this guy in a car that looks like a banana.*

After he passed, she made a quick U-turn and maintained a comfortable distance behind. Traffic was light through town, and the big truck was easy to see, even when separated by several vehicles. Becker made his way to Marine Drive and headed west. Traffic became nonexistent as they left the city, and she was forced to hang back even further. The constant drizzle was a blessing, but she was still cautious about getting too close.

Still focused on her target, she tried to imagine where he was headed. Then she saw a sign announcing they had crossed onto the Lummi Indian Reservation, and it dawned on her: *Lummi Island. The son of a bitch is headed for Lummi Island.*

She called Wilkie as soon as she'd figured it out. When Roger saw who it was, he put it on speaker. "He's on his way to Lummi Island, Roger; that's got to be it."

"Can you stay with him, Kate?" Wally asked.

"Yeah, but the ferry to the island is tiny; it only holds twenty cars."

"Is that a problem?"

"It is if you're driving a '69 yellow Mustang GT. I didn't plan on tailing the guy to Lummi Island. *Shit.*"

It was quiet for a few seconds, then Roger asked, "I'm guessing BPD doesn't have anyone there, right?"

"Right, and it's not part of the Lummi Nation either, so there's no tribal police."

"What are our options?"

"Only two, as far as I can see. I either let him go, and we try to pick him up when he leaves again, or I take a chance and ride over on the ferry with him. Maybe he'll think I'm a visitor or something."

"Is he dangerous, Kate?" Wally was concerned.

"I can't say. He's a big guy, and he *did* kidnap Buzz, so there's that. As far as I know, though, besides threats and abductions, he's a stand-up guy. I'm leaning toward following him; we may not get another chance."

Wally smiled. Even in the face of danger, his new girlfriend still dispensed the sarcasm. He said, "Be careful then, Kate. We're about forty minutes out. Keep in touch and let us know what's happening."

"Copy, guys. I'll get back when I know something."

She watched as the big Ford truck pulled up to the ferry line. It was a weekday, so it appeared there would only be a few cars on the boat. Turning onto the shoulder, she pretended to be on the phone and let three more vehicles get between her and Becker. The drizzle had subsided, and the sun threatened to show—an unfortunate event if one in a yellow GT wanted to remain unnoticed.

The ferry landed, discharged its vehicles, and loaded those headed to the long, skinny San Juan island. Kate spent the six-minute crossing, scrolling on her phone and pretending to be occupied. An occasional glance at Becker saw him talking on his cell phone and aggressively gesturing with his hands. She'd give anything to know what he was saying and to whom.

The journey was a blink, and disembarking was accomplished in minutes. As an artist colony and part-time vacation spot, the island's population was only half that of the summer months. It seemed the vehicles were evenly split, heading north and south on Nugent Road, and unfortunately, she ended up directly behind Becker's pickup.

Although the posted speed limit coming off the ferry was twenty-five, Becker seemed in a hurry, and in short order he was over a hill and out of sight. She sped up until she saw him taking a curve and relaxed, thinking he'd be difficult to lose on this narrow two-lane road.

She continued through several curves, which opened up to a straightaway without anything moving. She panicked and stepped on the gas until the road reached a T and still no Becker. *What the hell? He must have turned off, but where?*

She swung the wheel hard left, stepped on it, did a power U-ey, and headed back the way she'd come. About a half mile back, just before the curve, a gravel drive led into a dark canopy of Douglas fir and western redcedar. She turned onto the narrow driveway and pulled her car off to the side where it would be out of sight. Next, she tucked her service weapon behind her back, grabbed her Nikons, and tried calling Wilkie.

Of course there's no service—shit! With the island's elevation varying from sea level to over fifteen hundred feet, it was common to experience geographic cell phone outages.

Not willing to risk losing Becker, she left her vehicle and walked carefully along the side of the narrow drive where the crunch of the gravel would be muted. The air was freezing and heavy with humidity; she was glad she'd worn her heavy denim jacket. After almost four hundred yards of uphill walking, she saw a cedar-shingled cabin in a small clearing. A black Ford Super Duty pickup was parked alongside it.

She used one of the giant firs for cover as she peered through her binocs and focused on a large window on the right side of the porch. She watched for several minutes, hoping to see some movement. Then she heard a branch snap behind her—then a shotgun shell being racked into the chamber.

"Hands in the air ... now!"

She complied, seriously pissed that she'd allowed him to get behind her.

"Keep facing the tree, reach behind you with two fingers, and put the gun on the ground. Put your phone next to it, too."

She did as instructed, then turned around and faced him.

"Did you think I wouldn't see a yellow Mustang following me?"

She said nothing.

"I picked you up just after I left Sable's place. I wondered how you knew I'd be there, but then I thought about how strange the name change on the property was. After I left there, Orla phoned me to let me know what had happened. She overheard Sable telling Thorn about the plan, and, stupid me, I fell for it."

"Why don't you let Buzz and me go, and you can get on with your life? I'm sure you can convince him not to press charges, and I won't. C'mon, let's forget about this."

If Kate had had any hope of convincing this man, it was quickly dashed. His cruel smile and arrogant manner were enough of an answer.

"How about you turn around and get that cute little ass of yours up the hill to the house? I've got just the place for you inside." He picked up her gun and put a bullet through her phone, the boom shattering the stillness in the forest.

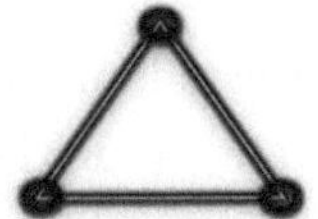

THIRTY

We hadn't heard from Kate since she'd reported that Becker was headed to Lummi Island. Still twenty minutes from the ferry landing, we kept trying to reach her, and Wally was looking more concerned by the minute.

"What if he made her, Rog?"

"I guess he could have, but from what I've seen, she seems like a resourceful cop. Agree?"

He nodded his assent but still looked worried. We arrived at the dock as the gate was starting to come down, but when the attendant saw our cruiser, he waved us on.

We got underway immediately, and Wally was out of the car questioning the deckhand almost before I had the thing in park. Their conversation was short, and Wally was back inside in less than a minute.

"He said he was sure there was a yellow Mustang on the 1:30 crossing; that was forty minutes ago, and she hasn't returned."

"So she's somewhere on the island?"

"Yup. The guy said cell service sucks on Lummi too, so maybe that's why we can't reach her."

Lummi was not very big as islands go, but it was densely forested, especially on the south end, with only a smattering of residences. The difficulty was in trying to guess where Becker had gone. We hoped to stumble across Kate's yellow Mustang, but we both knew this was a long shot.

In twenty minutes, we'd driven the island's length with no success, and I could see Wally was becoming anxious. "Any ideas?" I asked.

"This isn't working. We know she's here somewhere, and so is Becker, so how do we find her?"

"My guess is he's somewhere isolated, or someone would have picked up his plates by now. There's gotta be a few hundred homes scattered in the forest here on the south end, but short of knocking on every door, I'm not coming up with anything."

Wally considered this depressing approach for a few minutes and said, "If he's here, which we *know* he is, then he's got to be in a cabin or house that's out of the way."

"Yeah ... so?"

"What if we list all the seasonal homes and check to see if any of them are rentals? We can check with the post office, get a list of the places that forward mail or have it held, then find out if any of those places are rented out."

"I like it, but first, let's stop by the Whatcom County sheriff's office and tell them what we're up to. They have jurisdiction over Lummi Island, and I'm sure they have a better handle on the residents than we would."

"Will they be pissed that we're here without their knowledge?"

"Only a little bit. Remember, we didn't know we'd end up here, and neither did Kate. I'm sure BPD and the sheriff have a good relationship; hell, their offices are only a block apart, and we can use the help from their deputies."

We took the next ferry back to the mainland, called ahead to the sheriff, told him what was happening, and asked him to update BPD on Kate's disappearance. If my guess were correct, we'd soon have more boots on the streets of Lummi Island than had been there in some time.

***

Buzz was seated at the small kitchen table munching on a bowl of Cheerios when he heard the gunshot. A minute later, when Becker shoved Kate Mahoney through the door, he jumped up and managed to spill half the bowl.

"Get your ass in your room, Buzz; we've got a guest joining us."

He pushed the shotgun into Kate's back and directed her to the room he'd partitioned off for Buzz. "In there, both of you."

He locked the bolt on the door while Buzz stood there, eyes staring at Kate but appearing dazed and confused.

"Hand me your keys and your ID," he directed Kate.

"Kate Mahoney, huh?" he read after she complied. "It says you're a detective … wow, who'da thought a pretty little thing like you would be a cop? How about you two get to know each other? I'll be back in a few minutes. We can't have that fancy car attracting anyone, can we?"

As soon as Becker had left, Kate introduced herself: "I'm Kate Mahoney with Bellingham Police, and you're Buzz Aldrin, right?"

"Um … yes. Who … why are you here?"

"I'm working with some deputies from Whidbey Island. We've been trying to find you."

"How come? Who knew— Wait, was it that Wilkie guy who stopped by my place?"

"Yup, he's the one that got things rolling, and your mother has been helping too."

"My mother?"

"Yes. She's worried about you. She said she hasn't been much of a mother, but she seems genuinely concerned."

Buzz seemed to take this in while Kate used the opportunity to assess the space they were confined to. There was a bed, a toilet, and a sink. Right away, she was thinking how much fun this was going to be, just her and Buzz … The plywood wall was impenetrable, as was the hog wire. Although the wall was only eight feet tall, the razor wire topping it eliminated any thoughts of climbing over it. For now, she was stuck here.

***

Darkness had arrived. The two captives were sitting on opposite sides of the bed, looking through the hog wire at Becker, who had returned and was now scrolling and texting on his phone.

Kate interrupted him. "You can forget about it, Becker; there's no service here."

"Shut up, Mahoney. You don't know what you're talking about. I've got service as long as we're on this hill. It's down on the road where the signal's blocked that nothing works."

"What are you planning to do with me?"

"I haven't decided yet, but one thing is sure: you're not going anywhere soon. At least not until Buzz here takes care of business for me."

Buzz seemed tired of sitting on the sidelines and finally spoke. "I don't think I can do what you want, Alan. None of the talismans work. Either that or I don't have the power."

"Bullshit. I saw how you were when we were at Ebey's Landing. Did you think I missed that? Something there got to you; what was it?"

Buzz said nothing, afraid he would finally have to give in to his father's wishes.

"*Hey* ... I'm talking to you ... *Buzz* ..."

"I, uh ... I don't know. There's an energy about that place that I can't explain."

"I'm giving you until tomorrow morning to figure something out. If you can't, maybe I'll have to pay your mother another visit."

***

Several hours passed with minimal conversation among the three people. Becker had passed the dinner staple—chicken pot pies—to the two prisoners, an encouraging thought to Kate since he wasn't starving them to death. *Of course*, she thought, *maybe he's simply doing it to ensure Buzz's cooperation.*

Shortly before nine o'clock, a vehicle could be heard approaching the cabin. The snapping and crunching of the gravel eventually ceased, and the faint hum of a car engine stopped. Buzz looked at Kate, who glanced at Becker, who seemed unconcerned about the sound.

All three turned to the door when, without so much as a knock, it swung wide open. A slim, gray-haired woman slammed it shut and walked over to Becker, who stood to embrace her. Both Buzz and Kate stood, surprised at what was happening.

"You'll have to excuse our rudeness," Becker said sarcastically as they disengaged. "Buzz, just in case you don't recognize her, this is your aunt, Orla. Mahoney, I think you've already met."

"What are we going to do with her?" Orla looked concerned.

"I don't know. So far, we haven't done much except take Buzz away from his home and try to get him to do some magic for us. I can't see him pressing charges, and anyway, who's gonna believe he's a witch or warlock or whatever?"

"Yeah, but we've got a cop locked up. I don't think they like that."

"Let's see how we make out with your nephew here, and then we can decide."

"You figured out the name on the county website is bullshit, right?"

"Yup. It was just to get me off the island so Mahoney here could follow me."

"What next?"

"Buzz can't seem to get anywhere, but when we got to Ebey's Landing, he seemed different, like there was some energy about the place."

"Has he tried that old ear?"

Becker looked confused. "What are you talking about?"

"The ear, the goddamn ear."

"Orla ... what the *fuck* are you talking about?"

"Sable had this shriveled-up ear that she kept in a little box. She said it was from the guy who settled Ebey's Landing, and it was passed down from her Indian great-grandmother. She thought it had special powers but was afraid of it, too. She forgot it when we left the island, and when we went back to look for Buzz, it was gone from the yurt. She assumed Buzz had taken it."

After this revelation, the two looked through the hog wire at Buzz, who seemed distracted by something on the floor. Kate, too, was now looking at him.

"Oh, Buzzer?" Becker seemed to sense a shift in the cosmos.

Still looking down, he answered, "Yes?"

"Is this true? About the ear?"

"Um ... yes. My mom said it was connected to her past and Isaac Ebey's spirit. She *was* afraid of it too because of its power."

"And you never told me this? Why?"

"Cuz it's gone. I kept it on the shelf in my house, but I saw it was missing that day you burned the place down."

"How could it be missing? You were the only one there."

"No ... I think that cop stopped by after you kidnapped me. When I went inside to get my things, it wasn't there, and it smelled like someone had been inside."

"It smelled? You're kidding, right? That place smelled like a sewer."

"I could tell ..." He still hadn't raised his head.

"Why would the cop take it?"

"I don't know."

Becker turned to Orla. "Do you think this thing could work?"

"Who knows? All I'm sure of is that Sable treated it like gold. She was beside herself when we couldn't find it the last time we were there."

"How do we get it?"

"Hell, I don't know. If the cop took it, then maybe it's in his office at the station. He probably has no idea what or whose it is."

Becker turned back to Buzz and said, "Why don't you do some magic or a spell or something and get the ear back here?"

"It doesn't work like that; the ear *is* the talisman. It's the sacred item that causes things to happen, but nobody can cause anything to happen to *it*."

"Suppose we can get it. Will it be enough to get this done?"

Buzz looked tired and sounded even worse. It was as if he wanted this chapter in his life to end. He finally looked up at Becker and Orla and capitulated. "If you can get it, I think I can make it happen, but I'll need to do it from where the ear originated."

"Ebey's Landing?" Becker asked.

"Yes. I think it could work."

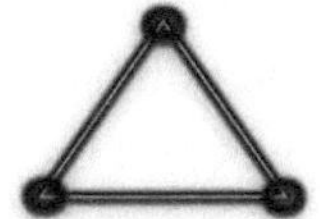

Thirty-One

Wally and I elected to stay in Bellingham for the night. Sheriff Davis, our fearless leader in Island County, had granted us permission and placed several off-duty deputies on call for the South Whidbey district. Lawbreakers rarely went on a rampage on our island, so we were confident things were under control.

After meeting with the BPD chief and the Whatcom County sheriff, it was agreed that Bellingham Police would lead the effort because Kate was one of theirs. The sheriff would provide backup, and Wally and I would assist where needed since this whole thing had started in our neck of the woods.

The computer geeks at BPD had listed all the seasonal homes on the south end of Lummi and were contacting the owners to see how many had rented out their places for the off-season. Only a handful of owners answered since it was after nine o'clock at night, and only one reported having a renter. Unfortunately, an older woman was now living there year-round, and the home was immediately removed from the list.

Over fifty residences were classified as seasonal, and although the owners were identified, any hope of contacting them would have to wait until morning. We stayed at a nearby hotel and agreed to meet for breakfast at four the following day. Wally probably wouldn't be getting much sleep, and when I told him most of the property owners were two or three hours ahead of us on the West Coast, he insisted we get an early start on the phones.

The Whatcom County Sheriff's Department paired with the BPD in two-person teams to begin knocking on doors at daybreak regardless of the progress or lack of it with the phone campaign. The forecast for the following day was clear skies—a rarity at this time of year—and temperatures in the mid-forties. The promise of a day without clouds and rain had the task force chomping at the bit; Kate Mahoney was one of their own, and they were determined to get her back safely.

***

My phone alarm jolted me from a sound sleep at 3:45. Before I turned the lights off, I'd spent some face time with Andie, bringing her up to speed on the state of the investigation. Her questions, perceptive as always, spurred me to reconsider what was driving Becker. Now that Kate and Buzz were missing, I began to consider whether he was a lone wolf in the crime spree.

I met Wally at the self-serve breakfast bar, where he was slurping down a sixteen-ounce cup of black coffee. "Sleep well?" I asked.

"What do you think? I keep thinking about this guy; it's not like he's a hardened criminal or anything. Sure, he's a blackmailer and probably an asshole, but why go to all this trouble for a piece of land?"

"Yeah, I've been thinking about that too. I'm also wondering how he does this stuff by himself. He's got a place somewhere on Lummi, Buzz to deal with, and now Kate's missing. That's a lot of balls in the air for one person."

We were quiet for a few minutes, me trying to understand what was happening and Wally, I was sure, thinking about Kate. Then my phone dancing on the table startled us.

I saw the number and immediately took the call.

"Yes? ... When? ... What did they take? ... Are you sure? ... Okay, let me talk to Wally, and I may get back to you. Otherwise, we'll check it out when we get back."

Wally was staring at me as I disconnected. "What?"

"That was Sheriff Davis. It seems our Freeland office was broken into last night."

"Broken *into*?"

"Yep, that's a first for me. Usually folks want to get away from the cops. Thing is, Davis said nothing was taken."

"That makes no sense. Someone breaks into a sheriff's office for fun? Bullshit."

"I agree, but the two deputies on duty were cruising somewhere, and when they got back, the door was busted in, and the alarm was blasting. They called Bruce in to see what was missing, and he said nothing."

Wally looked tired, and I was sure Kate was on his mind. The break-in was bizarre, but until something else popped up, I'd have to put it on the back burner. "Okay ... let's get over to BPD and start making some calls. Maybe Bruce will discover the reason for what happened when he's had a chance to wake up."

We got to the squad room at five and were given a list of Lummi Island homeowners from the Eastern time zone to call. Some numbers didn't exist, and a few weren't answered. We left messages where we could and tried various searches for those property owners we couldn't reach.

It was tedious work, but there weren't any shortcuts. The teams on the island had reported no results so far. At nine, we broke for coffee and stale donuts; Kate's associates' glum faces showed their frustration.

As we returned to our workstations, my phone buzzed with a number I'd seen before, but I couldn't recall its owner. Thinking it could help in our search, I answered it.

"This is Wilkie."

"Deputy, this is Sable Aldrin."

"Hi, ma'am. We're kinda busy here; there's a missing detective. She was following Becker and we lost contact with her."

"Remember when I said Orla was acting strangely?"

"Um ... yes, but I need to get back to work."

As if I hadn't said anything, she continued, "Well, she's been gone a lot lately, and now she's been missing for forty-eight hours."

"If you're worried about her, you should file a report with the Bellingham Police, but I need to get back to work."

"I think she's with Alan Becker."

"Listen, ma'am ... what did you say?"

"I'm pretty sure she's with Becker and they're holding Buzz until he can deliver for them."

Wally overheard my end of the conversation and stopped beside me, sensing something was up.

"Why do you think that?"

"Deputy Wilkie, I may have lost some of my powers, but I know my sister. When I was in that relationship with Alan years ago, Orla was quiet about it, but I could tell she was jealous. She has always been in my shadow, and her resentment flares up occasionally. I think she's been seeing Alan for some time, and now that he's making his move with Buzz, I'm certain Orla is working with him."

If Sable had been correct, we would have had a completely different situation, but I needed to be sure. "Sable, do you have a picture of Orla?"

"Yes ... why?"

"Will you text it to me? It's not that I doubt you, but I need confirmation on this, and I think I know how."

"Okay, I'm sending it now ... and Deputy?"

"Yes?"

"Will you let me know when you find Buzz?"

"I will, and thanks for the call. This helps a lot."

"Wait—there's something else."

"Yes?"

"When we left the yurt camp, I left something behind, and I think Buzz has it. Whatever happens, you can't let Alan find out about it. It's the most powerful talisman in my family's history, and with it, he can force Buzz to do almost anything."

Uh-oh. My gut clenched as the puzzle pieces began falling into place. I dreaded the answer to my next question because I already knew it, but I asked anyway: "What is it, Sable? What is the talisman?"

"It's the ear that belonged to Isaac Ebey. Don't let them get it."

I didn't let on that I thought that ship had sailed but thanked her and said goodbye.

"Talk to me, Roger; what was all that?" Wally was primed for action.

"We've got problems, but first, I need you to show this picture to Becker's neighbor. Have him confirm who was hanging out there."

"Rog ... that's Orla."

"It is, and Sable says she's in this with Becker."

"What about here? We need to find Kate."

"We will, Wally, we will, but this is the fastest way. Get this confirmed. It should only take— Wait ... can you reach Montgomery on his cell and text it?"

"Sure."

"Okay, do it now. Then let's get the team updated."

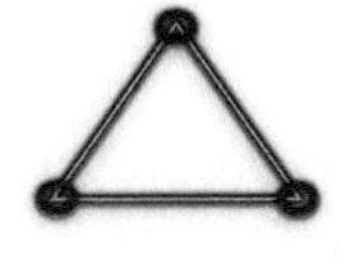

THIRTY-TWO

The cabin was cold. The dial on her smartwatch said it was close to midnight, and the only light in the place was courtesy of the full moon shining through the window on the far side of the divided room.

Orla, Becker, and Buzz had taken off a little after ten, and within minutes of their departure, her prison was plunged into darkness. She assumed that whatever the power source was, it had run out of fuel.

She felt terrible for Buzz. His years in the forest had taught him plenty but very little about the ways of the world and the avarice of some of its inhabitants. He seemed almost trance-like, responding robotically to the directions from his father, and appeared unaware of any consequences his actions would bring.

On the other hand, Orla was energized by the prospect of a happily-ever-after scenario with Becker. It was certain both of them were delusional in their expectations. What was disturbing was their belief in the magic Buzz could perform. Kate had been taught there was no effect without cause, that nothing happened for *no* reason, and that talk of magic was pure bullshit.

That Wally was open to such nonsense bothered her somewhat, but she was sure she could eventually convince him otherwise. She wished like hell he was with her now. Based on the conversation between Orla and Becker, the three of them were on their way to burgle a police station to steal a goddamn shriveled-up old ear. *What the fuck is wrong with these people?*

They'd treated her like she wasn't there when they let Buzz out. According to their discussions, after they obtained the item from the police station, they would go to Ebey's Landing, where Buzz would perform some ritual that would magically show Becker was the valid and original owner of some land on Whidbey Island.

And she was now a prisoner in some stupid freezing cabin on Lummi fucking Island. She'd always had a temper, and now she could feel it rising. She was pissed that she'd let Becker get the drop on her, pissed that she'd let him lock her up, pissed that they were taking advantage of a guy who wanted nothing but to be left alone, and royally fucking pissed off that she was on the sidelines for who knew how long.

She had assessed the makeshift cell when she was first forced into it. The three-quarter-inch plywood walls were tightly screwed and impossible to penetrate. The hog wire was brutally strong but climbable, except for the razor wire fastened to the top rail of the wall. No windows were on her side of the cabin, and the walls were spruce logs over a foot in diameter. She fed her anger and determination to escape for fear that a tiny spark of panic might threaten her resolve. *There has to be a way out of here.*

She began by doing fifty push-ups, fifty sit-ups, and fifty squats, followed by a five-minute plank. When she had finished, she was exhausted and sweating but no longer cold, and her mind was clear. If there was no way to open the bolted door or penetrate the plywood or hog wire, then all that remained was to scale the wall—the one topped with razor wire.

Her cell contained a bed, a sink and toilet, and a small refrigerator, none of which was much help ... unless ... The mattress on the bed was flat with no springs, similar to that of a futon. If she could find a way to hold it in place, covering the razor wire, then scaling the hog wire would be a cinch.

She pulled it off the bed and attempted to throw it to the top of the wall, but it was too heavy, and she ended up under it every time before she gave up. The damn thing had to weigh forty pounds and was far flimsier than innerspring mattresses. Her idea was sound, but the execution needed improvement.

With no light save for the moon glow, she felt her way around the now-naked bed and was surprised to feel that the frame wasn't wire or slats. It was a rope bed. The construction had been popular in the 1800s and early 1900s when money was scarce before the widespread use of box springs. A single rope was woven back and forth between the two sides to create a semi-rigid platform to support the mattress.

It took some time, but by feeling, she traced her way to the foot of the bed, where the rope started and stopped. The material felt rough and was probably woven hemp or sisal, which made it difficult to untie the aged knots fastening it.

After an hour of frustration and broken nails, she managed to untie the knots and fed the rope back and forth until it lay in a twisted pile at her feet. Kate had been so engrossed in her task that she hadn't thoroughly thought through her plan. She considered simply tossing it over the top and hoisting the mattress up to cover the razor wire, but now she understood if she took that approach, the razors would quickly cut through the rope.

Now, with fragments of an alternative plan, she put the rope between her teeth, stood on top of the small fridge, and climbed the hog wire until she could reach the top row of squares. She fed the rope through and over the wire, then jumped back down with the loose end in hand.

The mattress was about six and a half feet long, three feet wide, and six inches thick, and nowhere was there a place to tie the goddamn rope. There was plenty of it, just no straps or openings where it could be attached. *Screw it*, she thought. *I'm gonna get this done.*

She wrapped the rope around the mattress about two feet from the end, pulled it as tight as possible, and tied it. Although she couldn't see it, she assumed it now looked like a giant white Gumby. She stood it against the wall and pulled the rope taut through the hog wire.

Rather than functioning as a pulley, which would have allowed her to hoist the mattress to the top of the wall, the rope's coarse fiber was immovable against the galvanized hog wire as she attempted to winch the dense cushion vertically. *Jesus, this isn't working.*

Sapped of energy, she sat down, leaning against the now-upholstered wall with the rope's end in one hand, keeping the mattress vertical. She sat there catching her breath, thinking about Wally Turpin. She wished he were here now; he'd know what to do. Picturing his impish smile hardened her resolve. *Okay, girl, get off your ass and make this happen.* She stood up, grabbed the mattress by hugging it around the middle, and lifted it several inches while at the same time tightening the rope she held. Now the damn thing was at least off the floor, but there was another five feet to go before the top of it was above the razor wire.

Lifting the heavy pile of compressed cotton and wool a few inches at a time and securing it by tightening the rope was mind-numbing and exhausting. She was thankful her time in the gym had prepared her for what could have been a new Olympic event—the mattress lift—but she was physically drained and a puddle of sweat by the time the top of the mattress was a foot over the razor wire.

It took several hours, and the rope's heavy texture blistered at first, then tore and cut the palms of her hands. After finally securing it, her white Gumby now floating against the hog wire, she slumped to the floor, leaning against the small fridge. Thankfully, it still held several bottles of cold water, which she extracted and drank greedily, steeling herself for the next step in her escape plan.

She hadn't thought much about the time but noticed the room wasn't as dark now as before, suggesting the first hints of daybreak. She was shocked to see her watch showed it was a few minutes before seven. It would be easy to collapse on the floor, as depleted as she was, but without knowing if or when Becker might return, she collected herself for her final assault on this goddamn wall. *At least now I can see what I'm doing.*

Standing now, she could see the results of her all-night efforts. The mattress floated against the wall and extended a foot above the razor wire, the top barely leaning over the lethal-looking blades. She peeled her sweaty T-shirt off, tore it into strips, and used it to wrap around her bleeding hands, then donned her denim jacket and zipped it up tightly. Standing on the small refrigerator, she began climbing the hog wire to the mattress's right until she was level with the wall's highest point. From this position, keeping her right foot on the wire, she reached over to the top of the mattress and pulled herself up until her stomach crushed the futon-like mass over the razor wire.

With the bulk of her weight now past the top of the wall, she slid headfirst toward the floor on the other side.

This is fucking perfect, she thought. *I spent the entire fucking night finding a way over this goddamn wall, only to crush my brains on the other side.*

At the last minute, still upside down, she grabbed the hog wire with painfully damaged hands, flipped over with a piercing scream, and dropped to the floor on her feet.

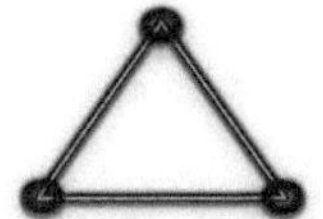

THIRTY-THREE

It took Mr. Montgomery ten seconds to identify Orla Aldrin as the frequent visitor to Becker's rental on Lake Whatcom. I should have seen this, but I was so involved with the urgency of the investigation that I failed to step back and ask the tough questions.

The fact that Becker knew Sable's powers had ebbed, the history of the Morgan/Aldrin family, and the magical powers of Isaac Ebey's missing ear had to come from someone close.

Because Orla had been missing for more than a few hours, it had to mean she'd met up with Becker, which also meant things were accelerating. It was a certainty that the break-in at the Freeland office was because the ear was there, although how he knew it was there was still a mystery.

"That was Bruce," Wally said. It was after nine, and now that we knew Orla was an accomplice and was undoubtedly part of the break-in, we could expand the search to Whidbey Island. Wally had just put his phone down.

"And?"

"He said he looked around carefully, and the only thing missing was that little wooden box from your desk."

"Of course it was."

"Is that a problem?"

"Sable says it's powerful, and if *she's* worried, then I sure as hell am too."

We called the team together and told them what we had learned. The plan was to keep searching for Kate and also alert the deputies on Whidbey that there was a good chance the fugitives were in their vicinity.

As we finished the briefing, Wally's phone began buzzing; he looked at it quizzically.

"Strange number," he mouthed as he answered.

He looked startled, then relieved as he almost shouted, "Kate ... where ... but how did you ... okay, stay there. We're on our way ... are you sure? Okay, see you soon."

"Was that her?"

"Yeah. She's on her way here. Somehow, she got away and said there's a lot to tell us, but she couldn't because she was on the cell of some guy next to her on the ferry; she doesn't have hers."

"How did she sound?"

"Great ... but tired. I can't wait to get my hands on that asshole."

I understood his feelings, but right now, he looked like the most thankful man on the planet.

Most of the task force had overheard Wally and me interacting, and one by one, they began to clap until the entire room was on its feet. I let Wally tell them what he knew, and soon after, several came over to pat this man they barely knew on the back. When a fellow cop was in danger, it was but one family.

It was ten a.m. when the bright yellow Mustang pulled into the lot. Wally had insisted we wait outside until she arrived, and I was glad he did. She pulled into the nearby handicapped spot, chirped her brakes, and turned the powerful engine off. My deputy had her door open and started to pull her from the car until he saw the blood seeping from her hands.

"Jesus, Kate, are you okay?"

Her answer was to stand and squeeze him until I thought he might pass out. As they separated, she left bloodstains on the sleeves of his uniform jacket.

"Just fabulous. I had a few issues escaping from my dorm room, but I'm fine."

"Kate," I interrupted, "we're glad to see you in one piece ... well, mostly. Let's get you inside and see what we can do to fix you up. You can tell us what happened then."

After donning a clean T-shirt from her locker, she sat while one of the BPD officers who had served as a medic in Iraq began first aid on her hands. He cleaned her blistered and bloody hands gently, then applied antiseptic ointment and completed the procedure by wrapping them both with several layers of gauze.

While being treated, she related the events from the cabin on Lummi Island. She told of the conversations between Becker and Orla, the discussions about the ear and its importance, and Buzz's concession to go along with their plan.

After explaining how she'd escaped and her resulting injuries, she said, "What I can't understand is why these people actually believe in this witchcraft shit. It's like they're part of some cult with no factual tethers."

When Wally raised his eyebrows and looked my way, Kate noticed our unspoken exchange. "Don't tell me you guys are buying this crap."

"Let's just say we're keeping an open mind, Kate. Some of what we've seen doesn't make much sense, so we'll wait until the dust has settled before we commit to anything." I wasn't sure what to believe myself, but finding Buzz was the priority right now.

"You said something about Ebey's Landing?"

"Yeah—Buzz seemed to think they needed to be there for the spell—or whatever—to be effective."

"Well, since that's our patch, we'll handle it. You should try to get some rest; you've got to be running on fumes."

She looked like I had punched her in the nose and jumped to her feet. "If you think I'm gonna stay here while you and Wally go after this asshole—the one who locked me up, by the way—you're seriously fucking mistaken."

As soon as she spoke, she glanced at the BPD chief, her boss, who smiled, shook his head, and nodded his approval. Wally looked at her, bursting with pride as if she'd just been crowned Miss America. I knew when I was overruled.

"Okay, but you're not driving. You're coming with us."

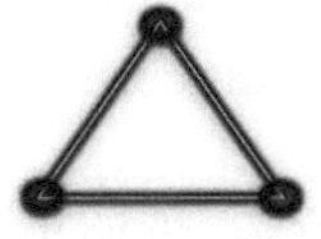

THIRTY-FOUR

Buzz waited in the car—they'd taken Orla's instead of the big truck—while Alan and his aunt broke into the sheriff's office in Freeland. He thought about running but didn't know where he'd go, and maybe if he could do what his father wanted, they'd leave him alone.

His spells and magic had evolved through trial and error using the scrolls and incantations his mother had left behind. He'd never dared to use the relic from Isaac Ebey and never even knew its provenance. What he was positive of, however, was the power it held. It was as if the appendage generated its own force field, causing his fingers to tingle and producing a thrumming in his gut, increasing in intensity the closer he was to it.

It was similar to his experience at Ebey's Landing but more intense. When he told Alan he needed to return there to be successful with his magic, he was sure it was the proper venue, even if he didn't understand it. Sure, he had the words and blueprints his mother had used. Still, his achievements in wizardry resulted from his intuition and heritage, heightened by his solitary years of communing with nature. The confluence of his life experiences and genetic makeup had produced a power the three sisters from Fulton and Scott would have envied. Buzz Aldrin, whether he knew it or not, could shake the foundations of logic itself.

The break-in was easy. The building was small, poorly lit, on a dark street, and had no cameras or alarms. This was Whidby Island, after all. Who breaks *into* a police station?

Orla saw the item on the desk in the only private office and grabbed it. She and Becker were back inside the car in under five minutes. The smashed lock on the door was unfortunate collateral damage, but with rooms full of valuable computers and police equipment untouched, it was doubtful there would be any serious investigation.

By the time they reached Ebey's Landing, it was daybreak, and the sun had just appeared. Cemetery Road led to the parking area near the trailhead, where Buzz directed them to park. The forty-degree temperature forced clouds of vapor from the trio as they traversed the trail, finally making it down the 300-foot bluffs to the beach.

"Why do we need to be here, Buzz?" Orla's question seemed more like a complaint.

When her nephew failed to answer, Becker filled the void. "If he says this is the place, then it is. I saw what happened to him the last time we came here, and it wasn't an act."

Out of breath and tired from no sleep, they paused to look at the majestic presentation of the sun-kissed, snow-capped Olympic Mountains on the far side of Puget Sound. That a pair of kidnappers and their prisoner would stop to take in such a beautiful display of nature was a testament to the grandeur of the place.

"We need to build a platform." Buzz broke the silence.

"What are you talking about?"

"If we do this, Alan, we've got to construct a triangle with circles at the three points. Each circle must be six feet in diameter, the centers approximately a hundred feet apart."

"How are we gonna do that?" Orla whined.

"Rocks," Buzz answered. "Start collecting rocks and use them to make the circles."

"Like we had in the yurt camp?" Alan asked.

"Just like that, but they need to be farther apart. A hundred feet."

"How come?"

"Because if you want to change history, we need access to that period before the property was in the Aldrin family. This is the only way to do it."

"This is gonna take all day, and I'm tired."

"We're all tired, Orla. Stop bitching and start picking up rocks." It was clear Becker was still focused on his end game.

***

Kate slept in the rear seat during the entire two-hour drive to Ebey's Landing. The clear skies would have made for a spectacular drive through Deception Pass, then south to Coupeville, if Wally and I hadn't been picturing what we'd do when and if we found Becker.

The case was an odd one. We had a kidnapping that nobody had reported, done by a miscreant who had imprisoned a police officer. Other than threatening Kate with a shotgun and confining her, his history with law-breaking was limited to blackmail. The threat of violence seemed to be there but had never been acted upon.

Then there was the witchcraft aspect; I wasn't sure what to believe. Kate thought the whole thing was absurd, but my interaction with Sable gave me pause.

I parked my thoughts and glanced at Wally, who seemed to be entertaining similar feelings. "Sup, Pods?"

"This whole thing is bizarre. Too many players and just too much weird shit. Give me a robber or killer any day; then I know how to deal with it. This stuff is creepy."

I laughed at his simplification but was much more in his camp than I let on.

By the time we reached Cemetery Road, it was almost two. Even though it was February, the sunshine had coaxed a sizeable number of hikers to the historic reserve, judging by the number of vehicles parked at the trailhead.

As soon as I turned the ignition off, Kate woke up. Her expression suggested she was reliving her captivity, but she was back in the present within seconds.

"Okay, Kate?" Wally had seen it, too.

"Yeah ... yeah, just thinking back to my fun night. I'm good, though. Where are we?"

"We're at Ebey's Landing, and if Bruce is correct, that little Audi over there belongs to Orla Aldrin. At least that's her plate."

171

We followed the path to its end, several hikers passing us as we walked. At the cliff's edge, hundreds of feet below, we saw three people arranging rocks in circles. There were a few onlookers, perhaps wondering what they were doing, but it *was* Whidbey, where folks let folks be who they were.

"There's that son of a bitch. That's Buzz and Orla with him." It was clear Kate harbored ill will toward her abductor.

"It looks like they're making a giant version of that circle arrangement we found near those remnants of the yurts, and Buzz is directing them," Wally said.

I agreed and asked, "How long will it take us to get down there, and can we do it without them seeing us?"

"They seem preoccupied, and the trail that winds down the bluff is hidden in some places. I think we'll be good until we reach the bottom. Besides, it looks like some of the hikers are watching too."

"Yeah, and then?" I asked.

Wally reached behind his back and replied, "I'm carrying. You two?"

"I'm good," I answered, "but if it comes to that, remember there are other folks around."

"I'm not. The prick took my Glock and smashed my phone on Lummi."

"So you think he'll shoot?"

"Hard to say. He's an asshole for sure, but other than bossing his kid around, extortion, getting the drop on me, and sticking me in a cell, I haven't seen any overt violence from him."

"Yeah, we were thinking the same thing. Let's assume the worst, and we should be fine."

We reached the halfway point of the downhill climb in less than twenty minutes and stopped to see what was happening on the beach. The threesome still looked tiny from our location, but it appeared Buzz was outlining a smaller circle in the center of the triangle made by the three larger ones while Orla and Becker observed.

"Looks like they're almost done with what they're doing. Let's see if we can move a little faster."

Wally and Kate nodded and picked up the pace.

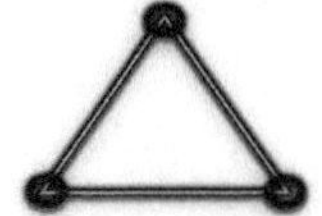

THIRTY-FIVE

Orla and Becker were tired and stood by watching Buzz. Visitors to the historic reserve spent as much time on the beach as they did on the trails, so it wasn't uncommon to see small groups chatting and observing the actions of others. None among them, however, had ever seen such a strange arrangement of stones and rocks, and the handful of onlookers were curious to see what came next.

With the triangle now complete, Buzz arranged the smaller center circle, which would be the resting place for the talisman and the location for the recitation of the chants. If he was right, whatever the outcome of this moment, the ear long ago removed from Isaac Ebey's head would cease to exist. As a result of his focus, he was unconscious of the group of spectators, which had doubled in size.

He instructed his father and aunt to light the fires in the three larger circles and join him inside the triangle near the center circle. As the fires were lit and the ritual began, a hush replaced the conversation among the observers.

Buzz told them, "I need you and Orla to sit on the water side of this center ring."

"Can't we just stand here?" Orla whined.

"No, you can't. I need to be the tallest person inside the triangle, and my recitations will take a little time."

"Orla, just do what he says. The sooner he gets on with this, the sooner we won't have anything to do with him anymore." Then he looked at Buzz and asked, "And why do you have to be the tallest in the triangle?"

"I, uh ... I don't know, but that's what the instructions say."

"Wait a minute ... you're using *instructions* for this?"

"Well ... not really instructions. One of the incantations stipulates that if the administrator—that's me—doesn't look down upon the recipients of the benefits—that's you—then miscalculations can occur. I can only look down on you if you're seated."

Still grumbling, Becker and Orla sat in the sand facing the bluff, with the water behind their backs. Buzz placed the shriveled ear in the center ring and stood facing the seated couple and the Puget Sound. He unfurled a yellowed and brittle parchment and began speaking familiar words, but in no order that made sense to anyone who could hear them.

The recitation continued for almost fifteen minutes when those observing began to lose interest in the happening. They chalked the incident up to simply another curious event perpetrated by an odd group of Whidbey Islanders. They started moving away to continue their excursion on the splendid winter day.

***

We made it to the beach just in time to see the hikers who had gathered around the three fires start drifting from the proceedings. Buzz and the other two were so focused on the matter at hand that they barely noticed.

The spectators became a perfect screen for our descent and were even better at disguising our approach. We could hear Buzz mumbling familiar words, but somehow, they made no sense. I even thought I overheard a Latin word occasionally.

As if the crowd knew we needed their cover but decided not to assist, they began departing as soon as we got within fifty feet of the fires. When the last of the onlookers had left, only the three of us were there.

We covered the distance to the center of the triangle in seconds but not fast enough to avoid Orla registering our presence. "Alan, look!"

When he noticed Kate, he began to stand, but Wally was ready.

"Stay down, Becker; please give me a chance to use this. Hands behind your backs, both of you." He had pulled his gun and hurriedly positioned himself behind the couple.

Kate and I followed, with the BPD detective doing the honors with the zip-ties. I noticed the ones she installed on Becker seemed to be pulled extra tight.

While subduing our quarry, we failed to notice our astronaut friend was still mumbling words and phrases. Because none of it made sense, it seemed just background noise, but Kate shared a concern.

"Something's wrong with him. He's in some trance."

Buzz was across the center circle from us, and Kate was right. It was as if he were alone. Not sure how to proceed, we looked at each other for suggestions.

That was when Buzz's voice doubled in volume as he took three steps toward the circle and tossed a handful of something into it. A green plume of fire erupted, and the dense smoke reeked of something I'd smelled before—when I was in Buzz's shabby little house on Lone Lake Road. Then I passed out.

***

It was the smell I noticed first. It wasn't the foul odor from Buzz's; it was the freshness of the salt water. Then I heard the gulls and the gentle lapping of the water. I felt the sand on my face, but it was warm. I started wondering how the sand could be warm in February, and then I opened my eyes.

Kate was sitting across from me, looking dazed, and Wally was flat on his back but looked unhurt.

"Look," she said, pointing to the bluff.

My focus seemed a little off, but I saw two figures climbing the trail to the top of the bluff. "That Becker?"

"I think so. By the time I came around, they were already on their way. What the fuck just happened?"

Still gathering my senses, I stood on shaky legs and looked around. Aside from the two tiny figures climbing the bluff trail, the place was deserted. Buzz was missing, as was the small crowd of onlookers that had begun to walk away.

I said the first thing that popped into my mind. "How come it's so warm? It was in the mid-forties when we arrived, and now it's gotta be close to seventy."

"I don't know … maybe a freak warm front?"

"Don't think so … let's get your buddy up. Maybe that big brain of his has the answers."

We shook Wally until he moved on his own and could stand. "What the fuck just happened?"

"You two are spending too much time together. Now you're repeating each other's words."

"No … come on … what *did* happen?"

"We're trying to figure that out. The last thing I remember is Buzz throwing something in the center ring when it burst into flame. Then I must've passed out—you two also, I guess—and here we are."

"Yeah, and there was that awful smell." Wally and I nodded in acknowledgment.

"Damn, it's hot … how come?" Wally took his heavy jacket off, still trying to make sense of things.

"We don't know. Hey, let's see if there's cell service here. We can alert BPD that Becker and Orla are on the move."

We pulled out our phones but needn't have. Among us, the two Androids and one iPhone displayed the same thing—a blank screen.

"Huh … weird," I said. "Let's get back to the car and get going. With any luck, we'll be able to get the word out to both Island County and BPD."

We arrived at the base of the towering cliffs, where the trail began, when Kate said, "Something's different."

"Yeah, it's almost thirty degrees warmer."

"No, Wally, something else. It smells different and more organic, and look at the growth along the trail. It's taller, and now it's almost a tiny path. Remember how worn and traveled it was? Another thing is the sun; look where it is. It's much farther north than it was … like in the summer months."

Wally nodded, unwilling to acknowledge the obvious or too unnerved by the inconsistencies. After Kate had clinically listed the differences, only one conclusion made sense: whatever had happened, we were now in the summer months. As far as the growth of grasses along the trail went, I had no answer,

We trudged up the trail in single file, mostly quiet with our confused thoughts, finally arriving at the summit, carrying our jackets and sweating.

Since I was the first to clear the top of the ridge, I was also the first to see the parking area where we'd left our vehicle. Except it wasn't there—nothing was.

"Okay, you guys, this is getting weird. Jesus … what the *fuck* is happening?"

"I'm not sure, Kate … I don't know."

"Look—over there." Wally pointed to a patchwork of fields in the distance. "Whatever they're growing is green, not brown like in the winter. Also … it looks like they're plowing it with a couple of horses instead of a tractor."

The field in question must have been a half-mile away. The vistas from Ebey's Landing covered such great distances that it was difficult to estimate.

All of us were anxious, but with little in the way of alternatives, we headed for the guy with the horses. It turned out to be slightly farther than we'd thought; of course, the guy kept moving, so that didn't help.

When he saw us approaching, he pulled on the reins with a loud "Whoa" and turned to face us. He appeared to be a farmhand dressed in a flannel shirt and corduroy trousers held up by wide suspenders. His thick leather boots looked hot and uncomfortable, but he didn't seem to mind. A skinny guy with a dirty but kind face peeking from under a wide-brimmed straw hat smiled cautiously as we approached.

"Howdy … help you folks?"

I was afraid of the answer, but I asked anyway. "Have you seen any cars over by the bluff?"

"Cars?"

"Yes. We parked there this morning, and now it's missing."

The farmer looked at us like we were speaking in tongues, and a look of concern crossed his face.

"Folks, I don't know much about cars, and I never seen one. I heard they were trying to make something that could carry folks without horses, but I don't think it'll ever happen."

It dawned on us that something mind-numbing had occurred, and we could see this man was beginning to feel uneasy.

"We're sorry, sir, I think we got a little confused. Can you tell us where the nearest town is? Is it Coupeville?" My change of approach seemed to settle him somewhat.

"Yep, it sure is. You follow that road for a mile and it'll take you right into town." He pointed the way and we took our leave.

We passed several farms on our journey, all being tended by people with horses instead of tractors. Just as we reached the outskirts of town, Kate finally voiced what we knew to be true. "We're not in Kansas anymore, guys, are we?"

That she could maintain her sense of humor throughout our dilemma spoke volumes. I knew Wally was glad she was with us, and so was I.

"I'm afraid not. Somehow, we got caught inside that triangle, and now we've taken a trip back in time. Let's figure out exactly where we are—what year it is—and then maybe figure out some way to get back."

Wally had been quiet but turned to Kate. "So, what do you think about this witchy stuff now?"

She rolled her eyes and flipped him off, then grinned. "What do you think, smartass?"

The friendly banter was enough to quiet our nerves after the shock of finding ourselves in another century, and now we had to devise a plan. We arrived on Front Street, Coupeville's main business strip, and went to the general store. Our unconventional dress drew some stares, but most folks seemed okay with it.

It was approaching six o'clock, and although there was plenty of daylight left, we thought it prudent to find a place to spend the night. Then Kate threw a wrench into our plans. "Ruh-roh."

"What is it?" Wally asked.

"What do we do for money?"

"I've got plenty of cash, and it should be worth much more now."

"I'm not sure that's gonna work," I said.

"Huh? Why?"

"Because, silly, our cash looks a lot different than theirs," Kate explained.

Wally acknowledged the fact and asked, "Okay, what do we do?"

"Are you still wearing that Rolex your dad gave you?" I asked. He looked at his wrist and nodded. "Let me have it. I'll take it to that jeweler across the street and see what they'll give me."

"Ah, geez ... it's engraved and everything."

Kate put her arm around his shoulders and squeezed him. "Listen, Sporty, I know that means a lot to you, but I don't see much choice here. I'll do my best to make it up to you."

Her reassurance seemed to do the trick, and they waited outside the general store for me while I tried my luck with the town jeweler. When I joined them after almost an hour, they looked up expectantly.

"Well, how'd you make out?" Wally asked.

"It seems the owner had heard of wristwatches before but had never seen one. I had to wait while he took it apart to examine the mechanism. It didn't hurt that the case was gold either."

"How much?"

"Two hundred dollars. He said it was the most he's ever paid for anything, but I guess it's pretty special for this date on the calendar."

"Speaking of," Kate said, "what *is* the date today?"

"Yeah … the guy had a newspaper in there. I looked at it while he was appraising the watch. The date on the paper said July 25th, 1889."

My announcement shut down any conversation for several minutes until Kate, obviously the practical one among us, said, "Well, boys, how about we find a place to stay for the night … you know, now that we're flush with cash?"

"We can't just stay here … in this century, I mean …"

"There's not much we can do this minute, Wally. Kate's right; let's clean up, find some rooms, and have dinner. Maybe after that, we can come up with a plan."

We headed a block up the hill to the Coupeville Inn, a Victorian affair offering a huge wrap-around porch with a harbor view. We managed to afford two rooms for the exorbitant cost of $1.50 each per night and told the proprietor we were indefinite about the length of our stay. I offered to share my room with Wally, but he suggested a better option was for him to bunk with Kate to ensure she'd be safe. I almost said it was more likely the other way around, but wisely held my tongue.

We had an early dinner with barely any conversation. I think we were coming to grips with our dilemma, but even more, our energy reserves were depleted, especially Kate's. We agreed to meet for breakfast when, hopefully, inspired and refreshed, we'd have found a way out of our dilemma.

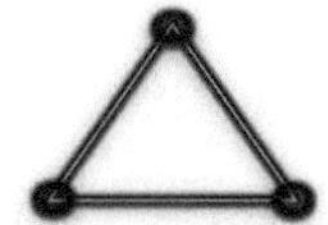

Thirty-Six

After polishing off a hearty breakfast, we were on our second cup of coffee when I broached the subject. "Any thoughts, you two?"

Kate and Wally looked at each other; then, she nodded at him, encouraging him to speak.

"I was thinking ..."

"Yes?"

"Remember that research I did on the Aldrin family, tracing it back to that house in San Francisco?"

"I do, and I also remember Buzz's great-great-grandmother had a very strange name."

"Yes, it was Gyaaxa Gwang and she was Haida."

"Okay ..."

"According to the historical background on Ebey's Landing, the Haida stormed the bluffs and decapitated Isaac Ebey. You said that Sable told you the ear belonged to Isaac, right?"

Wondering where this was headed, I said, "Yes, that's correct."

"What if Sarah—formerly Gyaaxa—was related to the Haida party that killed Ebey, and maybe that's why the thing was so potent as a talisman? Why else would it be passed on through generations of that family?"

I could tell Wally had run this by Kate a few times because she followed easily, and I was still trying to grasp its direction. "Okay, let's say she is related. How does that help us?"

Kate picked up the thread now. "If we're right, then if we could find this Gyaaxa or Sarah or whatever, then maybe she'll have some idea how we can get back to the future."

"Okay, I see where you're going with this, but wouldn't this person be a youngster now?"

Wally answered, "Yeah, we thought about that too. We agree it's a long shot, but we're fresh out of witches or warlocks without Buzz here."

I wasn't sure if or how a young girl could help us, but there weren't many other options. I asked, "Do you have any idea how we might locate this person?"

"No—we thought we'd get your opinion before we did anything else."

"Let's do this. We'll walk around town, maybe buy some clothes that fit in a little better, and try to get a handle on the day's news. The newspaper should help, but listen to the shopkeepers and customers. If nothing else, we'll look a lot less like outsiders. Remember, this town was named the county seat less than eight years ago, so we're not the only strangers here."

We agreed to meet back at the hotel later in the afternoon.

***

After walking around the small commercial district a few times, I had lunch at a small café on Front Street and picked up a new outfit at the general store. On my travels, I passed Wally and Kate and was glad to see they, too, had managed to update their wardrobes. Kate wore a tight blouse with a high neck and puffy sleeves and a flowing skirt that might have been at home on the set of *Gone with the Wind*.

The weather was spectacular, with bright sunny skies and temperatures in the mid-seventies. I caught myself looking at my cell phone several times to check on the forecast or look for emails, but the screen was dark. The number of people bustling about the small island town surprised me, but at least now, with our new clothes, the locals accepted us as simply visitors from off the island and not from another time.

It was mid-afternoon when I decided to head back to the hotel. The warm breeze beckoned me to one of the wooden slatted chairs on the porch. It was similar to an Adirondack chair, but I was uncertain if those things had even been invented yet. I ordered a lemonade and settled back to contemplate the future.

I must have dozed for more than a few minutes because I awoke to the sound of two men seated only a few feet away. A small crowd of folks were now enjoying the warm temperatures and the peaceful view, but it was the two nearest me whose conversation I could hear.

"The site Ferry wants looks fine, but his idea for the new courthouse is ridiculous."

"You're the architect; I'm just the governor's chief of staff. Remember, if statehood goes through in November like we think it will, the county seats will have more say in state government. I'd say if Elisha Ferry likes something, then that's what you should build."

I hadn't been a big history buff, and now I was living it. It seemed the Washington Territory became a state in November of 1889, five months away. I vaguely remembered that Elisha Ferry was the first state governor, and it appeared he had opinions on how the courthouse should be constructed.

"You're signing my vouchers, so I'll do what he wants."

"I knew we could count on you."

"On another subject, does Ferry have anything to do with those Indian schools? It seems cruel that we take away the kids and stick them in a boarding school so they'll learn English."

"Hey, Thomas, they're goddamn Indians. If they can't speak English and learn a trade, then tough. We're better off without the savages anyway. At least we have most of those Haida kids at the Tulalip place now. The little fuckers won't be cutting any more heads off. But to answer your question, no. Those policies come from the Feds, and I'm glad they're taking care of business."

After overhearing this outburst, I glanced at Thomas, who seemed to find something interesting on his thumb. Then he said, "They are people, Edgar. What they did in the past was the result of our pillaging and stealing their land. I don't condone the way we treat them, and if you took the time to get to know them, I think you'd feel differently."

"Tell you what, Thomas, you stick to your architecture, and I'll take care of the governor. And as far as those Indians are concerned, I hope I never see another one; they're less than human." After his latest rant, the state official stood up and left the architect alone.

I waited a respectful amount of time before rising and taking the seat vacated by the state official. Thomas, the architect, was gazing over the peaceful waters of Penn Cove.

"Excuse me, sir. I apologize for interrupting, but I couldn't help but overhear your conversation with that fellow from Olympia."

The architect seemed slightly annoyed that I had eavesdropped but then looked quizzically at me, perhaps noticing my speech was not in cadence with the times.

"Yes? Did you have something to offer regarding our discussion?"

"Only that I agree with you about the Natives and how they're being treated. I can't imagine how I'd feel if invaders stole my land, then restricted me to a fraction of the property I'd once owned."

He reached his hand out to me and introduced himself. "My name is Thomas Gray. I'm designing the new courthouse for the town here. You sound like you're not from the area."

"Um … yes. Roger Wilkie. Some friends and I thought we'd see what this island has to offer. You must enjoy working here; it's a beautiful place."

He gazed at the water for a few seconds before he spoke. "I do, and you're right; it *is* a beautiful spot. There are times, though, when I find it difficult to interact with folks with no compassion or empathy for others, especially those we've wronged."

"But you have to?"

"Only if I want to stay in business. Most of my work is in the government sector, and while many officials are kind and thoughtful, others, like Edgar, refuse to see the damage we've done to these poor folks."

"What's this about the Indian schools?"

"The federal government thinks we need to erase the culture and language from the natives, and they're removing children from their families."

"Do they get to return to their families?"

"Sometimes, but usually, by the time they've gone through six or eight years of indoctrination, they're so messed up that they don't know where they belong. It's a tragedy."

"Are there schools on Whidbey Island?"

"No … none here. The closest—where most of the Haida kids are—is across the pond in Snohomish County. Right now, it's being run by the Catholics, but I'm sure the Feds will take over before long. I don't know that it makes any difference."

I figured he wouldn't mind me asking since he'd brought it up. "Was that the group who killed Isaac Ebey?"

He nodded, then spoke quietly. "Yes ... yes, it was. That was a tragedy. I think it resulted from years of settlers being given land that the government took. The natives tried to be reasonable, but it seemed every treaty they entered into was broken. Ebey was influential in the Washington Territory government, so he became a target. After the raid, the tribe was hunted mercilessly, and now the remaining families have had their children taken away."

I agreed that the condition was appalling and thanked him for the conversation. Then, I returned to my room to freshen up before meeting my fellow time travelers for dinner.

***

"I thought politics were nasty in 2024. What's going on here makes our time in history seem tame by comparison."

We were sitting at a table by the window overlooking the porch and the view of the cove, listening to Kate's observations. They were much the same as mine and Wally's; then he picked up the conversation. "I agree. We had extremes on both the right and the left to deal with, but these folks are stuck still thinking Native Americans and folks with dark skin aren't even people."

"Right, but I did run across someone who thought the natives—who used to own all this land, as you know—were getting a raw deal." I proceeded to recount my conversation with the architect designing the courthouse.

Kate and Wally had heard about the Indian schools but were aghast when I explained the degree to which these poor people had been exploited.

The three of us focused on our meal and retreated to our thoughts. I wondered why the hell people did what they did, and I assumed Wally and Kate were thinking along those same lines.

We were having coffee and a slice of apple pie from some place called Whidbey Pies when Kate asked the question we were all thinking. "So ... what the hell do we do next?"

"This visit to a simpler time and place is neither," Wally answered. "Let's find a way back home."

"Geez, you sound like Dorothy. Maybe we can find a Yellow Brick Road somewhere."

"Good one, Kate; weren't you the one who said the whole witch thingy was a bunch of crap?"

"C'mon now, kids, can't we all get along?" It was easy to spot the genuine affection these two had for each other, but that didn't stop me from teasing them. "Any suggestions other than trying to find Buzz's great-great-grandmother, who is currently a young teenager?"

My two associates looked at each other, then at me, and, at the same time, answered, "Nope, Boss."

"I guess that means we need to find a way off the island and visit the Indian school across the water on the Tulalip Reservation. Let's get some sleep—and I *mean sleep*, you two—and be ready first thing in the morning."

It was rare that I managed an embarrassed blush from my friends, but this was one of those times. I supposed they weren't aware that I'd seen them holding hands under the table. I was glad for them, although it made me miss Andie even more.

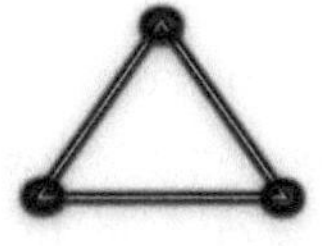

THIRTY-SEVEN

I t was only a short walk from the hotel to the harbor, and it was another sparkling sunny day. We weren't sure what we'd find in the way of transportation to the mainland, but we had plenty of money.

Robertson's Wharf appeared to have the most activity, so that was our first stop. We'd been told at the Coupeville Inn that many of the vessels of the Mosquito Fleet—an armada of steamships providing ad hoc off-island service—could be found there.

More than a dozen steamboats, mostly side-wheelers but a few sternwheelers, dotted Penn Cove on moorings, with several tied to the heavily trafficked wharf. People and supplies moved back and forth in what appeared to be a haphazard fashion, but I suspected the participants knew where they were going.

"Busy place, eh?"

Wally was a master of the understatement. I was astonished at the frenetic activity in the town I knew from 2024 as a sleepy tourist destination. Even though routine ferry service had yet to be established and the Deception Pass bridge was almost fifty years away, Coupeville was one of the major commerce centers of Puget Sound.

Heading toward the pier, Kate nudged me and pointed to the left. "There—harbormaster's office. Let's see if we can find someone to take us to that boarding school."

We got in line inside the office behind several others looking for transportation. When it was our turn, and we told the man our destination, he looked strangely at us.

"Not many folks go there, but you may be in luck; one of the smaller boats returned earlier than expected from repairs due to a collision suffered when a fog bank rolled in. See that guy at the end of the dock pestering people? He's the captain, and I'm sure if you offer him cash for a trip across the passage, he'll take you."

We made our way the hundred yards or so down the timbered, creosote-soaked dock to the gentleman attempting to find fares for his small steamboat.

The captain, smallish in stature, wore a long black coat that seemed too warm for the weather. His white, high-collared shirt was open at the neck, and his derby hat reminded me of a black-and-white Laurel and Hardy movie I'd once seen.

As we approached, his weathered and bearded face took on an expectant look. "Howdy, folks, are you taking a trip today? Captain Timothy Swanson at your service."

"Yes. We'd like to get to Tulalip Bay," I said.

His closely set, dark eyes squinted as he responded, "You sure? Lotta Indians over there. They got the kids in one of them schools there to make them come around to our way of living."

"Yes, we know that. Should we try to get someone else to take us?"

"No ... no, of course not. I'm happy to oblige, but I just wanted you to know where you're going."

"How long is the trip?" Kate asked.

"We'll be fighting the currents for most of the trip, so it'll take at least three hours by the time we get you on shore. The dock in that cove is quite small, so we'll need to take you there in the tender. Will you need to return to Coupeville?"

I had no idea what we'd run into at the Indian school, and I wasn't sure if we'd be able to find transportation back to Whidbey Island, so I answered in the affirmative.

"The round-trip fare for the three of you will be eighteen dollars; is that acceptable?"

Wally raised his eyebrows, apparently still not accustomed to the value of money in 1890, but I answered before he had a chance. "That seems about right, sir. When do we leave?"

***

It was almost noon by the time we got underway. The temperature was in the low seventies, but the brisk sea breeze made it feel ten degrees cooler. I could see why the captain wore his heavy wool coat. Under different circumstances, it would have been a beautiful day on the waters of Puget Sound. As it was, we found ourselves well over a century in the past, unsure of what we could do to reverse the spell that had propelled us here.

We sat on deck chairs for the entire trip, standing only when the captain steered the steamship into Tulalip Bay. Several docks dotted the shores of the small cove, but the captain ignored them and made a sweeping turn before giving the order to drop anchor.

"It's best to be pointed back to open water before we shut down," he said when he approached us. "I'll have the first mate take you in as soon as we lower the tender. How long do you think you'll be?"

I had no idea how long we'd be if we were coming back or what century we might be in, so I punted. "We should be done by nightfall, but I'm not sure."

Captain Swanson didn't seem satisfied with my response. "I'll tell you what I'll do. You've paid for a round trip, but I can't wait here indefinitely. I'll give you until tomorrow morning, but then I must leave; I have other customers to serve. My mate will return after dropping you off, and you can signal us when you're ready to depart."

"How will we do that?" Kate asked.

"Use a torch if it's dark. We will keep watch from here."

"Wouldn't having your first mate wait on shore be better?" Wally read my mind.

"Too many Indians to take a chance. It was a risk taking you here, but I'll not be tempting fate by having my mate stay ashore during the night."

I wanted to engage the captain in conversation about the plight of the Native Americans, but I held my tongue. My perspective from 130 years in the future wouldn't compare to this era, where wars and butchery were recent memories.

I agreed, and the three of us joined the first mate in the oversized dinghy, which he proceeded to row to shore. We pulled alongside a small dock and climbed up. Kate's ridiculous wardrobe made the procedure difficult, but I guessed the women of this era weren't expected to act in such a manner.

As we said goodbye to our escort, he looked at us as if we were crazy. I hoped he was mistaken.

***

After the roar of the steam boilers and the frequent blasts of the whistles, the silence we now experienced was eerie. It seemed that none of us wanted to be the first to make a sound. We sat quietly on the dock, gradually picking up the lapping of the water against the pilings and then the chattering of the squirrels and birds in the forest.

"So ... how about those M's?"

"Good one, Wally. You pick that up from O'Malley?" It was one of O'Malley's favorite go-to's for breaking the ice or changing the direction of a conversation.

"Ahh ... thought we could use a little levity, Boss. What do we do now?"

At first, the shock of being whisked back in time was numbing, and thoughts of returning home were intentionally shuffled to the side. Now, though, the reality was setting in, and the real possibility that we might not make it back was front and center. I thought about Andie and our home and how much I missed her. I thought about how worried she'd be not knowing what had happened to us, and I wondered what would happen if we weren't successful in finding a way back.

With these thoughts running through my mind, I took a deep breath and tried to act like I knew what I was doing. "We're where we need to be. Let's get moving and see if we can find our way to this school."

THIRTY-EIGHT

We weren't sure who the dock belonged to but assumed there'd be a road or path leading away from it. It was a path. We followed it for several hundred yards until it met up with a rutted two-track dirt road that appeared well-traveled.

"Do you Think we'll make it back home, Roger?" Kate asked. I was certain Wally had the same thought running through his mind.

"We're sure as hell going to try. Hopefully we can locate the Haida girl and maybe get some direction."

The words were barely out of my mouth when we heard the sound of hoof-beats and someone's deep voice singing in a foreign language. We hurried off to the roadside, aiming for concealment behind an ancient cedar when Kate's voluminous skirt snagged on an exposed root, and she tumbled.

"Goddammit, how can people wear these fucking outfits?" she shouted, oblivious to the approaching horse-drawn wagon. We bent to help her up just as the carriage stopped less than twenty feet away.

The three of us looked up to see who was driving, but with the sun directly behind the man—from his size, it had to be—it was difficult to make out any features. Except for the horse's snorting and the wagon seat's creaking, there was no other sound.

I stood, held my hand over my brow to shield the sun, and said, "Excuse me, sir, my friend took a little spill, and once we help her up, we'll be out of your way."

There was no response from the man, although now I could make out his appearance. His face was creased from the elements, and his complexion was reddish-brown. His nose was broad, his cheekbones prominent, and his eyes a piercing greenish gray. He wore an animal skin jacket, and his comportment was severe.

"You are not from here," were his first words.

"No, we came from Coupeville," I answered as Wally helped Kate get back on her feet.

"No ... you are not of this time."

We looked at each other, unsure of his exact meaning and fearful of what might happen next.

Saying this was awkward and terrifying would have been an understatement, so I thought it best to agree with him and let the chips fall where they would.

"Yes, you are correct. My name is Roger Wilkie, and this is Wally Turpin and Kate Mahoney. We came here looking for someone."

The man said nothing but climbed down from his perch and strode purposefully over to us. He appeared fiftyish and had to be at least six-four with shoulders like an NFL fullback.

We tensed as he approached within a few feet ..., and then he extended his hand. "I am Koyah." He shook my hand, then Wally's, and then made a little bow in Kate's direction. "White people do not visit here often. Who are you trying to find? Your spirits are peaceful, and I know much about this place. If you tell me your story, perhaps I can assist."

I looked at both Kate and Wally to see their reaction to Koyah's proposal and took their expressions to mean *What the hell? What could go wrong?*

I began by telling the story of Buzz and the history of the Aldrin clan. I told him about Becker's attempts at stealing the property, then Buzz's ceremony on the beach with Isaac Ebey's ear when attempting to change the original title on the land.

He stood by, expressionless, as I continued the saga, including the three of us being caught in the center of the triangle just as the fire burst from the circle. Then I turned to Wally. "Tell him what you found out about Buzz's great-great-grandmother's history."

Wally started with Sarah Morgan, formerly Gyaaxa Gwang, and how we thought she went to San Francisco and was taught by the witches on Fulton and Scott Streets.

As he continued reporting on his research, the giant man's demeanor changed from suspicion to amazement. He leaned against the wagon while he listened to the tale.

When Wally had finished, I said, "We thought if somehow we could find this Gyaaxa, we might be able to find a way back to our time."

Kate had been quiet the entire time but stepped toward the big man. "Do you think we're crazy? That we could be from the future, or we made this up?"

Koyah appeared stunned for a few seconds, then recovered. "Excuse me—women in my world are not as forward as they seem in yours.

"I can tell by your accents and how you wear your clothing that you are strangers. Some of my people think I can speak to the spirits, and while I cannot, that doesn't mean I am unaware of their existence; I can sense when someone of great power makes contact with them. During the past few days, the spirit world has been active and confused, and it seems you three are the reason. That is why I think you are not from this time.

"I can see both good and evil in people, and there is no shadow of evil or malice among you. It is why I will help you, but you need to hear more from me."

I wasn't sure whether it was the spirit world, magic, or witchery, but whoever this Koyah was, he seemed to have at least some answers. With the sun sinking lower in the sky, the temperature had begun to drop, and a slight chill was in the air. Our new acquaintance took his horse by the reins, turned him into the woods, and told us to follow him. The man's appearance might have seemed threatening, but his countenance convinced us otherwise, so we followed.

We walked less than fifty yards and came to a small clearing with what appeared to be a fire pit in the center. Our escort directed us to sit on the stumps that ringed the pit while he efficiently built a fire. Without a single wasted motion or utterance, he had a blazing fire going in less time than it would have taken me to warm up my truck—if I'd had one.

He sat on one of the vacant slabs of fir across from us, stared into the flames, and began his story.

"I am Haida. Our tribe's ancestral territory lies off the coast of Vancouver Island. Thirty years ago, when I was very young, we saw the white man invade our land and parcel it out to new settlers. Our people had lived on the land for over twelve thousand years, yet in a fraction of that time, we were run off our property and killed by men with superior weapons. When we were killed by their guns and the diseases they brought, our only choice was to surrender or to move further away from civilization. In both cases, it made little difference. If we moved, they chased us and murdered us. When we surrendered on their terms, they broke their treaties.

"We met with officials on a US Navy steamer in the spring to negotiate a relocation agreement, only to see our chief and twenty-seven of our people slaughtered. It seemed the white man would only be content if we were annihilated.

"We moved to the land they gave us, but we did not forget their treachery. In the late summer, the strongest and fittest members of our tribe made a long journey by canoe, looking for retribution. We heard there was a high-ranking official who had been given Indian land on Whidbey Island.

"I was the youngest of the raiding party then, but I was included because of my size and strength. I did what I was told but was scared of what I might be forced to do. We landed on a sandy beach and climbed the high cliffs to the home of the white chief. When we arrived at his home, the older men went crazy, shooting guns and screaming. I was told to find the women and children and bring them to the cliff.

"I saw them running to the blockhouse, but I let them go; executing the white chief for what they did to my people seemed to be a fair trade, but I chose to leave the family alone. When I returned to the man's home, I saw he had been shot, and one of my tribe had taken his head. I was told we would use it in the future in ceremonies, paying respect to those of us who had died in combat."

He stopped at this point but continued to stare into the fire. We looked at each other, stunned at this first-hand account of the raid on Ebey's Landing.

Listening only to the crackling of the fire for what seemed an eternity, Kate finally broke the silence solemnly. "That must have been awful. You are correct about us. We are from over a hundred years ago, and I wish we could say people have learned how to get along better. In many cases, they have, but some still judge people on the color of their skin, their language, or their sex. In the United States, like now, we still have a few politicians who care about folks, but many are in it for something else.

"It has taken a long time, but most of us are aware of how poorly the Natives in America and those in Canada were treated, and there are movements to find some way to make reparations. It doesn't help you now, though. If I may, sir, why have you told us this story?"

It was the most I'd heard Kate speak at once, and I was grateful for how she'd expressed the same feelings I think we all had. We didn't have to wait long for his answer.

He looked directly at Kate, a small smile briefly appearing. "I am beginning to see why the women of your time have become powerful.

"There is more to what I have told you," he continued. "After the raid killing Isaac Ebey, the relocation of my people increased until almost all of the Natives were assigned to reservations. The Haida live on their ancestral lands on the Queen Charlotte Islands, but I did not choose to live there.

"During the attack on Whidbey Island, the two others on my canoe were killed. I was the last to leave the beach and lost sight of those ahead because it was just me rowing. I became disoriented and traveled south instead of north. A sudden wind capsized my boat and dumped me into the freezing water. We were told to avoid the water because even though the summer was warm, the water was still very cold.

"I made it to the shore, shivering and thirsty, and lay down on the sand to catch my breath. The next thing I remember was a beautiful woman pouring water into my mouth. She helped me to her home, a small shack in the woods, and told me to sleep.

"I learned she was a house servant for one of the wealthy landowners on the island. While I stayed with her, she taught me English and the customs of the white man. Even though she was white, she felt that we were being wronged and our lands stolen. She continued her employment, and I learned to farm her small plot of land. We grew most of our food and used her wages to buy what we needed.

"For a long time, we lived a wonderful life, but we were never able to conceive a child. After eighteen years, we were blessed with a daughter. It was a difficult birth, and the woman I loved died the following day.

"I raised my daughter, taught her the Haida customs and language, and managed to get odd jobs to earn money for necessities. Our lives were comfortable, and others on the island left us alone.

"One day, on my daughter's seventh birthday, a Catholic nun came to visit. She said to pack some things and that she would be taking her to the Indian School on the Tulalip Reservation and that I had no choice in the matter. When I told her no—to leave—she said she would be back with the sheriff and someone from the federal government, and if that happened, I would go to jail. She said I belonged on the reservation and not on Whidbey Island.

"They took her to the school. My life without her was empty, so I moved to the reservation to be nearer. They only let me be with her a few weeks a year, but it is better than nothing."

"I'm so sorry, Koyah. How is your daughter being treated?" Kate asked.

"They can no longer speak their native language and are punished for doing so. The girls are taught to cook and sew and are forced to work to earn money for the school. The boys are taught fishing, farming, carpentry, and must work."

We were aware of the scandals and the terrible history of these schools, but to be in the presence of one of the victims was devastating.

"We are sorry for this unforgivable tragedy, Koyah, but all we can do is try to make amends when and if we get back," I offered.

"There is one other thing I have not told you."

"What is that?"

"My daughter bears a Haida name. She is Gyaaxa Gwang."

The sun had recently dropped below the horizon, and the fire's warmth had diminished. And the four of us sat there ... thinking about a young teenager forced to live a life away from her father.

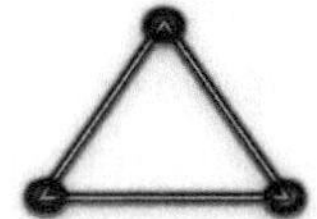

Thirty-Nine

The woman who had begun the legacy of the Aldrin clan was Koyah's daughter. Our only hope for a return to our lives in 2024 rested with a very young woman who had no idea what the future held.

Koyah rose from his perch and wordlessly tossed a few more logs on the fire. Then he looked at the three of us, each in turn, and said, "Will you stay here until I come back? There is something I must do."

I looked at Wally and Kate, who were both looking at me, waiting for a response.

"Yes, of course. Will you be long?"

"Maybe, maybe not," he answered as he turned, patted his horse on the rump, and disappeared into the dense woods.

"Well, Boss, any words of wisdom?"

"If I had any, I'd tell you, Wally. I think all we can do is try not to screw up the future. Based on your research, this Gyaaxa or Sarah learned her craft when she got to San Francisco, which means she won't be able to help us, at least right now."

"Don't get me wrong, I love hanging out with you two, but I'd rather not wait twenty years to return to where we came from."

"Good one, Kate; pretty sure we're on the same page there." Wally was quick with the reply and managed to reach over and squeeze her hand as he delivered it.

Overwhelmed by the events of the past few days, I began to feel the sprouts of futility seeping in. Buzz and Sable were in another century. The only person we knew with any powers was still a child. It appeared Koyah had some mystical abilities but was nowhere near powerful enough to be of any help.

"I don't know what's going to happen or where we'll end up, but if I've learned anything from O'Malley, it's to put one foot in front of the other and make the best decision about each step. He may not be the brightest star in the universe, but that philosophy has gotten him outta more shitshows than you can imagine. Let's stay positive and do what makes sense a step at a time. If we focus on the now, hopefully, the future will take care of itself." I wasn't sure if my little speech offered solace, but it was all I had.

We stared at the fire, each lost in our thoughts, while the warmth from the flames made us drowsy. A snapped branch startled us to attention, and we saw the massive hulk of Koyah stroll back into our little camp. We stood when he reached the fire.

"I have spoken to the spirits, and I have reached a decision," he announced.

"I thought you couldn't speak to them," Wally reminded him.

He smiled at this and said, "I was not completely honest with you. I speak to them often, but they mostly do not listen. This time, they did."

"What did they say?" Kate asked.

Koyah took a deep breath and answered, "They said Gyaaxa must live her life as intended. If, as you say, she traveled to San Francisco and became a witch, then she must do that. Do you have a way to help her escape?"

"What about you?" I asked.

"There is not much I can do to help her. The government funds the school and watches everything, and if I try to remove her, they will put me in jail. Most of the people who run the school know who I am, and, as you can see, it is difficult for me to go unnoticed."

"If she goes to San Francisco, you may never see her again."

"The spirits say I will, but maybe not for a long time. It is more important that she gets to live the life she was created for, so will you help?"

"Yes, of course we will. We have a boat waiting to take us back to Whidbey Island, but I'm sure the captain will alter his schedule if we make it worth his while. What is the best way to do this?"

The Haida giant handed me a folded paper and said, "Give this to Gyaaxa. She will know I sent you, and she will do what you tell her to do. If you follow this road, it will take you to the school. Wait until early morning, before daylight. Her bunk is on the second floor of the dormitory with the other girls."

"How will we know her?" asked Kate.

"She is allowed a gift from her family. I gave her a box with two sand dollars when we were last together."

"And how will we find those?"

"It is not the sand dollars. I wrapped the box in a white ribbon. She told me she keeps it tied to her bed to remind her of me. There will be a full moon later tonight, which should help you to see it."

"Suppose it's not there, or we make a mistake?" I was worried that we could abduct some other poor child.

"She will be the only one who will understand the letter, and she has a small mole under her left ear."

While discussing our plans to rescue Gyaaxa, we heard a horse approaching, and a look of fear overcame Koyah. "What is it?" Wally asked.

"It is US cavalry. They enforce the curfews on the reservation. If they find you, they may detain you, but they will surely escort me to my dwelling. If they see me another time tonight, I will be placed in the stockade. It is best to hide, and I will let them take me."

As the hoofbeats came closer, Wally and I shook hands with him and promised we would watch out for his daughter. To his surprise, Kate hugged the large man, wiping a tear from her eye. As they separated, I thought I saw the same from Koyah.

We hurried into the woods while the Haida man brushed our footprints aside, ensuring he would be seen alone. We heard a stern command from the soldier but couldn't make out the words. From our location, we saw the faint glow of the fire disappear as our protector smothered the flames. We heard the seat squeak as the big fellow climbed onto it, then snicked the horse forward, obediently following the trooper.

When the sounds of horses had faded, we were left alone with crickets and the distant call of owls. The temperature had dipped to the low fifties, and without the fire, the cold began to have its effect.

"Now what? I'm freezing my ass off." It was nice to see Kate still had the mouth of an army sergeant.

"Now we wait. We still have five or six hours before we try to find Gyaaxa. According to Koyah, the moon should be up soon, and we can follow the road to the school."

We stayed close to each other for warmth but still shivered. When the moon showed its face, we started down the dirt road, glad of the warmth of the movement. After thirty minutes we saw the compound ahead, on the top of a slight rise.

The school was a cluster of buildings laid out in almost military precision. Most of the structures were single stories, but two were three stories high, with peaked dormers jutting from the roof.

"Those two have to be the dormitories," I said. "Which one is the girls'?"

"The one on the right, silly," Kate answered.

"And you know this how?" asked Wally.

"Look closer, dummy."

"What?"

"The clotheslines—look what's hanging outside the one on the left."

"Trousers?"

"Yep. Nothing on the ones on the right. Can't be having girls' undies hanging outside. Right?"

Wally looked at me, and I shrugged. "Hey, she's your girlfriend. I'd listen to her."

"Girlfriend?"

"That's what I'd call her, but it's up to you. Let's snag some of the boys' blankets to keep us warm while we wait."

My two companions looked at each other, seemingly embarrassed that I'd spoken the obvious.

"Well ... come on, you two, sheesh."

We figured that it was approaching midnight, so we needed to hunker down for a few more hours. Scattered lights were visible in a few smaller buildings, so we steered clear of them, grabbed some blankets off the line, and retreated behind one of the small workshops.

"Hey, look." Wally had turned the knob on the door and found it unlocked.

Once inside, the smell of sawn lumber told us it was a carpentry shop. With what we could make out from the moonlight streaming through the windows, we saw scattered pieces of furniture in various stages of construction. Several piles of straw and cotton upholstery material were the perfect nest for us until we moved.

I volunteered to take the first watch while the two lovebirds caught some z's. They didn't complain.

I felt my shoulder being shaken as Kate whispered, "C'mon, Roger, it's time."

Taking one of the blankets, we left the workshop and went to the girls' dormitory. The moon's brightness gave us excellent visibility until we entered the building and saw a staircase to the left of the entrance. I told Wally to stay by the door in case of any unexpected visitors. I wanted Kate with me to try to lessen the shock of strangers waking the child in the middle of the night.

When we arrived at the second-floor landing, we saw at least thirty beds stretched across a high-ceilinged open room. The high windows allowed enough light for us to make out the little bodies in various positions, all of them sound asleep.

I wasn't sure where to begin when Kate whispered, "There ... in the corner. See the ribbon at the foot of the bed?"

She led the way to the far corner, where a young girl was lying on her side, hugging her pillow. Luckily, she was lying on her right side, and the tiny mole was visible.

I hated to wake her by holding her mouth, but it was the only way to ensure she didn't wake the others. I thought it better to have Kate do the honors, and I whispered to her to do it.

As soon as she gently placed her hand over the girl's face, her eyes opened wide, and she let out a muffled shriek. Kate leaned to her ear and spoke softly for a few seconds, and Gyaaxa relaxed, but only slightly; her eyes were still filled with fear. Kate held her hand out, and I opened the note Koyah had given us and passed it to her. She held it before the young girl's eyes until she realized her father had sent us.

Kate wrapped the blanket over Gyaaxa's shoulders while I grabbed a pile of clothing and shoes from the foot of the bed. We made our way back down the stairs, where Wally waited. At the sight of yet another white man, Gyaaxa froze until Kate reassured her that all was fine.

Rather than take the time to get her dressed and get her shoes on, Wally carried her to the tree line, where Kate got her dressed. We still had the better part of an hour to get to the dock, and I wasn't keen on running into any US Army types.

Wally and I led the way while Kate held Gyaaxa's hand behind us. We made it to the dock without incident, and I lit the torch we'd left behind to signal Captain Swanson. It took longer than I'd hoped, but the first mate arrived, and the captain was with him. He saw we had an additional passenger and that she was likely of Native American descent.

As soon as he was on the dock, he said abruptly, "We don't have enough room for another passenger."

Kate's patience must have been wearing thin, and she must have been tired. This had to be the reason for what followed.

Still holding Gyaxxa's hand, she strode up to the captain and got within an inch of his face. "Listen to me, you prejudiced little shit. You'll take the four of us to Tacoma, or we will make sure you never sail again. Here's fifty dollars. After we drop her off, you will take us back to Coupeville. You will treat her like royalty on the trip, and if I see otherwise, I will personally fuck you up."

If Captain Swanson had been spoken to like that before, I was certain it hadn't been by a woman. His shock was so extreme that he could only nod and look at his first mate—who seemed to have found something of interest on his shoe.

The hierarchy having been established, we made our way through the dawning skies to the steamer. It would be the last time Gyaaxa Gwang would see this cove.

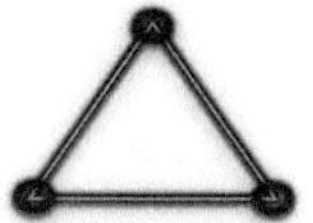

Forty

Alan Becker and Orla Aldrin were the first to regain consciousness. Becker may have been a charlatan and an opportunist, but that didn't mean he was stupid. He understood what Buzz was attempting to do, and the awareness that he was now in a different century slowly dawned on him.

Orla had just begun to come around, but the three cops were still out cold. He tried to get her attention. "Orla ... Orla, over here."

She looked in his direction, obviously disoriented. "What ... where ... what the fuck just happened?"

"Orla, you still have your keys?"

"Uh ... yeah, think so."

"Get over here and cut these ties off with that little knife you have on there. We need to get moving."

Still dazed and stumbling, she did as she was told. Slowly coming to grips with their situation, she asked, "Did Buzz send us back in time?"

"Looks that way. I'm not sure how he planned to bring us back to the present, but while we're here, I will make sure we get that property."

"How?"

"If I'm right, much property is still available for homesteading. All I need to do is file a claim with the county for that land off Lone Lake Road. When we're back, the records will show I've been the legal owner. I guess that little shit knew what he was doing after all."

Orla's vacant look suggested she still hadn't grasped the full import of what had happened, but she followed Becker as he headed for the bluffs that led to the road, which took them to Coupeville—the Island County seat.

***

Buzz slowly came around. He remembered some people watching the ceremony, but they had wandered away. Two of them, a man and a woman, were standing over him.

"Sir ... sir, are you okay?' the woman asked.

"Uh ... yes, yes. I must have dozed off."

"What about those other folks that were here?"

"You mean the tall guy and the woman? They left."

"No, there were three others—two men and a woman. They looked like cops."

Buzz knew that when he was caught up in a spell, it was often an out-of-body experience. It sounded like Kate and that Whidbey cop, Wilkie, had been there. He wasn't sure about the third one.

"I, uh ... I think they left too."

"You're sure you're okay? We can call someone if you'd like."

"No ... thank you, but I'm fine. Thanks again." His dismissal had its intended effect, and the Good Samaritans left.

Buzz wasn't sure what happened, but he had a good idea. At first, he thought he could rewind history by changing the original names of the land settlements. Then he'd realized the only way that could happen was if a person were there to *make* it happen. He'd thought of sending Becker and Orla back to the time before the property was settled. He figured if they were successful, then fine, and if they got stuck back then, who cared? He hadn't planned on three other innocent people being caught in the triangle when the spell triggered.

Now standing, he surveyed the three circles and the triangle they created. The fires had died, and the smaller center circle was charred and black with soot, except for a tiny patch in the middle, which was light brown and haloed by the beach sand, almost like a donut.

He knelt and peered at the anomaly. It was the talisman, the ear; it hadn't been destroyed. He reached for the grisly item and put it in his pocket. He wasn't sure what to do with it, but he thought he might know someone who could help.

Although he was wasted, he could still conjure up a ride to Wilson Street in Bellingham, and so he did.

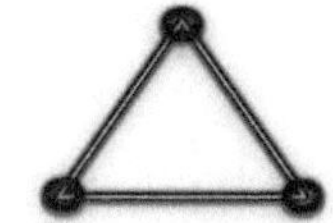

Forty-One

I f we were in the era of automobiles, the drive from the Tulalip Reservation to Tacoma would take about an hour and a half; by steamboat, it would take us an entire day.

We made good time, according to Captain Swanson—which meant about eight miles per hour—for the first few hours. The weather was clear, and traffic on the sound was light in the early morning. Since Kate's discussion with the captain, he went out of his way to avoid her. She had taken Gyaaxa forward to gaze at the city of Seattle as we passed it while Wally and I relaxed aft on the promenade deck. He came to update us on our progress while Kate was out of sight. It was as if we were a tiny boys' club who knew who the real boss was.

When he asked if we'd mind stopping to take on a load of lumber headed for Coupeville, Wally couldn't resist needling him. He was secretly thrilled that he was dating such a badass woman.

"It's fine with us, Captain, as long as it's on the return trip, but maybe you should check with Kate first."

"Um ... no, that's fine, I'll get it on the next trip."

"You sure? She might say it's okay with her."

He stood quietly for a few seconds, perhaps running through scenarios of how his conversation might go with Kate, and seemed to think the lumber could wait.

"Next time," he said and headed for the stairs.

"A little mean to the captain, weren't you, Wally?"

"Hey, Kate gave the little dick a small fortune for this trip. Serves him right."

"Wally?"

"Yeah?"

"You think she's pretty special, don't you?"

"Yeah, Rog, I do."

I clapped him on the back and said, "So do I, buddy, so do I."

***

Kate felt terrible for the girl. She had been pulled from her home, away from her father, and forced to abandon her heritage. *What the fuck is wrong with these people?*

She said nothing during the first part of their journey, but as they were passing Seattle while Kate sat with her on the forward deck, she stood and pointed and said, "City ... city."

"That's Seattle," Kate said. "You will be traveling to a much bigger city—San Francisco."

Gyaaxa's eyes grew bigger, and she repeated the words: "San Francisco?"

Kate was at a loss about what or how much to tell her. She knew how her journey played out and was reluctant to meddle with history. On the other hand, maybe she was supposed to explain everything to her to ensure no unintended consequences. The whole thing was too chaotic and seemingly random to wrap her head around, so she did what she thought made sense; so far, that had worked for her.

"Yes ... San Francisco. What did your father's note say, Gyaaxa?"

"He said I should go with you. The spirits told him that you and your friends would help me escape the white man's school. He said I would see him again if I did what you told me."

"He did?" Kate was surprised.

She looked sad as she said, "He said it would be in the spirit world. He said they would watch over me on my journey and to trust the wisdom they gave me."

Kate squeezed the girl's shoulder and thought, not for the first time; *these poor people we have persecuted know more about life and tradition than we could ever hope to, and these ignorant assholes in the government are driving them out of existence.* She promised herself that if she managed to return from this voyage through history, she would do anything within her power to expose the mistakes made by the people of this time.

It was almost six o'clock when they nudged up to the 300-foot wharf owned by the Northern Pacific Railroad. Primarily used for offshore coal bunkers, steamships were allowed to tie up for a minimal fee, and those traveling to the Bay Area were in and out every other day.

Swanson told his passengers they would spend the night at the harbor, and the staterooms on the lower deck were available if they wanted them. The three time travelers and their young companion walked the length of the wharf and gorged themselves on hot dogs and a newly imported beverage called Coca-Cola. When they returned to the boat, overcome with exhaustion and lack of sleep, they bade each other goodnight and retired to their stateroom. It was understood that Gyaaxa would bunk with Kate while Roger and Wally shared a room.

After ensuring Gyaaxa was comfortable, Kate collapsed on her bed and instantly fell asleep. At some point in the very early morning hours, Kate woke, startled by the silence in the room. She lit the oil lamp on the nightstand and saw that the other bed was empty save for a small scrap of folded paper on the pillow. It was the note Koyah had given to his daughter. The writing was in a language she couldn't understand, but when she looked at the other side, she saw a child's unpracticed handwriting with the words "thank you."

She folded it, put it in her pocket, and sat still, tears for the young girl rolling down her face. Knowing what the future held for the matriarch of the Aldrin family didn't make her departure any easier, and her absence left a sadness that would take some time to heal.

***

The next morning brought another bright and sunny August day. I still had difficulty adjusting to the weather since only a few days ago, we were in the middle of winter.

Wally and I were already on deck, and the captain was steering us away from the massive wharf when Kate met up with us. I could tell by the look on her face that she was alone.

"She left in the middle of the night; this note was on her pillow."

She handed Wally the note, who read it and passed it to me. Then he embraced her and said, "Kate, we knew this was the way it would happen. You've made a difference in her life, and she'll continue to have a full one thanks to you."

"Yeah ... but I didn't think I'd get so attached, you know?"

"I do, Kate ... I do."

I left them alone and walked over to Captain Swanson, who was headed toward us. "Good morning, Captain."

"Same to you, Mr. Wilkie. I wanted to let you know we should be in Coupeville by six or seven this evening. The currents are favorable, so that will help. It's just the three of you now?"

"Thanks for the update, Captain. We look forward to getting back to Whidbey Island."

Swanson may not have been my kind of guy, but he knew his business, and we pulled into the Penn Cove dock a little before six. It was daylight until well past nine in mid-summer, so we opted for an outside table at the Front Street Bistro for our evening meal.

The beer we ordered was a local brew and excellent, if a bit warm. It reminded us that we were no longer living in the twenty-first century.

"I don't know about you two, but I can't wait to hit the sack. Good move keeping our rooms at the inn, Wally."

"Yeah, I figured it made sense at the prices we're paying. What's next, Boss?"

As he asked me this, he looked at Kate. I was struck by how much they were in sync.

"I wish I knew. Gyaaxa, or Sarah, should be on her way to San Francisco soon, but unless we want to wait fifteen years, we need to find another way to get home."

"Yeah, but what if we don't?" Kate asked.

I had avoided thinking of that possibility for days, but the longer we lived in the past, the more likely it was to become permanent. It would be difficult for all of us, but at least Wally and Kate had each other. I missed my wife fiercely, and the thought of a life without her was intolerable.

"I don't know, Kate, I—

"Roger! Across the street—look!"

I turned just in time to see the backs of a tall man and a woman seated on a horse-drawn wagon. The guy had just grabbed the reins and was about to head out of town.

I jumped up and shouted, "Becker … Orla …"

They turned and looked at us; then he smiled, and with a flip of the bird, they headed up the hill and away from town.

"Son of a bitch," Wally said.

"I'm not sure what they were up to, but I'll bet it had something to do with the land office over there," I said.

"What do you think?"

"If I were to guess, Kate, I'd say he was signing papers to allow him to home-stead the land that Buzz used to live on. He probably thinks by doing so, his name will be on the deed and it will never have belonged to the Aldrin family."

"Will that work?"

"For now … I think so. How this plays out through the next hundred and thirty years … I have no fucking idea."

"Should we go after him?" Wally asked.

"And do what? As much as I'd like to see the guy get what's coming to him, there's not much we can do. He hasn't broken any laws here, and we're not cops anymore. Let's pretend he doesn't exist and focus on what we do next to go home." I was weary of Alan Becker and his antics. I wanted to return to the Whidbey Island of 2024 and be with my wife.

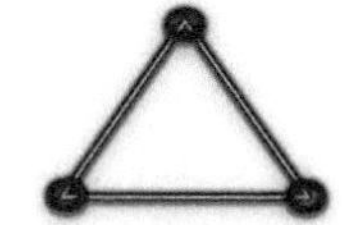

FORTY-TWO

The door was almost twice as tall as Buzz. The confused driver had left him at the curb of the Aldrin house; he shuffled his way up the walk to the imposing entrance. He hesitated for a few seconds before reaching as high as he could to grasp the ring in the lion's mouth. As he lifted it, it slipped from his hand and slammed against the back plate. The clank startled him, and it took all his willpower to stay where he was.

He heard footsteps, growing louder, approaching the door. His stomach roiled as he listened to the deadbolts slide from their slots. The door opened several inches, followed by a woman's gasp.

As it swung wide, he heard a voice he hadn't heard in over two decades. "Buzz ... Buzz, it's you."

Sable embraced her son while he stood motionless. After several seconds, she realized that her son had mixed feelings about this reunion, and she stepped back.

"Come inside, Buzz. Let's get you out of the cold and have some tea."

He followed his mother down the sweltering hallway and into the parlor, where she showed him a seat on the sofa.

"Have a seat while I put the kettle on."

Buzz unzipped his jacket and looked around the house where his mother lived—one he had never been to. He had chosen to stay in the woods off Lone

Lake Road but was only a kid then. Sure, he'd hidden from them, but if his mother loved him, she would never have given up looking for him. He couldn't understand her feelings or reasons for abandoning him, but it would be impossible to put it behind him.

She handed him a cup and sat across from him, but before she could speak, he said, "I need some help."

Sable wanted to say her piece but sensed this wasn't the time. Her last contact with the police, who were chasing Becker and now Orla, was when Wilkie had spoken to her on the phone. Now that Buzz was free, she wasn't sure what else could be the problem. She held her tongue.

"Alan kidnapped me from Lone Lake and burned my home."

"I know that, Buzz."

"You do?"

"Yes, that policeman—Wilkie is his name—and two others were here trying to find you. I told them that Alan might be after you to get to the property."

"He took me to some house on Lummi Island, and I tried to cast some spells that would alter the ownership of the property, but I failed. He said if I didn't keep at it, he would make everything about our family and ancestors public."

"So you tried to help him steal your *home* ... to protect us?"

"Yeah."

If it were possible to feel any worse as a mother, Sable Aldrin now did. Somehow, her son, the one with the name of an astronaut, had lived alone with only nature and the elements to teach him and had turned out to be a more caring and thoughtful person than she deserved.

"How can I help?"

"One of the cops looking for me was a woman—Kate something—and Alan locked her up in the house, too."

"Yes, I met her."

"Anyway, I didn't know what to do because none of my spells were working, and then I thought about the ear you always kept."

Sable began to feel uneasy at the mention of the powerful talisman.

"I told him it might help me, but I thought the cop—Wilkie—had taken it. He and Orla took me to the police station in Freeland, and they broke in and found it. He left the lady cop locked up in the house on Lummi, but I guess she got away."

While unsure where her son was headed, Sable wondered what her life would have been like if she'd never heard the name Alan Becker.

"And what happened after you took the ear?"

"We drove to Ebey's Landing. We went there because I was there once before and felt something I'd never felt before. It seems like a sacred place or maybe a spiritual one."

Sable knew the relic was essential and had been passed down through generations of Aldrin women. She wasn't entirely clear about its importance, only that her mother had stressed keeping it safe.

"Go on, Buzz ..."

"We went down to the beach, where I created the triangle of fires. I read about its power in the scrolls I found in your yurt. I told Alan and Orla to sit in the middle and began reciting the sacred verses I had memorized. I had gathered the items I needed beforehand and tossed them into the center circle while saying the words that would erase the years and allow the property to transfer."

A sense of dread came over Sable, and she asked, "What happened?"

"Well ... I must have passed out. When I came to, there was a couple there who had seen most of it. Alan and Orla were in the triangle, but I hadn't seen the three cops. I guess they came to arrest Alan and Orla and were caught when I threw the talisman into the sacrificial circle. All of them were gone."

Buzz slurped his now-lukewarm tea while Sable stared into hers. Although her powers were at a low point, her years of practicing the occult had given her insights that few of her kind shared. She had a good idea of what had happened on the beach at Ebey's Landing, but first, she needed more information.

"How would you like me to help, Buzz?"

"I need to know what happened to the police who were trying to help me. I want to know where they are and how to rescue them. They tried to help me, and something I've done has hurt them. I need you to help me do that."

"You have become one of the most powerful practitioners of the magic arts, and I believe it's because of your connection to the natural world. I'm not positive, but I think what you have accomplished is transporting these individuals back in time. We need to do more research to pinpoint where they are and then find a way to retrieve them."

"Can it be done?"

"I don't know, but then I wasn't sure they could be sent there in the first place. Why don't you get some rest while I think about this? It may take some time."

Buzz stretched out on the sofa and was asleep within minutes. While he snored peacefully, Angela gazed at the chubby little man and reflected on her poor choices throughout her sixty years. Yet despite them, her son had turned out to be a kind, caring person who only wanted to live life on his terms. Then Alan Becker intervened and turned his world upside down.

She knew she could never make up for the lost time with her son, but maybe they might grow closer if she helped him through this. She walked over to the kitchen table, opened her laptop, and began researching the era of donation claims and the Homestead Act.

When Thorn walked into the house, she was shocked that over three hours had passed.

He saw the person sleeping on the sofa and asked his sister, "That Buzz?"

"It is; how did you know?"

"Who else would you let fall asleep on the sofa? How is he?" Thorn was a quiet, reflective sort, but that didn't mean he was unaware of Becker and the upheaval he had caused.

"He's exhausted … and worried."

She shared her son's story and explained what they were attempting to do. Thorn knew his sister's abilities well, and little about her life was unknown to him. His life, even in these older years, had always been one of support. Never married and with no desire to do so, he was content living with his sisters. Most people sensed they were an odd family—of course, they were—and left them alone. He knew Orla had secretly been jealous of Sable's relationship with Becker early on, and it was no surprise that she had gone over to the dark side earlier last year. His relationship with Buzz was far less than that of a distant uncle, but maybe that was about to change.

"What can I do to help?"

She passed her notes to him and told him to concentrate on the historical data for the late 1800s. She would dig through old notes and papers passed down from her mother, which might shed more light on acquiring the Lone Lake Road property. She accepted what Becker had told her about her great-grandmother was the truth, and now it needed verifying. Because of her aversion to witchcraft as a youngster, she had never cared to study the entire history of the Aldrin family, but it appeared that was about to change.

It was after six when Buzz finally woke from his slumber. From his prone position, he saw his mother poring over piles of yellowed papers and Thorn hunched over a laptop. They both looked at him as he stood.

"Good sleep?"

"Yes … sorry, I didn't mean to crash like that."

"Not to worry. Your uncle and I have been trying to figure this thing out."

"Hi, Thorn. Thank you for helping."

"My pleasure, Buzz. I hope we can rescue your friends."

"They're not friends; I hardly know them."

"Did you say they tried to help you—that they tracked down Becker?"

"Yeah ... they did."

"Then I'd call them friends.

"Have you found out anything?"

Sable looked up and said, "My grandmother, Angela, purchased the property from the original owners, who obtained the land under the Homestead Act in about 1910 or close to it. Thorn discovered they must have filed for the property between 1886 and 1890. We need to visit the Island County seat to see what records they still have. If your spell wasn't specific regarding the exact date, it might be difficult to find these folks."

"The incantation I used was meant to allow Becker to erase the Aldrin name from the land so he would own it in the present. I didn't pay much attention to specific dates. Is that going to be a problem?"

She looked at her notes and answered, "We won't know until we try to make contact. We'll go to Coupeville tomorrow and see what they've kept from that far back."

She stood up, her age beginning to wilt her tall frame, and walked over to her son. "I'm glad you're here, Buzz. There's nothing I can say or do that will make up for my failings as a mother, but I will commit to doing everything possible to help recover these people. Let's have a bite to eat and then get some rest; we have a busy day tomorrow. You can use Orla's room."

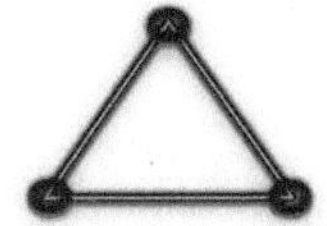

Forty-Three

Andie Saunders finished feeding her three pygmy goats and closed the door to her home office. The class she taught at the University of Washington only met two days a week, and her home lab and office allowed her to continue her research without messing with the ferries daily.

She missed Roger—she always did when he was out of town—but she never felt far away, because he always kept her abreast of his investigations. When he'd called to tell her he wasn't sure when he'd be home, he'd also told her about the break-in at the Freeland office. She thought it odd, but she knew Roger would figure things out.

But that was hours ago, and it was now dinner time. She knew he was busy, but he always answered his texts, and she'd already sent several. Her calls went straight to his voicemail, but after her first message, she hung up. She was worried.

At seven o'clock, she called Sheriff Davis, who answered immediately. "Hi, Andie."

"Tom, have you heard from Roger?"

"No ... he's not back yet?"

"No, and I can't reach him."

"Geez, that's odd. They got Kate Mahoney back, and the last time I talked to him, they were headed to Ebey's Landing. Something about the break-in made them think Becker might be there. Let me make a few calls, and I'll get back to you."

She took her phone and went to the barn to be with her goats. She loved the little guys, and they always made her feel better; she did her best thinking while talking things over with them. It buzzed about ten minutes later. It was Tom Davis.

"Hi, Tom. Did you reach him?"

"Uh ... no, I did not; I couldn't reach Wally either. I called the chief at BPD, too, and asked about Mahoney. Nobody can reach her either."

"Tom, I'm worried. What's happened?"

"I don't know. There's not much we can do tonight, but I'll get a couple of cars to Ebey's Landing first thing in the morning. Another thing, Andie ..."

"Yes?"

"That Becker guy has disappeared too. Kate said he was with Orla Aldrin at the house on Lummi. We've got BOLOs out on his truck and her car, but nothing yet. I'll call as soon as I know anything, and if you hear from him, ring me."

She tried to keep busy cleaning and dusting the same things again and again, but it was no use. She was sure something had happened. The TV was on some silly rom-com but offered no success in distracting her. She started her nightly routine and was getting ready for bed when her phone buzzed. She answered ... hoping ...

"Andie, it's Tom. I know I said we would wait until morning, but I sent a car out to the trailhead at Ebey's. They found Orla's car there, along with one of ours. That place is enormous and dangerous at night, so we'll keep a team there through the night and send in a couple more tomorrow to search. We're getting some help from BPD as well."

"I'll meet you there, Tom."

"Maybe you should wait until we see what's what."

"I'll see you there."

She would get very little sleep tonight, but at least they knew where to start looking.

***

She left at first light, about seven during the waning days of February, and made it to the trailhead in forty minutes. Two Island County sheriff's vehicles and a BPD cruiser were on site.

She parked and walked over to a group of uniformed deputies and police, listening to Tom Davis give instructions. He wrapped things up quickly when he saw her, and the assembly broke up and headed for their assignments.

"Andie, sorry we have to meet under these circumstances. Nothing happened overnight, and the search teams are just getting underway. I don't have to tell you how big this place is; it'll take some time to go over all of it."

"How could they just disappear? I mean, their cars are right here."

"Yeah ... I don't know. I know you wanted to be here, but it's probably not a good idea for you to be wandering over these cliffs while we're searching."

She wanted to do *something*, but the sheriff was right; she'd likely be in the way.

"Why don't I head into town and pick up some coffee and donuts for the team?"

Davis looked relieved at the offer and said, "That's a great idea. These people will love it after traipsing around in a forty-degree drizzle. Maybe we'll have something to report when you get back."

She drove back to the little historic town of Coupeville, hoping the distraction would keep her from worrying and unsure whether she wanted the team to have anything to report or not.

It took the two-person teams a while to make it down to the beach, and when they did, there was nothing to see. There were remnants of several beach campfires that looked to be arranged geometrically and scads of footprints. As a unit of the National Park Service, the historic reserve was a favorite hiking destination even during the inclement winter months.

It was still early in the day, and while there were a few early visitors, the only sounds came from the seagulls and the chattering eagles overhead. After two hours, it became apparent there was nothing to find, and the searchers headed back up the bluffs.

Andie arrived as the teams, now cold and wet, were reassessing the situation. They were grateful for the refreshments she brought, and all expressed their concern for Roger.

Tom was explaining their next steps to her when an ancient VW Westfalia camper chugged into the parking area. The couple, well into their fifties, appeared well-equipped to hike the reserve's bluffs, woods, and beaches. They looked surprised at the number of law enforcement folks milling about and weren't bashful about interrupting Sheriff Davis.

"Wow, what's goin' on? Someone fall?" the woman asked.

Looking annoyed, Davis replied, "An officer is missing, and we're searching the area."

He turned away, sure that his abrupt response was all that was needed to send them on their way.

"This have anything to do with that odd little guy who was here yesterday?"

The man's question silenced every murmur within hearing distance. The couple now had the sheriff's, Andie's, and several other deputies' complete attention.

Davis faced the couple and said, "I'm Sheriff Tom Davis, and this is Andie Saunders, and you are?"

They looked at each other, perhaps thinking they'd be hiking now if they had kept their mouths shut.

"I'm Tony, and this is Toni too, but with an 'i.' The last name is D'Angelo."

"You both were here yesterday, then?"

"Yeah. There was this little guy, kinda chubby, down on the beach doing some sort of ceremony." Toni with an "i" seemed to be the talker in the family.

"What kind of ceremony?" Andie asked, oblivious to her layperson's status in the investigation.

"He had these three fire circles going. They were far apart but, like, in a triangle. There was another couple with him—big guy, older than us—she was a little younger and smaller. Anyway, they were kind of in the middle of the thing while the guy was saying things in some weird language. We thought it was some cult religious thing, so we started to walk away with the others."

"What others?" Davis asked.

"Other hikers," the other Tony answered. "There's always a bunch around, especially when the weather's nicer."

"Not like today, right?" Back to the female Toni.

"So that was all you saw?" Andie pressed.

"No. When we started to leave, two guys and a woman were sneaking around the other hikers; one of the men wore a uniform. Just when the little guy's voice got louder, the three of 'em got behind the couple, and it looked like they put cuffs or ties on the guy."

As her story continued, most of the deputies and officers gathered around. There was a sense of a breakthrough in the air.

"And then?" Andie tried to hurry the woman along.

"We were still kinda walking away, but when we looked back, it seemed like the dude threw a bunch of stuff into the smaller circle, and then ... poof!" She waved her hands. "A greenish flame and a bunch of smoke blew into the air."

"What about the couple and the other three?" Davis asked. "Dunno ... they must've scurried away while we were watching the smoke. There was a bunch of it, and it smelled awful," the male Tony answered.

"Did you see them after that?"

"Nope ... we thought it kinda weird how they all just disappeared, but we were a little herbed up at the time and just figured we missed them." The woman looked annoyed at her partner, perhaps thinking he might have shared too much.

She quickly picked up the thread. "The little guy was lying on the ground, and we thought he might have passed out or something, so we ran back over to see if he was okay. When we got there, he was moving around, and he seemed disoriented. We asked him if he needed help, but he said no, and then when we asked about the other folks, he said they must have taken off."

"You never saw the couple or the other three again?" asked Davis.

"Nope. We assumed we missed them when they took off. The guy *was* a little weird, and we were glad to be on our way."

With no more new information coming from the hikers, the sheriff took their contact information and thanked them. Next, he told the BPD police they were free to go and told the Island County deputies to return to their duties. Andie watched as everyone returned to their vehicles and vacated the scene, leaving only the two of them.

"Are you calling off the search, Sheriff?"

"I don't know everything that's been going on with Roger's investigation, Andie, but I have been getting updates from him, and I gotta say, this whole case gets stranger every day. I know about the Buzz Aldrin kidnapping, and I know there's been talk of witchcraft involved. He's forwarded his conversations with Sable Aldrin, so I know the whole family thing."

"What are you saying, Tom? Are you calling off the search or not?"

"I'm saying I think we need to go to the horse's mouth on this one, and I think that person is Buzz Aldrin."

"How can we find him?"

"From what Roger's reported, his house is burned down, and the person who kidnapped him has disappeared; I can only think of one place he might go."

"His mother's?" Andie had already made the connection.

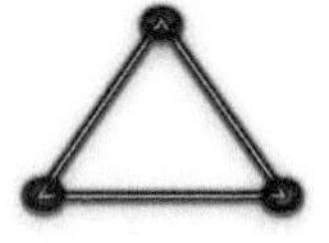

Forty-Four

We turned in early and made plans to meet for breakfast to discuss our next moves. Our only prospect of returning to the future was on her way to San Francisco, and she wouldn't even be aware of it for at least a dozen years.

We must have been tired because I didn't reach the dining room until nine, and Kate and Wally hadn't arrived yet. I was on my second cup of coffee when the two lovebirds joined me at the table. Their obvious infatuation with each other reminded me of the loss I felt at the uncertainty of being united with my wife. I was happy for them but, I had to admit, just a teensy bit jealous.

"Hey, Rog, come up with any ideas since last night?" Wally asked.

"Not yet; I figured I'd wait for the two of you to come up with something."

"Geez, Roger, we can't do everything for you." Kate was a bit of a ball-buster.

I smiled and shook my head as they sat down. "I suppose we should have known that Gyaaxa, or Sarah, wouldn't have been able to help us at her current age anyway."

"Yes, but maybe if we hadn't made sure we got her to Tacoma, she wouldn't have been the matriarch of the Aldrin family."

"If we weren't here, someone must have helped her because she *was*," Wally chipped in.

"The whole thing is too confusing to get my head around. Maybe we accept what *is* and move on. How do we get back?"

It was no wonder Kate was a good cop. She was clear on the issue, accepted it, and went on to find a solution. The three of us were quiet for a moment; the only sounds were murmurs from other tables and the tinkling of glasses and silverware.

"Buzz did something that threw us back when the property became registered, right?"

"Yes, Kate—so?"

"And he did it from Ebey's Landing, right?"

Wally and I nodded.

"Why from there?"

"It had to have something to do with the ear. The thing supposedly belonged to Isaac Ebey and was taken, along with his head, when he was killed back in 1857. Maybe Buzz chose that place because that's where Isaac was killed."

"So what? If he had the ear, why not do it anywhere?" asked Wally.

"Shit, I don't know. I'm not a goddamn witch. Maybe you should ask the Aldrins when we get back. *If* we get back."

"Okay, kids, let's settle down now." Our predicament was unprecedented and a fascinating first-hand look back in history, but the fear of being stuck in the 1800s was real. We had no idea if we would make it back or what to do to try and make that happen.

"I think you're right. Something about that place is spiritual or has energy or something else. How about we go back there and see if anything happens? It's only a couple of miles away; it's a nice day, and hell, we've got nothing else to do. Right?"

My two associates agreed as they looked at each other and grinned.

We made it to the bluff a little before noon. I'd been to Ebey's Landing often, yet every single time, I was stunned by the magnificence of the view. It was the same in this time—over a century in the past—as it had been in the twenty-first century. The scale and scope of this meeting of land, sky, and sea surpassed anything I'd ever seen. For a brief few seconds, I forgot why we were here.

We wound our way down to the beach and walked to the site of our transportation. The beach was deserted save for dozens of seagulls riding the ocean breezes and a pair of eagles at the water's edge, working on the carcass of something no longer alive.

"Look," Kate said, pointing to an anomaly in the sand.

"I can see it." Wally hurried over to Kate's position.

The faint outline of a circle was visible in the sand. There were no stones, nor was there a defining perimeter. It was almost a shadow that vanished the closer they got to it.

I was farthest away, but the distance helped me to make out two others. "Come back over here," I said. "You can make out all three of them. They've got to be the ones Buzz used."

We stood on a large stump of driftwood and gazed at the shadow of the triangle that had been our spaceship to another century.

"Okay ... now what?"

"I don't know, Wally. Let's stick around for a while. At least we know the exact place where we landed."

We did that. We spent several hours wandering the beach, throwing stones in the water, and lying in the sand before we climbed back up the bluff and returned to the hotel.

Acknowledging the fate of our future was entirely out of our control was a tough pill to swallow, but we had begun to do that. With no other options available, we committed to visiting the site for a few hours every day. What we'd do in the remaining hours would be a challenge. Whether temporary or not, we were stuck in 1889.

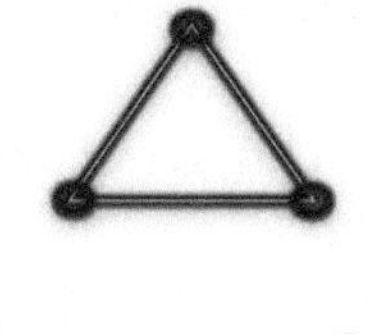

FORTY-FIVE

Andie parked her car at the sheriff's office in Coupeville and rode with him to Wilson Street in Bellingham. Although she was strictly a citizen and not a cop, he valued her input and proximity to the case. He called BPD along the way to explain what he was up to, and they offered any help he needed. He told Andie that he thought it made more sense to visit the Aldrins without calling first. If Buzz was there, he didn't want to spook him.

They pulled up to the curb in front of the Victorian architectural wonder a little before noon. Neither had been to the home before, and both looked at each other wide-eyed at its presentation. They strode up the steps to the massive front door, again looking at each other, both taking deep breaths; then Sheriff Tom Davis reached the ring in the lion's mouth and slapped it against the back plate.

They heard someone approaching the door seconds before it was opened, but only a few inches. A tall, gray-haired woman could be seen on the other side. Davis was not in uniform, and Andie was dressed in jeans and her Gore-Tex hiking jacket. Sheriff Davis held out his ID and introduced them both.

"What do you want?"

Standing in the drizzle on the stoop, they could feel the heat from inside the house, and the accompanying odor was difficult to ignore.

"Are you Sable Aldrin?"

"Yes."

"I think you know why we are here."

"No ... I don't," she answered, although her downward cast revealed the lie.

"Ma'am ... we don't mean anyone any harm. Roger Wilkie has kept me in the loop on the entire investigation regarding Buzz and his father. He, along with his deputy and a detective from Bellingham Police, have gone out of their way to make sure Buzz wasn't harmed and was rescued. We're concerned for the safety of our friends and fellow officers. This is Andie Saunders, Roger's wife. Please try to help us."

The woman at the door took a deep breath and then opened it fully. "Please come in." She closed the door, and they followed her down the hallway. They entered the living room, where a short, chubby man sat on a sofa, and an older man wearing reading glasses sat in a nearby Queen Anne chair. They both stood as the trio entered the room.

"Sheriff and Ms. Saunders, this is my brother, Thorn, and my son, Buzz."

The four of them looked at each other and nodded while Sable continued, "Buzz, this is Deputy Wilkie's boss and his wife. They're here to talk about what happened to the people who tried to help you." She turned to her guests and asked them to be seated.

"Thanks for seeing us. We've just come from Ebey's Landing, where we found your sister's car and Roger Wilkie's patrol car. He's been missing for almost two days, and we can't reach him, his associate, or a detective from Bellingham. We think you can help us."

It took a full minute before Buzz stood up. His demeanor was that of a schoolchild being called before the principal, but he seemed to gather courage as he began his story.

"Kate tried to rescue me in the house on Lummi Island. Alan kept her with me, and then Orla showed up. She's my aunt. I needed a talisman that had been handed down through our family, but Deputy Wilkie had it in his office."

"The ear?" Andie asked.

"How did you know?"

"I saw it. When Roger discovered you were gone, he took me to your house. I think he took it to find out who it belonged to, to maybe get a lead on where you were."

"When I went back for it and saw it was missing, I knew it had to be the deputy that took it. That's when Alan burned my house down.

"I wasn't sure what to do. Alan was threatening my family, and he had Kate locked up. I thought if we got the talisman and I could do what he wanted, he'd leave us alone, and somebody could rescue Kate. After he broke into the sheriff's office, we went to Ebey's Landing because that's where the energy was strongest. I didn't know why, but now I understand it."

Thorn and Sable were looking at Buzz during his narration with a hint of pride and respect on their faces.

"When we got to the beach, we constructed the triangle and the center altar—the small circle in the center. I was trying to change the original deed on the property so Alan would be the owner. I was focused on the point in time when the land was transferred from the government, who took it from the Natives to the first settlers to homestead the property.

"I know how to do *some* things and cast everyday spells and curses, but this was something I'd never tried before."

"That's because it's never been done before, at least by anyone I know of," Sable interrupted.

"So, I recited the words I knew from the scrolls I found in the old yurt. When I said them out loud, something I'd never felt before came over me. Alan was in the triangle because I was trying to make him the owner, and I guess Orla joined him. I was so caught up in the ceremony that I never saw Kate and the others, but they must have entered the triangle before I executed the spell."

"What happened to them?" Andie asked.

"I think, instead of rewriting the deed on the original date, all those inside the triangle were sent back to that date."

"You mean they went back in time? That's ridiculous," said Davis.

Sable was amazed at what her son had accomplished, even if there had been complications. "It may sound ridiculous to you, Sheriff, but I'm confident that is what happened. If not, how do you explain the absence of these three, and why are their vehicles still there? Do you think Wilkie up and left his wife?"

"I think he's telling the truth, Tom."

"How is it possible, Andie?"

"I don't know, but I'm a scientist, and there's a bunch of stuff I don't know." She turned to Buzz and asked, "Do you know how to get them back?"

Sable answered, "We were discussing that when you came. Buzz feels terrible about this but has more power than anyone I've ever met. If it can be done, he can do it."

"What can we do to help?"

"We still have the talisman, so that's good. What we need are the precise dates of the property transfer. We were going to research the records at the county to see how far back they were kept. We must also review everything Buzz recited on the beach and find a way to reverse the incantations."

"When will you be ready to try if we can handle the property dates?"

"If we spend the afternoon studying and you can get us the dates, we should be ready to go in the morning. Right, Buzz?"

"Yeah, but I think it's better to do it on the beach at the same time. By the time we had everything ready, it was around two thirty or three."

"Okay, we'll meet you at Ebey's late morning. That should give us time to get everything together." Sheriff Davis seemed to have reconsidered his opinion of time travel.

With all in attendance at the Aldrin household on the same page, Andie and the sheriff headed back to Whidbey Island, where they would attempt to uncover the history of the hundred acres of land just off the curves on Lone Lake Road.

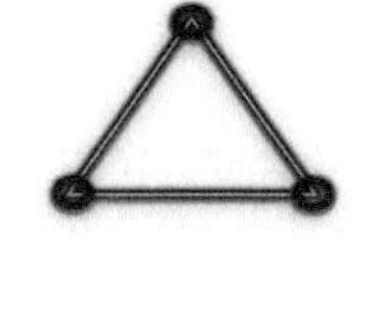

Forty-Six

Coupeville is a small town of about 1,900 souls. It was established as the county seat in 1881 mainly because of its central location on Whidbey Island and its importance as a commerce hub in Puget Sound.

Sheriff Davis called the Auditor's Recording Department while en route to the waterfront town and informed them of the documents he was looking for. The clerk said they still had historical records dating back to the 1850s, and she'd start digging through them to find the notes for that particular parcel.

They arrived at the County Office building on Seventh and Main an hour before closing. Davis's office was only a block away, and his familiarity with the county employees allowed immediate access when they entered the building.

"Go on downstairs. Heather has already pulled the stuff you're looking for," the front desk clerk directed them.

They descended to the basement, and the smell of musty paper and perhaps a hint of mold greeted their arrival. Heather Foote was behind the front counter at a sizeable Formica-topped table with a mess of yellowed papers spread about.

"Hey, Tom, sounds like you're working on something interesting, eh?"

"You have no idea, Heather, no idea at all. This is Andie Saunders. She's Roger Wilkie's wife, helping me out."

If Heather thought a civilian involved with an investigation was curious, she didn't let on. Instead, she got right to the point. "You said you needed the dates on the initial transfer of the property on Lone Lake Road, right?"

"Yes—the exact date is important."

"Okay ... there was a filing on August 23rd of 1889. It was a homestead filing from the Washington Territorial Government to an individual."

"Not from the state?"

"No—Washington didn't become a state until November of that year. There's even a time stamp on the filing; it was done at four p.m. on a Friday."

"Who filed the claim? Asked Andie.

"Looks like a guy named Alan Becker was the recipient."

Davis and Andie looked wide-eyed at each other, each mouthing the exact words, "Holy shit!"

"He did it, Tom. He managed to get Becker's name on the deed."

"I'll be damned ... he did."

Heather stared at them with a look reserved for those outside looking in. She said, "Are we done here? Is that all you need?"

"That's it. Great work, and thanks a million."

"Yes, Heather, you don't know how much this helps," Andie said.

They hurried up the stairs, leaving a bewildered Heather Foote to pack away the brittle documents from over a century ago. She wasn't sure how she had been of such great help, but the appreciative look on her customers' faces made her smile.

They called Sable and Buzz with the breakthrough information as soon as they returned to the sheriff's office. Sable sounded proud of what her son had accomplished, but when Buzz spoke, he sounded concerned.

"Are you sure it was the 23rd?"

"Yes. At four o'clock."

"You're sure about the time too?"

"Yes. Is that important? Andie asked.

"I, uh ... I'm not sure. This thing we're trying to do ... there's no formula for it. I'm taking hundreds of years of notes—some of these from the witches of Fulton Street—and trying to distill them into a single moment. I think we'll be ready to go tomorrow."

As they disconnected, Andie turned to Davis with a worried look. "I sure as hell hope he knows what he's doing."

"Yeah, me too. Right now, though, he's all we've got. Try to get some rest tonight, and I'll meet you at Ebey's Landing around noon."

Andie's mind was so riddled with questions, fears, and doubts that the half-hour drive to her home on Lone Lake—the lake at the south end of the road—passed in a blink.

She welcomed the chores of feeding her goats and letting them out for a romp. She wondered what Roger was going through and was scared she would never see him again. She managed to brush the thoughts aside briefly and fired off a note to her department head that she needed a few more days off.

The next day was frightful to think about and her sleep was fitful. Finally giving up, she rose at five and puttered about, cleaning everything again. Now that Becker had become the deed holder, she wondered what ramifications that would have for the Aldrin family and their history with the property. Would it cease to exist? Would Buzz never have lived there, or would he even be alive? The whole thing was too random and bizarre to comprehend, so she parked the thoughts, fed the goats, and then began the drive to Ebey's Landing.

When she arrived, the sheriff's cruiser and five or six other vehicles were parked at the trailhead. It appeared Roger's and Orla's cars had been taken away.

Standing at the top of the bluff, she could see activity three hundred feet below on the beach. Several hikers had already passed her, and several more were making their way down the trail. Thankfully, the weather was cooperating, with clear skies and temperatures in the upper forties.

When she arrived at the site for the ceremony, Tom Davis, Buzz, and two other deputies were busy moving stones and preparing what would soon be fires inside the rings. Buzz was directing while his mother stood off to the side, watching. It seemed she had become the understudy to her son, whose gifts had surpassed anything she had known.

"Hey, Andie. Do you want to help with the rings?" Davis asked.

"Sure, just tell me what to do."

It took another two hours to arrange everything, and Buzz finally told them it was ready. Like before, curious hikers stopped to look but moved on when the workers didn't engage with their questions. They were used to odd goings-on and the eccentricities of the islanders and considered their activities more a curiosity than a fault.

Shortly before three, Buzz asked those helping to stand to the side with Sable. He told them to be sure none of the gawkers managed to stray inside the hundred-foot triangle.

He stood before the center ring and began to chant in a sing-song voice using words known only to him. He swung his arms high in the air and then low, still reciting unintelligible phrases. When his voice raised higher, he reached out and dropped whatever was in his hand into the smaller circle. It burst into flame, as before, released foul-smelling smoke, and he collapsed to the ground.

No one moved for a few seconds until the smoke had cleared. Andie rushed over to Buzz just as he began to stir. She helped him sit up, and he asked, "What happened?"

By this time, the others, including his mother, had encircled him. Andie said, "You collapsed after the flames erupted from the altar ring."

"Nothing else?"

"No."

"I'm sorry. I failed. I thought it would work in reverse, but I was wrong."

"Buzz, maybe you needed something more than the ear could provide," offered Sable.

"I don't know ... I just don't know."

Andie was out of her league but tried to look at the situation holistically.

"Hey, Buzz, now that Becker is listed as the original deed holder, would that change anything? I mean, before, you were trying to *get* his name on the title. Now that it is, maybe you need to do or use something else."

"Yeah ... maybe ... I don't know."

He was depleted, and she didn't think pressing him on anything at the moment would be productive, but, goddammit, she had to find a way to get her husband back. And she would.

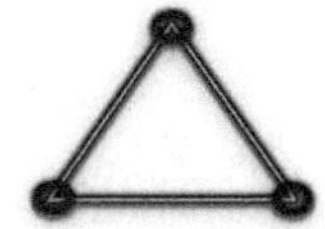

FORTY-SEVEN

It was the third day in a row we had made the trek to what would eventually become a National Historical Reserve. Ironically, such a stunning landscape, once occupied by Native Americans but claimed by the US Government, was now celebrated for its cultural and agricultural traditions.

If nothing else, the hikes up and down the bluffs had kept us in shape. We walked along the beach on another beautiful summer day.

"How long do we keep this up, and what if we never get back?" Wally asked the same thing I was thinking.

"I don't know. I guess at some point, we need to find a job."

"What? A job, Roger?" Kate asked.

"If we're stuck here, like, forever, we'll need to find a way to buy food and clothing and shelter. We've still got a little left from Wally's watch, but that will run out soon."

"Maybe we could invent something. We know a lot more than these folks."

"Hah, we could, but that might take some time. I guess we could always become cops."

"Not me. Have you seen the way these men treat women? Can you imagine a lady cop telling them what to do?"

I hadn't thought much about that. It took years for women to be treated as equals, and many places in the world still considered them less than.

"You're right, Kate. Let's at least think about some options. We should be good for another week of leisure before making any decisions."

"Hey, Boss?"

"Yes?"

"Do we have enough money for me to buy another outfit? These goddamn frilly things are getting heavy with dirt and muck. I don't know how these women did it."

Wally and I laughed at the truth of the matter, and I said, "Sure, let's do that when we get back to town. I don't blame you."

When we returned to town, she headed straight for the general store. While most of the women's clothing of the era was made to order, a few items were available for immediate purchase. While looking for something other than the frilly Victorian garb, she noticed a garment that wasn't quite a dress but was also a far cry from slacks or pants. She'd already purchased a blouse and skirt but was curious about the strange-looking item.

"What's this?"

The clerk's mouth frowned in distaste as he answered, "Oh, you don't want those. Some woman ordered them, then changed her mind. One of those women who aren't too feminine, if you get my drift, invented them, but I doubt anyone in this town will want them. I made the lady pay for them anyway." He smiled conspiratorially.

"What do you call it?"

"Bloomers. Some woman back east, name of Bloomer, came up with them. She thinks women should vote, too. Hah, that'll be the day …"

"I'll take them."

He appeared surprised for a few seconds, then bit his cheek and walked her to the counter to settle up.

"That'll be six dollars, ma'am."

"I'll give you three."

"The tag says six, ma'am."

"Yes, it does, but you told me the woman already paid for them. Didn't you?"

"Well, uh … yeah."

"So if I give you three, that means you'll be selling them for nine instead of six, right?"

He took a deep breath but knew when he was beaten. "Okay, okay … three it is."

Kate paid the man and took her new purchases back to the Coupeville Inn.

At dinner that evening, I sat with Wally while we waited for Kate to join us. When she entered the dining room, heads turned. She wore a white blouse with leg-o-mutton sleeves, a tan A-line skirt that came to her knees, and a pair of white poofy pants underneath that came to her ankles. Wally's eyes popped out of his head as she sat with us at our table.

"Woo-hoo … hottie at the table," he said as he gave her a peck on the cheek.

A slight blush crept up her face as I complimented her on the new attire. "You look lovely, Kate."

"Thanks. It seems some of the other patrons think differently, though."

"They'll come around in another century. Don't worry."

She laughed and said, "They're not jeans, but they're a hell of a lot more comfortable than those silly frilly skirts and dresses. They're bloomers, and I got a killer deal on them."

We congratulated her on her score and settled in for another dinner in a world that only existed in the history books. The next day would bring another hike to the beach and the bluffs and another return to the hotel. I was afraid our discussion about what to do next would have to come sooner rather than later.

FORTY-EIGHT

Andie was tired from the day's activities and the lack of sleep the night before. She knew little about witchcraft; she was a microbiologist and a scientist and dealt with data and facts, not magic. Her research required her to focus on the minutest details while never losing sight of the big picture. The tiniest clues could affect the overall outcome, but the combination of all the little things ultimately solved the equation or produced the desired result.

Trying to see things from Buzz's perspective was challenging. Not only because he was a warlock and she wasn't a witch but also because he was too close to the problem and riddled with guilt over what had happened.

His approach made sense, she conceded, but his reliance solely upon the ear seemed to fall short. Yes, the ear had a connection to his great-great-grandmother; she was Haida, after all. However, the stimulus for the entire state of affairs was the property on Lone Lake Road. How did Ebey's Landing and the ear connect with the hundred acres in question?

She thought about it for hours before falling asleep and awoke at five with an idea. Despite the early hour, she called Tom Davis's cell.

"Hey, Andie … it's early."

"Yeah, I know, Tom—sorry. I need a phone number for Buzz. I've got an idea."

"What is it?"

"Never mind. If it doesn't make sense to him, then it won't matter. Just give me the number ... please."

"Okay ... I guess. I've only got Sable's; I'll text you."

She called the number as soon as she received it. It rang and rang, then dropped. Not surprisingly, there was no voicemail. She called again with the same result and repeated the process. Finally, on the fifth attempt, Sable answered.

"Yes?"

"Sable, it's Andie Saunders. I need to speak with Buzz about something."

"It's early."

"Sable ... it's my husband we're talking about. Let me talk to Buzz. I'll let it go if he doesn't think it makes sense."

She heard a heavy sigh through the phone and pictured Sable carrying it to where her son slept.

"Here he is. I just woke him up."

"Hel ... hello?"

"Buzz, it's Andie, Roger's wife. I had an idea and wanted to run it by you."

"Okay ... what have you got?" His voice seemed stronger, more alert.

She asked him several questions, and when the answers were affirmative, she told him what she was thinking and why. After three minutes of explanation without interruption, she finished ... and waited for his response.

When she heard nothing, she wondered if he was still there. "Buzz ... Buzz, are you there?"

"Yes ... I was thinking ... and yes, I think it's possible. If we want to make it to the landing this afternoon, we need to get a crew to Lone Lake Road with a couple of pickups. If the tide's high, we'll need something to get them down the bluff, too."

"I'll get Tom to round up the people on this end; we'll worry about the bluff when we get there. See you there at noon."

Andie was back on the phone with Sheriff Davis immediately and explained what she needed and that Buzz thought it was possible. He promised the trucks, wheelbarrows, and a crew of twelve would be on site in two hours.

She dressed for the weather, which was drizzly and cold, fed her pals in the barn, and drove the ten minutes to the property off the curves on Lone Lake Road. Splashing through the puddles and ruts on the dirt road, she parked at the burned-out shell of Buzz's former residence. It was daylight, but only barely. The gloomy skies made her hike through the woods difficult, but she persisted, following Buzz's directions.

After passing the outhouse and then the remains of the yurt encampment, the woods became thicker and more difficult to negotiate. Another hundred yards took her to the ivy-choked remains of the original cabin—the one built by the property's first homesteader. The structure was in ruins, and the fireplace had crumbled into a pile of river rocks. She hoped it was much, much more than that.

By the time she returned to her car, Davis and his people had arrived. She told them to follow her and that some brush-clearing would be necessary. They broke into teams, two to a wheelbarrow, and followed her to the cabin's remains. The teams were instructed to collect as many river rocks from the fireplace as they could carry, wheel them back, and load them into the trucks.

Andie was shocked at the workers' speed, considering the mud, wet foliage, and uneven terrain. *Whatever Tom said to them has produced a workforce of dedicated, no-excuse, no-give-in people who won't stop until they're told ... enough!*

As they got ready to head to Ebey's Landing, Andie asked him how the teams could be so efficient.

"It was easy," he said. "I told them this was our last hope to get Wally, Roger, and Kate back, and we needed their help. Most of these folks were off duty and volunteered, even though they don't know exactly what we're up to."

She thought about the good-hearted people on the island and was thankful she lived there. If this last-ditch effort panned out, she'd find a way to thank them.

***

Getting the stones out of the woods was challenging, but a more pressing problem was finding a way to get them to the beach and positioned before dark. The tide peaked at 12:30 and would have receded enough to allow the construction of the triangle by three p.m. Unfortunately, the shallowness of the beach would not allow them to use the coast road to deliver the river rocks to the site, and they would be forced to find a way down the difficult trail from the bluff. Buzz and Sable met Andie at the trailhead when she arrived a few minutes ahead of Sheriff Davis and his crew.

"Are we going to make it before dark, Buzz?"

"I've got everything I need, and I think you're on to something by using the stones from when the property was settled for the circles. We had a connection to the Aldrin family with the ear, but the property was never part of the equation. Now it is."

"Yeah, if we make it down this trail in time."

Davis walked up, overhearing the end of the conversation, and said, "If we have to take these down the trail by hand, it'll take hours. We won't have time."

"Any other suggestions?" Andie asked.

"Hey, Buzz, look at what we've got in the trucks and tell me if we've got enough for the circles."

Buzz walked around the loaded pickups and circled back to Davis. "There's more than enough in there, Sheriff."

"So if we lose a few, it's no big deal?"

"Yes, that's safe to say."

"Okay. You, Andie, and your mom should go to the beach and clear any hikers away from the bluff. We'll get them down using the express lane."

Andie now understood his plan. "You're going to throw them over the bluff?"

"Yup. We'll probably lose a few, but they're mostly round, and the bluff is so steep, I think enough of them will make it. As long as you keep folks away, it'll be a hell of a lot safer than trying to take the trail with a bunch of wheelbarrows."

Andie and the Aldrins took the trail to the beach and made it in under twenty minutes. The weather had discouraged most of the hikers, so keeping the landing area clear would be easy.

"We're ready when you are, Tom; let her rip," Andie said over her cell.

The trucks pulled as close as they dared to the bluff's edge, and the crews tossed the river rocks over. It was over three hundred feet in height, and it took almost fifteen seconds before the first stones splashed into the sand after bouncing down the grassy bluff. After ten minutes, two truckloads of the stones used for building a fireplace on the Lone Lake Road parcel over a century ago were now on the beach at Ebey's Landing.

Once the danger from the tumbling stones had passed, Buzz began supervising the construction of the triangle. The ebbing tide had revealed enough of the beach to allow for the hundred-foot length, with the farthest circle on the still-wet sand. The assembly of the river rock circles was completed quickly when the balance of the crew arrived after making their way down the bluff.

By four o'clock, the giant triangle, complete with the empty center circle, was ready. Under darkening, rainy, gray skies, the day hikers had retreated up the bluff while the deputies and off-duty volunteers remained, curious to see what would happen.

Andie stood with Sable and Tom Davis on one side, with the others opposite. Buzz took his place in the center, making it clear that no one was to enter the triangle. Dressed in Thorn's old jeans with the cuffs rolled up by a half-dozen turns and wearing a soaked Patagonia parka, the sleeves bunched up to his elbows, he looked more like a homeless street urchin than a warlock with the power to thrust people back in time.

The drops spilled off his borrowed BPD ballcap bill as he took his place behind the center circle. The sound of rain dripping off those assembled, the whispering small waves of the ebbing tide, and the occasional high-pitched gull screech lent a mystical quality to the occasion.

Buzz raised his hands above his head and began to chant. Those who could hear him, especially the volunteers, looked at each other, wondering who this was and what he was mumbling. His voice became louder and higher pitched as he recited verse after verse of what all except Sable heard as gibberish. Just when the observers thought his voice couldn't escalate any higher, it did. That was the precise moment when Buzz tossed the ear into the circle. Green flames erupted from thin air, and a plume of rancid smoke settled over the entire triangle.

Forty-Nine

We had breakfast in the dining room, just like the previous five days. I was beginning to feel like Bill Murray from *Groundhog Day*. We had settled into the routine of eating breakfast, then hiking to Ebey's Landing and spending a few hours there. After that, we would walk back to town, where we'd split up—or rather, I would split up; Wally and Kate were joined at the hip—and either look for something to explore or nap.

Our mood had gone from shock when we arrived to excitement when we rescued Gyaaxa and took her to Tacoma. But now we were a hair short of full-out depression, thinking we might have to spend the rest of our years stuck in the past. At least Wally and Kate had each other, which helped soften their landing, but neither looked forward to a future in the dark ages.

Today, we decided to delay our trip until the afternoon to add a little variety to the routine. I was beginning to think the trek was a waste of time, but because it was our only connection to the future, we stayed the course.

We packed a lunch and reached the landing shortly after noon. Although the nearby farms we passed were bustling with activity, the beach was deserted. We traversed the bluff trail to the beach and found a mammoth cedar log that had been tossed to the base of the bluff during one of the frequent winter storms. It was a perfect perch for eating the sandwiches we'd brought.

It was another day of clear skies, bright sunshine, and sparkling seas. If our situation hadn't been so dire and Andie had been by my side, it would have been heaven. The three of us were quiet, probably all thinking about the future.

Wally left to walk up the beach where the triangle had been constructed while Kate and I talked about what we'd do when and if we made it back.

"Guys ... come here," Wally yelled into the sea breeze.

"He probably wants to show us a dead crab or something," Kate said. We walked over the warm sand until we reached Wally.

"Look!"

The faint outline of the triangle was no longer faint. The three circles were now well defined by dents in the sand where the stones forming them should be. Even the smaller center ring was visible.

"It's different, Rog; grooves in the sand connect the circles now."

"Hey, Kate, will you stand up on that small knoll at the base of the bluff and tell me what you see? It's hard to get perspective from this close."

It took her several minutes to climb up the ten-foot mound, but once on the top, she began waving her hands and shouting. The onshore breeze blew away whatever she said, and we waved her back.

"It's like the whole outline of the triangle is blinking or shimmering. You can't see it up this close, but it's obvious from there. Something's happening, guys. What do we do, Roger?"

"Shit, I'm not sure. Wally, any ideas?"

"All I remember is being on the other side of that smaller circle when I came to."

"Right," Kate said. "We were all inside the triangle getting the zip ties on Becker."

"Inside ... *inside* the triangle. Come on, you two." I pushed them ahead of me as we scampered inside the perimeter.

We stood there silently for a few minutes, hoping against hope that this wasn't a figment of our imagination. After five minutes, our excitement dulled while thoughts of home were dashed.

"What now?" Wally asked.

"Let's sit here on the sand for a few more minutes," I said.

As the three of us started our way down to the sun-kissed beach, a plume of foul-smelling smoke gushed from the center circle and surrounded us. I wondered why the sea breeze did not affect the stinky cloud as I tumbled face-first onto the salty sand.

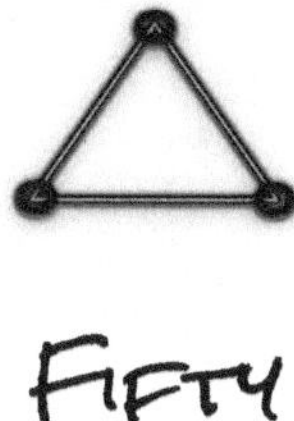

FIFTY

I was freezing. My face was numb from the cold sand, and the stink of the smoke was everywhere. I turned my head to the side, where Kate and Wally were barely visible through the haze.

I felt a cool breeze, and a light rain kissed my face as the smoke cleared. I heard people murmuring, then shouting, and then I listened to my wife screaming my name. Then she was holding me, squeezing me until I couldn't breathe.

We were back.

***

Sheriff Davis and the volunteers from BPD and Island County rushed to Kate and Wally as they came around. They left Andie alone with me. I had never been so glad to be back in the crappy Northwest weather.

I saw Buzz sitting on the wet sand, looking depleted, as Sable rushed over to him. I saw my boss and many of my associates, but most of all, I saw my lovely wife, who had tears rolling down her face to match those on mine.

I started hearing comments from the women volunteers asking Kate where the Halloween costume had come from. I expected it would be a long, long story over many beers before they would believe the full extent of our journey.

Sheriff Davis approached me when we were back on top of the bluff, getting into Andie's car. Not ordinarily a sentimental man, he gave me a quick hug and said how glad he was that we were able to make it back.

As I sat down, about to close the door, he asked, "Hey, Rog, what the hell happened to Becker and Sable's sister?"

***

It was a week before we understood everything that had happened, and we still weren't clear on much of it. As best as we could ascertain, we had spent over a week and a half in the summer of 1889, while only three days had elapsed in the present.

I was back in Tom Davis's office in Coupeville for a meeting with Heather Foote from the County Auditor's Office. They were both present when I arrived and, to my surprise, so were Wally and Kate, Buzz and Sable.

The sheriff began. "I can't imagine what an ordeal this has been for the three of you and you and Buzz too, Sable. This whole thing started with Becker kidnapping you, Buzz, to force you to get the property put in his name. When Andie and I met with Heather here, we found out that the first transfer of the property from the government went to Alan Becker."

This was news to me, but we had seen Becker come from the land office in 1889, so it made sense. I nodded, still not sure where this was headed.

Davis continued, "I told Heather to do a little more digging on this to see what the succeeding transfers looked like, and she did. Why don't you tell them, Heather?"

"As Tom said, Becker was the first owner of the property. He homesteaded the land, so basically, it was free. I looked at how the property was transferred over the years, and here's what I found. The first owner—Becker—apparently lived there for over twenty years. The records show he was delinquent in paying his taxes, so eventually, the state foreclosed on the property. When they showed up to evict the owner, they found he'd expired in his cabin. There's also a note saying there was a grave behind the cabin where it looks like his wife was buried.

"Angela Morgan, who later changed her name to Aldrin, purchased the property at auction in the mid-twenties, and it's been in the Aldrin family ever since."

After she'd completed her report, the room was silent. It seemed each of us was arriving at the same conclusion. Alan Becker had successfully acquired the property he'd been so keen to own. Unfortunately, he'd managed to do so by going back in time and staying there. I was sure if it was possible to identify the remains behind the old cabin, we would find they belonged to Orla Aldrin.

"Thanks for all your work, Heather. I guess Becker got what he wanted, but not exactly how he planned it." I stood to leave.

I thanked Tom Davis, embraced Wally and Kate, and told Buzz and Sable how much I appreciated their efforts. As I got to the door, I turned and said, "I almost forgot. We're having a get-together at our place next weekend. All the volunteers will be there, and you're all invited. Sable, we expect you and Buzz to be there. I'll text the directions."

***

Our home on Lone Lake—the lake, not the road, although it *is* at the end of the road—is of modest size, but the evening was mild for the first of March, so most of the guests were on the porch or in the barn visiting the goats.

Buzz and Sable were among the first to arrive, and it appeared they had found common ground during the past few weeks. She would always regret the past, but maybe moving forward, they would find sharing each other's company okay, too. They said there were plans to build a cabin on the property and that Buzz would even consider shopping for food rather than waiting for roadkill. For some reason, he had taken a liking to chicken pot pies.

The O'Malleys arrived, and Kevin had already begun pestering me for the details regarding my recent disappearance. I introduced him to Buzz and told him this was the little kid he had seen all those years ago. They walked away, discussing his plans for the new cabin.

The deputies and BPD officers were there with Tom Davis, and so was Bobby Waldron, who was thrilled to meet the guh-nome who used to live on Lone Lake Road.

Kate and Wally showed up last. Since their brush with time travel, it seemed they had grown closer, if that were possible.

"We're going to move in together, Rog; it was Kate's idea."

"The hell it was; he just won't leave me alone. I might as well save rent money." She punched him in the arm as she said this.

"Congrats to both of you," I said as I shook his hand. "Hey ... whoa, what's this?" The watch on Wally's wrist looked strikingly similar to the one his dad had given him.

"Kate gave it to me. She found it online—some antique Rolex dealer had it. They said it was from the 1800s. Once she saw the photo of my dad's initials on the back, she knew it was mine."

"Yeah, they wanted way more than two hundred bucks for it, too, but it was worth it for my man."

"I'm your man?"

"Okay, I'm done with you two. Go have fun."

It felt great having all the folks who were important to us sharing the evening, and even better when Andie came up and hugged me.

"Please don't ever leave me again," she said.

"It'll take more than a crafty warlock to keep me away, Andie. You're stuck with me."

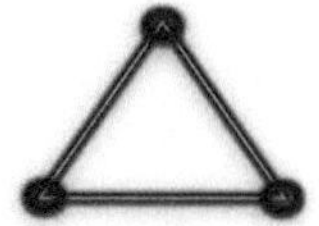

About the Author

Ted's observations and stories are formed by his stint in the Army, his sales, marketing, and entrepreneurial activities, and his life growing up as one of nine siblings in a typical Irish Catholic family.

Starting in New England, he managed to find his way to the Pacific Northwest, where he has lived for over three decades. He now lives on an island in the middle of Puget Sound with his wife and trusted GSD, Emma.

Feel free to reach out with any questions or comments to ted@tedmulcahey.com

Author's Notes

Lone Lake Road is a work of fiction. Any similarities to people, living or dead, are purely coincidental. The locations are real, and my hope is that I have been accurate in my descriptions of them.

Coupeville is the County Seat of Island County, and its historic and charming waterfront business district still reflects the buildings and character of a century ago. A stop at the Kingfisher Bookstore is essential.

The Westerfield house at the corner of Fulton and Scott in San Francisco has long been thought to be haunted. Built in 1889, the brooding structure once visited by Harry Houdini is on the National Register of Historic Places.

Ebey's Landing National Historical Reserve on the west coast of Whidbey Island is unforgettable. While its history reflects many of the injustices perpetrated upon the Native Americans by those with no awareness or conscience, it is still a testament to the beauty, power, and majesty of nature. No visitor to Whidbey Island should pass up the chance to stand at the top of the bluff, if only for a few minutes. It will be remembered always.

Among the more wicked things the early Americans chose to do to the People who lived here long before they did was to snatch their children from their families and place them in "boarding schools." Much of the history of that practice has come to light recently and has reminded us that other cultures, languages, and practices are to be celebrated, not discouraged or, worse, persecuted. It's the diversity that provides the strength of the country, and, unfortunately, it's taking us too long to realize it. We can do better.

OTHER WORKS

Bearied Treasure

Teed Up for Terror

Little Dirt Road

Juiced

Punch Down

Tanks